UNBROKEN

A DARK MAFIA SINGLE DAD ROMANCE

BRATVA KINGS

JANE HENRY

SYNOPSIS

Vadka Dragunov—Bratva executioner, cold-blooded tactician... and my sister's widower.

The man who built his empire in blood and protected it with silence. The man with a stare that holds me hostage—and a voice that cuts straight through me. I've avoided him, avoided all of them, as I've wallowed in my own grief following my sister's death.

But now there's no escape. I'm living in his world. I've been targeted. The Irish want war. And the only safe place left is under his watch... or under him.

He's a single father now—haunted, vengeful, and dangerous. A man who reads bedtime stories with the same hands that pull triggers. The man who would raze the world to keep his son safe.

He thinks I'm reckless, chaotic, unpredictable. I was only a child when we first met. He's always known me as little Ruthie.

But I'm not a child anymore, and I see what he hides beneath all that control—the obsession simmering just below the surface. The way he watches me like he wants to destroy me... or devour me.

And now the same loss that tore us apart is now pulling us closer.

Too close.

This was never supposed to happen.

I wasn't supposed to end up in his bed.

I wasn't supposed to want him to claim me like he owns me.

And I sure as hell wasn't supposed to be carrying the one secret that could burn everything down.

The Bratva is splintering. The Irish want blood.

And I'm falling head over heels for the man I can't have.

But is this love... or just what's left of us after everything else has been destroyed?

CHAPTER 1

VADKA

An empty bottle rolls across the floor, glinting in sunlight—sunlight?

Shit, it's daybreak. Have I been up all night?

The bottle stops against the toe of my boot.

I don't move.

My knuckles ache, bruised and split beneath crusted blood that isn't all mine. I stare down at it. Hell, I think *most* of it isn't mine.

Jesus. My head is killing me.

I don't remember how many men I killed.

The air reeks of body odor and whiskey. In the corner of the room, a woman's scuffed shoe lies, broken and crooked, shadowed by the doorway. My eyes catch on it, and for a moment, something lethal twists inside.

Memory grips me. A carefree night on the town. Mariah's hand on my arm to stop herself from keeling over. Her tinkling laugh and squeal when her heel broke, and she almost fell headfirst into the street. My wife, in my arms, her eyes twinkling at me. A little tipsy. Carefree.

So full of life.

I shove the memory down, out of sight, buried beneath too many feelings to name.

The Irish took my wife from me. And every last motherfucker will pay.

"Vadim."

Rafail's voice is low and rough. He hardly ever calls me my christened name. Everyone calls me Vadka, even him, when he's not pissed or serious, which is most of the time.

I don't look at him. I stare straight ahead… at nothing. Just me, here with my ghosts and demons.

"You *have* to stop this." Rafail's shadowy form steps in front of me, careful not to slip on the fucking gore that surrounds us. Dressed in a suit at the ass crack of dawn, he's either catching an international flight or hasn't gone to bed yet. "You *have* to fucking stop this," he repeats.

He crouches in front of me, serious eyes meeting mine. The eldest of his family, Rafail Kopolov, only celebrated his thirtieth birthday a few years back. The youngest reigning *pakhan* in Europe but one of the most feared. He's my *pakhan.* And my best friend.

"You're going to bring devastation I can't hold back, Vadka,"

Rafail says. His tone barely softens, but the fact that he's using my nickname means he's trying.

"They killed her." My voice is ragged. It never gets easier saying this out loud. *Never.* My eyes finally lift to Rafail's, my voice raw. "They killed my wife, Rafail."

His jaw flexes. "And what happens when you burn down every fucking city from here to Belfast? You think you'll find Mariah on the other side?"

The pain hits like a knife to my chest, so sharp and visceral I can't breathe at first.

"I don't fucking care," I manage to grind out. My chest heaves. "We'll find them."

"They're already coming," he snaps. "The Irish want war. Matvei is working on decoding the fucking flash drive we captured. They want blood for blood, brother, but you've given them every excuse." He leans in. "How many more innocents have to die?"

My mouth twists bitterly, and I shake my head. "They want war? Good. And I haven't killed *one* innocent, Rafail." I scratch at my chest to distract myself from the undeniable thirst for a drink. My voice is hoarse. "Not one."

"Not yet," he says softly.

Silence stretches between us. Rafail drags a hand through his hair and pushes himself to his feet, pacing. I almost feel bad for putting him in this position. I didn't want war. I never wanted to shed more blood than I had to.

But that was then. This is now.

They pulled the trigger and sounded the battle cry when they killed my wife.

My wife.

Rafail's gaze travels to the broken shoe on the floor. He swallows hard. This is when he tells me about the innocent lives at stake, how hard we've worked for peace, and reminds me of our limited resources. He might even pull rank.

But this time, he doesn't say any of those things. No. A flicker of genuine fear seems to run through his words when he says in a hoarse whisper, "Think of Luka."

The words hit harder than his fist would. My breath stops cold.

Luka. My boy. My miracle, asleep and safe.

Rafail presses harder. "Do you think Mariah died so you could abandon him? Or bring harm to him through your own recklessness?"

"Don't, Rafail." I drag a hand across my brow as a well of pain pushes at my chest, making it hard to breathe. *"Don't."*

"I have to. I can't let you destroy everything we've built and everything we hope for because of revenge. I can't."

I yank my hand away from my face and stare at him. "As if you wouldn't raze the fucking *earth* if someone killed Polina."

He flinches as if I slapped him. His jaw clenches, and he looks away. We both know the truth. He'd like to tell himself that he'd make decisions that would benefit the rest of his family and our Bratva. He likes to think he wouldn't cave to the temptation to murder the entire bloodline of any motherfucker who harmed a hair on her head. But we both know the truth.

He'd lose his fucking *shit*. The Rafail we all know and love would be gone and buried forever.

Just like me.

Just like me when I lost Mariah—my last link to sanity. Without her, the world blurs and ceases to have meaning.

"I won't abandon Luka," I tell him, my voice cracking. "I will cleanse this city of every trace of the Irish before they get within breathing distance of him."

He turns to go, and the empty bottle rolls and hits my foot. I'm seized with blinding, irrational rage. Without a second thought, I grab the bottle and hurl it across the room. Rafail watches, implacable.

The sound of glass shattering doesn't do what I hoped it would. It only makes what's broken feel irreparable.

"Then pull yourself out of this fucking quagmire and act like it," Rafail snaps, his limited patience fraying. "Because right now, brother, you're *drowning*. And you're dragging the rest of us under with you. Promise me. No more. Not until I give you the *go-ahead*."

I nod, my voice hoarse. "I promise."

I rise slowly, my gaze on Rafail. My breath still heaves with the effort of breaking the bottle. With the effort of not falling apart.

"Maybe we fucking drown them *first*."

CHAPTER 2

RUTHIE

I WIPE down the bar top for the hundredth time.

"You know," Zoya says thoughtfully, tipping her head to the side. "It's really okay to only wipe that down like fifty times. It's a bar, Ruthie, not an operating room."

At twenty years old, Zoya Kopolova is easily the youngest one here. Petite with dark-brown hair and brown eyes, she makes the room feel warmer and the crowd friendlier.

"That's what *you* think." My voice is flat, but my lips quirk up. "If you knew what truly happened at a bar, you'd realize it's not as far from an operating room as one might think." Here, hearts are broken and mended, pasts buried and surfaced. Here, couples meet and break apart. I have seen it all and sometimes fancy myself part therapist, part miracle worker.

The Wolf and Moon isn't a popular bar for young adults but an older bar with worn wood and comfortable seats saved for regulars. We're filled to near capacity on weeknights, and weekends are barely tolerable.

There are trendier places for the younger crowd to go, but Zoya chose here. She was always what my mother called "an old soul."

"Refill, please," Zoya asks sweetly, pushing her empty glass to me.

"Haven't you already had two?"

Zoya is everyone's younger sister and my close friend. I can't help it.

"I'm fine," she says, an adorable divot forming between her brows. "Hey. Seriously. The better question is, how are you?"

"Fine," I lie.

I'm here, aren't I? The truth claws at my throat. We don't need to talk about the sleepless nights, the anxiety attacks, the memories that surface like ghosts when I least expect it.

I hate working here now. Every time I set foot in this place, I remember everything that happened that night in sordid, nightmarish detail.

"How are they?" I ask Zoya quietly, not meeting her eyes. She knows exactly who I'm talking about.

I haven't seen Vadka or my nephew in weeks. Months, even. I can't. It's too damn painful, and honestly, I feel like a piece of shit because of it. Who abandons their dead sister's husband and child?

Me, that's who.

But it kills me every time to look at little Luka and see my sister's eyes. To see the raw pain in Vadka that mirrors my own.

"Luka is great," Zoya says quietly. "He likes to play with Stefan."

"Ooh. Perfect."

Stefan's sister Anya married into the Kopolov family.

"Stefan is so good with him. Honestly, they all are."

A lump rises in my throat. I know. It was one of the things my sister Mariah loved best about the Kopolov family, the family she married into by proxy. Found family. Immediate extended family for her son. Something neither of us could ever offer him.

"And Vadka?"

Zoya looks away for a moment, not replying. I hate how sometimes no reply *is* a reply.

My heart aches, and unbidden tears spring to my eyes.

"I don't know about Vadka," Zoya says softly, her face pained. She bites her lip as if she's said too much.

"What?" I lean in closer. "What are you talking about?"

It's been three months.

An eternity.

Yesterday.

"Well, he—he's not doing so well after Mariah's death, is all. He took it hard."

How could he not? He fell in love with her when they were young. They got married, bought a house, and had a child. And they were *smitten*. Madly in love. I didn't believe in fate until those two met.

My nose tingles, and my throat aches.

I can't think of this now. I have work to do.

So I turn halfway to the side so Zoya can't see me, even though I can't hide the husky tone of my voice. "Yeah? What's he doing?"

Zoya shrugs a shoulder. "He's kind of gone... well. Rogue, I guess you'd call it? If he wasn't Rafail's best friend..."

Rogue?

What?

My stomach knots.

"Well, is he taking care of Luka?" I ask sharply. My pulse feels too rapid, and there's a strange ringing in my ears.

Zoya flinches. "Yes, he said he hired a nanny or something? And Luka starts school in a few weeks, so..."

He does? How did I not know that?

My heart hurts. I have to check in on them. I *have* to. I turn fully away from Zoya to compose myself.

And that's when I see her. Corner table. Too young and too pretty for her own good, wide-eyed but... brittle. Next to a man leaning in too close. His knuckles are tight, whitened around the glass, flirtation barely covering aggression and violence.

I've seen this type a hundred times before. Once is too many.

Her smile doesn't reach her eyes. Her fingers worry the napkin. *Damn it.*

I know that look. I've *worn* that look. And my sister did, too, though never because of Vadka.

I'm kind of grateful for the distraction.

Without breaking stride, I cross to the stack of clean glasses behind the bar and grab a fresh one, just like I'm minding my own business. I wink at her behind his back and jerk my chin to the women's restroom. Her eyes widen before she sits up straighter.

Inside every stall and plastered to the wall of the women's restroom is our safety protocol: a number to text if you're in trouble or an order a woman could place. An "angel shot" means *I need help.*

I watch her excuse herself and head to the restroom. I nod to Zoya, who's watched the whole exchange. With a smile at me, she heads to the restroom a few seconds later.

Zoya loves helping a woman in distress, and she's good at it. Rafail, her older brother, would lose his mind that she's anywhere near a potentially volatile situation.

I watch the man tap his fingers nervously on the table, his jaw twitching, before he glances to the side and deftly pulls something from his pocket. *Bingo.* Son of a bitch slides the pill into her drink so quickly, anyone would've missed it if they weren't expecting this exact fucking move.

Thank fuck. You can't save a girl who doesn't want to be saved, and she hasn't called foul yet. But it's against the law to drug someone, so this asshole's just bought himself a ticket to hell.

Pulse racing, my hands stay steady enough to type a message to security.

Table six. Drugged the drink. Pull him

The response is almost instant. Seconds later, four of our bouncers close in. I watch the man stiffen, his gaze jerking up.

"Problem here?" Anton asks.

The man's face drains of color. "No, I'm fine."

Zoya exits the bathroom, the young woman behind her.

"Wh-what's happening?" she stammers.

"This piece of shit tried to drug you, darling," I say to her, my voice bright and sharp. "But not tonight." Before he can respond, Yuri hauls the man up by the collar and slams him into the side of the booth.

"You think we're blind here?" Yuri spits out.

"Yuri." My tone is tight. "Take him to the back before the Kopolovs hear about this."

Rafail's instructions are clear: Anyone drugs a woman at the Wolf and Moon, we tell him, and Vadka pays a visit.

My heart beats faster. I know exactly what will happen if Vadka catches wind. It isn't the man's life I'm worried about, but I don't want Vadka to get into any more trouble.

Rafail wants word to get out that predators aren't welcome in his city. Letting Vadka loose sends a loud, bloody message: This place is protected. Women here are under our watch. You try anything, you disappear. Reputation management through fear.

Rafail doesn't do it out of kindness. He's protecting his assets. His city. His reputation. But it makes him look like a protector, and he'll take that image—especially when it's Vadka's fists that do the talking.

Yuri hesitates, glowering at me. He *wants* to see Vadka deal with this motherfucker.

Sigh. So do I. But not tonight.

"*Go*," I snap. I've got company protocol on my side, and Yuri doesn't want to lose his job.

I turn to the girl. Her hands are shaking as she clutches her purse to her chest.

"You okay?" Zoya asks softly. She comes up to us as the rest of the bar goes back to their drinks.

She nods fast. "Y-yes. I think. I—"

Zoya places a hand on her shoulder. "Hey. You're not the one who owes anyone an explanation. Do you have someone you can call?"

The girl nods and swallows.

Zoya guides her to a quiet table. The bar holds its breath, watching the scene unfold, before glasses clink and voices pick up again.

I resume my work, filling orders, when my phone buzzes with a text. I expect it to be from Anton, telling me the predator's been handled. *Handled* means he won't be back. *Handled* means tonight, the predators don't win.

But it isn't Anton.

My heart thumps hard when I see *Vadka*.

My thumb hovers. My pulse picks up.

Stupid. It's just a name. Just a man.

Just a man with hands that could crush skulls and a voice that commands attention.

Just a man *who loved my sister*.

I go back to pouring drinks like my hands aren't shaking, trying to get my shit together. Like I'm not already answering him by pretending I haven't seen it.

Finally, when there's no one else to serve, I sigh and open the text.

> **Vadka**
> Are you hiding something from me, Ruthie?

I close my eyes for a beat, already tasting the fire in his words. He didn't fuck around *before* Mariah was gone, and now that she is, any semblance of politeness has vanished.

My heart beats faster, and my hands are immediately clammy. Which one of those bastards ratted me out?

> I handled it without you needing to add
> another tat to the collage, Vadka.

The Bratva mark actions with ink. He doesn't need another murder. Not on my watch.

> **Vadka**
> You deprived me of the chance of putting a
> predator in the ground? Why?

"Excuse me? Anyone here to take a drink order?"

"Be right there. Sorry, we had a bit of a commotion just now that I had to handle." I serve the three young women standing by the bar before I text Vadka back.

> Because you have a son and I won't let my
> nephew be motherless and fatherless.

Now my hands *are* shaking.

Son of a bitch.

I put my phone away and ignore the rest of the texts.

I ignore the real reason I don't want him here tonight.

Four hours later, when the bar's finally closed for the night, I still have the nighttime routine to complete, but I pull out my phone to check my texts.

I blow out a breath. I don't think so. I have work to do. He can wait.

I run through tomorrow's prep work and wipe the bar again. Clean enough for surgery now.

> **Vadka**
> You underestimate me.

Oh, no, I don't. That's the problem.

I grab a broom and sweep the floor, mindlessly pushing crumbs and dust into a pile. I sweep aimlessly, trying to get the job done.

I considered leaving the bar after Mariah's death, but this is the place I call home, and I hate to think I'm such a wuss I couldn't stand the pressure. Seriously. I'm an *adult*.

I turn my back to the bathroom, to the place that reminds me of Mariah. I can't think back on that night. No, not now.

I told myself that if I kept coming to work, if I kept putting one foot in front of the other, I'd eventually erase the memory of her vacant eyes and Vadka's screams of pain and devastation from my memory.

But I can't.

So this time, I don't try to. I face the vacant room and the whisper of Mariah's ghost. I let the tears fall silently and don't bother to wipe them.

"Why you?" I whisper into the stillness. If it had to be a random person, why did the universe have to pick *my sister*, the woman who was married and in love, the woman with a *child*? Why her? Why sunshine in human form and not *me*?

I was the one who was alone and barely lovable. I was only a bartender. Single, and probably would be for life. I had no children, and even my mother, god bless her, would look at me through the haze of dementia and still call me *Mariah*.

Why not me?

I choke on a sob and let my shoulders sag.

Why? Why am I still here, and the only person I've ever loved more than myself, erased from existence forever?

Why?

My phone rings. I hiccup through a sob and glance blearily at the screen.

Mom.

I let out a ragged breath and answer the phone.

I let myself hope that this time, she'll remember.

"Hello?"

"Hello? Who is this?"

"Mom. Mom, it's me. You called *me*, remember?"

"Ohhh," she says, and I cringe at what I know is coming next. "Mariah, honey, can you please bring me some groceries?"

"It's not Mariah, Mom. It's Ruthie," I whisper, squeezing my eyes shut against the pain that chokes me. I don't say the next sentence that's on the tip of my tongue. I don't have the energy to explain it again. I don't have it in me to make anything harder again.

It's me, Mom.

Mariah's gone.

CHAPTER 3

GRIEF IS STRANGE. I swear to god, it rots you from the inside, so you still carry the shape of who you were, but inside, you're just... hollow.

At least that's how it feels.

The house is too quiet, even when Luka's awake and pushing his trucks into walls, complete with sound effects.

I sit in the living room, slouched in my armchair. This was one of my favorite new purchases when I first got a job with the Kopolovs—a large, well-constructed, luxury leather armchair. My family never could've afforded anything nice like this when I was a kid, and it was the first thing my mother pointed out when she came here, her nose in the air, with a sniff. "Nice chair."

It's a good chair. Sturdy. Broken in just enough to feel like mine. I've moved it from place to place every time we packed up and started over.

I used to sit here with my laptop, doing work while Mariah lingered nearby.

We had a running joke about my chair. She knew damn well it was my space, which is why she'd plant herself in it—cross-legged, staring at me with that mock-defiant glint in her eyes if I worked too late and she missed me.

A challenge. A dare.

This is the chair where I'd nurse my drinks after the latest news from Rafail and where I rocked my newborn son to sleep so Mariah could get some rest when I could cajole her into giving him up for a little while.

I have a lot of memories in this chair.

But tonight, I can barely remember one.

I stare at the empty glass I left last night on the little table between my chair and the couch. It's almost cliché. Wife dies. Drown grief and sorrow in liquor. Become dead to the world.

I'm a fucking cliché.

But there's a reason. It *does* feel better when everything's numb for a little while. It helps me ignore every single fucking reminder of my wife.

Some nights, I swear I can still hear her putzing around the kitchen, banging pots and pans and singing off-key.

But we're alone here, Luka and me.

It's why I hired a damn nanny. I had to do something.

My failures tighten around my chest.

I'm failing as a father.

Failing as a man.

Failing as the backbone of the family.

I failed my wife.

I had just closed my eyes when the doorbell rings. I glance at the time on my phone. The nanny isn't due for another hour. I like punctual, and a little bit early is okay, but this feels borderline intrusive. Unwelcome.

I push myself to my feet and try to school the inevitable scowl on my face. I can't have the new hire running this early. If my reputation precedes me, I'll have to at least pretend to be friendly.

But the second I crack open the door, I realize I've made a mistake. It's not the new nanny. It's *Ruthie.*

And she looks *pissed.*

She doesn't even wait to be invited inside, just shoves past me, a firestorm in human form.

Goddamn it. Her eyes look like Mariah's when they're flashing at me like that—the same wide, almost innocent look flecked with danger.

I want to grab her by her sturdy shoulders and throw her the fuck out.

"Hey. What the hell are you doing here?" I snap. This is my house. "Didn't you work last night?"

She rolls her eyes. "Whatever. I can subsist on very little sleep. And anyway, I couldn't sleep because of what I heard was going on with Luka."

I blink in surprise. What the fuck is she talking about? "Something going on with Luka that I need to know about?"

She crosses her arms. "You really don't know? God, Vadka, my sister would've lost her *mind*."

When Mariah was here, I rarely saw it—hardly ever thought that Ruthie and Mariah looked alike. Mariah was taller and thinner, put together, and organized. Ruthie is smaller but curvier, chaotic, and impulsive. But now that she's standing in front of me spouting off about god-knows-what, I can see it—the same flash in her eyes, the same little upturned nose, the same defiant chin. She even has a little cowlick where Mariah did, right above her right eye.

I look away. I can't fucking think like this.

"What did you hear?" I snap, my voice sharp but low and even. That's how you keep control. Stay calm. Stay cold. Stay detached.

"You have no idea? How can you not know?" She takes a step toward me. My eyes zone in on her lips, full and glossy and nothing like Mariah's. Thank fuck. I look away again.

There's something in her tone—tight, brittle—that makes me straighten. My first instinct is to snap back, but I don't.

She exhales sharply, pacing a few feet into the living room before turning on me again. "That some stupid fuck tried to follow Luka's nanny home from the park last night. She panicked and quit."

I stare at her.

"What? What the fuck? She quit and didn't tell me?"

"No one told *me*," she repeats, her throat catching.

"Tell you what?" I shake my head. "Obviously, you knew since you just—"

"That you hired a nanny, a *stranger*, to watch my sister's kid! Zoya knew about the nanny. Apparently, she ran to the Kopolovs. Rafail didn't tell you?"

I run a hand through my hair and shake my head.

Ruthie plants her hands on her hips. "Where's your phone, Vadka?"

I check my pockets. Not there. Run a hand through my hair again and look around the living room. Jesus, it looks like shit in here. I walk over to the couch and move a basket of laundry, tripping over a pair of Luka's shoes.

"No one said anything to me. I would've handled it," I grit out.

"Would you?" Ruthie asks, moving aside papers and unopened mail, empty water bottles and paper plates. "Because from where I'm standing, it looks like you don't really have shit *handled*."

I stand up and straighten my shoulders. No fucking way does this little spitfire get to march in here and tell me off in my own fucking house.

"You're in my house," I remind her, my voice quiet but full of warning. "You don't get to march your ass in here and speak to me like that. Get out, Ruthie."

Her jaw tightens. "*No.* I want to see my nephew."

"Then fucking stop telling me off." I shake my head. "Jesus. A man loses his wife and can't fucking fall apart a little?"

"When you have a kid? *No.*"

Heat flares across my chest as we continue to throw shit around, looking for my phone. "Luka is *fine*. I'm taking care of my son."

She looks over at me—*really* looks at me, and something shifts. The fury doesn't vanish but flickers into something else. Something sadder.

"I know you're drowning, Vadka." Her voice lowers. "I know how that feels. But Luka isn't. And he needs us."

That lands like a fist to my ribs. My eyes burn, and my throat's too tight.

I open my mouth to speak but can't. If I do, I'm gonna sob like a goddamn baby.

Ruthie softens. "Here's your phone," she says, handing it to me.

Sure enough, it's dead and powered off. "Dead," I say with a sigh. I cringe as soon as the words hit my lips. "I'll charge it."

She nods and wraps her arms around herself as if she's cold. As if she's trying to hold herself together.

I know that feeling too.

"Where is he?" she whispers.

"Still sleeping if your temper tantrum didn't wake him up."

She rolls her eyes. "Well, I'll stay until he wakes up. Unless you're planning on calling in sick to work and telling Rafail you won't make it in today? When it's the end of the quarter, and someone threatened your damn nanny last night?"

I should tell her to leave. She has no right. This is *my* mess.

But Luka is her nephew, and I do have to see Rafail.

"Alright. I need to grab a shower." I look toward Luka's room on instinct. I haven't had a shower without worrying about where he was or what he needed from me in so damn long. It feels good to have another adult here, even if she's spitting venom at me.

I've known Ruthie for almost as long as I knew Mariah. And I know for a fact that she burns hot but fizzles out, and her heart's as big as they come. She'll calm down. Hell, probably did her good to tell me off.

I turn to go, and something in me tells me to stop. To turn around and ask her how *she's* doing. To maybe hug her or something, something... a brother would do. What if she needs that right now?

But when I turn back, she's halfway to the kitchen, broom in hand. I look after her, open my mouth to speak, then shake my head and walk to the bathroom.

I tiptoe into my room. Luka came in at some point in the middle of the night, sprawled out on his belly, all messy hair and tangled sheets. At four years old, I can already tell he'll be tall like me but wiry like his mama. I'm glad he's asleep. I love him so much it makes me ache, but right now, I don't want him to look up at me with his mother's eyes.

I leave the door to the bathroom partly open so I can still see him and keep an eye on him as I strip out of my clothes. God, I need a shower badly. I smell like I used to when I played sports in college. Mariah used to wrinkle her nose and tell me to hit the shower, so naturally, I'd tackle her and kiss her all sweaty, just so she'd fight me, and I could over-power her and kiss her. I smile to myself as I throw the clothes onto the floor and turn the shower on.

I look through the crack in the doorway to see Luka's still sleeping soundly. I close my eyes and pinch the bridge of my nose. God, my baby boy. So young to lose his mama.

I step into the shower, grateful for the hot, steamy water. Shampoo bottle's empty, so I squirt some weird purple toddler stuff onto my palm and make do. I clean fast, wanting to get back to my boy and get out of here so I can get to work. Ruthie isn't kidding. Rafail doesn't fuck around at the end of the quarter, and my cover job as owner and general manager of Black Line Security means I have reports to give him.

I mentally scold myself for losing it. Ruthie is right. My house is in shambles, I don't remember the last time I shopped for groceries, and Rafail will kick my ass for letting my phone die. I don't like feeling this out of control. I'm never like this.

I'll stare into space when something triggers a memory, then blink and come to hours later. Time passes weirdly when you're grieving, I guess.

How long does grief last? I would've thought I'd feel better by now. And Luka barely seemed to register the loss of his mama. He's asked for her a few times and cried when she didn't come home, but he's too young to really understand that she's gone forever.

And I know how this will go. He'll grow up with only vague memories of her. And then, eventually, he might even forget her. I lean my head against the wall as a fresh sob rips from my chest. It's safer to cry in the shower. I can hide the signs, and it's harder for anyone to hear.

The grief hits me like a tidal wave. The fact that she's gone, that I'll never hold her again, never talk to her again, never see her witness all my son's firsts ever again, feels like a reality that's too hard for me to swallow. My shoulders shake, and something loosens in my chest. The grief feels wrenched from me, raw and so painful it kills.

I cry until relief finally comes. My father used to beat the shit out of me for crying. Ironic. Maybe it's why I feel the need to hide when I do. But goddamn, a man's got to let some of this out.

I let the water splash on my face and wash away my tears, wipe my eyes, and peek through the curtain to see Luka still sleeping soundly.

Fuck. I'm all stuffed up and snotty, and my head aches. I hate this. I can't let myself fall apart every time I step in the fucking shower.

I turn the water off and reach for a towel when I realize I didn't bring one in with me. I grit my teeth and look at the gross clothes I tossed on the floor and the tiny hand towel that's askew, probably needs to be changed, and wouldn't even dry my shoulder.

Gah-reat.

I don't want to wake up Luka, but—

"Ruthie," I hiss, pulling the shower curtain around me for some privacy. I can hear her in the kitchen, but it isn't that far away. "*Ruthie.*"

Luka stirs. I freeze. The kid needs his sleep.

Shit.

I could jump out of the shower naked, run to the hallway where the clean towels are, and risk letting my sister-in-law see me streak through my house soaking wet.

Or not.

I roll my eyes and let out a low, sharp whistle. Luka doesn't move, and the sound in the kitchen ceases. I whistle again. A few seconds later, I hear the telltale sound of her footsteps heading this way. I look over to see Luka rolling over but still snoring softly.

"Did you *whistle* at me?" Ruthie hisses from the doorway.

"I forgot a towel."

She snorts at me, the little brat. "And?"

"*Ruthie.* Get me a towel."

"Say *please.*"

I grit my teeth. After her ass is out of here, I'm changing the locks. "*Please.*"

"And give me your credit card."

"Are you blackmailing me for a towel?" I hiss. *Jesus.*

"No, you need groceries," she says, smug as sin. "Hang on."

I hear her footsteps retreat, slow and unhurried, like she wants me to freeze to death or suffer. Probably both.

But she doesn't hand me a towel. She fucking drapes it, deliberately, on the hook by the curtain, just out of reach.

She knows what she's doing.

"Here you go," she says, tilting her head at me. "Don't ever say I never gave you anything."

I glare through the steam, water still streaming down my body. "You could've passed it to me."

"I suppose I could have. And you could've acted like a grown-up and remembered your towel. Seriously, Vadka. You had one job."

That smile. That wicked, sweet smirk of hers, that's all Ruthie.

"You really want to play this game?" I growl. I wrap the towel around my waist and shove the curtain aside. Her eyes grow wide, and in a second, she quickly sweeps her eyes down the length of my bare chest, over my inked shoulders and torso, before she realizes what she's doing. Her cheeks flame red.

I see the moment she realizes I was crying—her own eyes well with tears, and she looks away.

"Come on," she whispers. "Get dressed. I made breakfast."

We both look over to the sleeping form of my baby boy.

"He always sleep in your bed?"

I shake my head. "Nah. Just a lot since Mariah's been gone though."

She nods, eying my dirty clothes strewn on the floor. My eyes linger on a pair of socks. I wasn't this sloppy before she died. I'm a grown-ass man who likes his shit clean. And Mariah would lose her *mind* over the fucking socks. Every time I left them on the floor, she'd act like I dropped a live grenade in the living room.

I remember the last time we fought over them—sharp words, tempers flaring. I backed her against the wall and kissed the fight out of her, then did every stitch of damn laundry in the house while she watched, smug and beautiful.

Ruthie's voice cuts through the memory.

"Trash is full," she says over her shoulder as she leaves the room. "Take it out on your way out. I'm cleaning the fridge; you can handle the trash."

I grunt but don't reply. Instead, I salute her back. I'll do it.

I grab clothes out of the drawer and put them on top of the dresser. "Here's my card," I tell her, taking it out of my wallet.

"On second thought, keep it," she says, still whispering. "Use it for a haircut. Maybe even shave while you're at it."

I raise an eyebrow at her.

"My sister liked you clean-shaven," she whispers. Her voice shakes. It hits me in the chest, bright and honest.

"Yeah." I turn away. "She did."

Ruthie leaves, and I get changed and run my fingers through my too-long hair.

I don't shave. I bend and give Luka a kiss on the top of his tousled head before I go.

"He wakes up grumpy. Make him pee. Don't give him any juice until he eats."

"Are you giving me orders?"

"Who, me?" I splay a hand across my chest. "Never. How long are you staying?"

She swallows hard and looks away, turning back to the stove. "As long as you need me. Shift starts at six p.m., and I need to get home to get ready for it."

I nod. "I'll send someone to relieve you much sooner than that. And I'll interview more nannies today."

She looks over at me, her eyes welling with tears and her lower lip trembling. I can't help it. I walk over to her and reach for her to give her a big hug. She fits in my arms and rests her head on my chest, but she doesn't cry.

"I miss her," she whispers. "It's hard being here. I'm sorry. It's why I haven't come."

I can't help myself. I kiss the top of her head.

Why did I do that?

Ruthie freezes as if she doesn't know how to respond.

"I know. You don't have to stay. I can take Luka to the Kopolovs; someone will be there." They're my extended family now.

She shakes her head. "No, I miss him too. I want to see him. I need to. I'm sorry, Vadka."

It's right around then that I realize I'm still holding her. That she smells good, and she's curvy and pretty and... vulnerable.

Like me.

I let her go like she's on fire.

Step back. Turn away hard.

"I'll be back as soon as I can," I say, the door slamming shut behind me.

Grief makes people do crazy things.

I leave before I do something I regret.

CHAPTER 4

VADKA

As soon as I get to the bike, it feels as if a weight's been lifted. Luka's nanny was a middle-aged woman who taught him to sit at the table politely and chew with his mouth closed. But she was stern and a little detached, and even though I knew Luka to be safe, he cried every time I left.

He'll be thrilled to see Ruthie when he wakes up. He loves her.

My phone connects to the Bluetooth on my helmet, revealing so many missed calls and texts from Rafail, I cringe.

He's gonna kick my ass.

He might be my best friend, but Rafail does not fuck around when it comes to the brotherhood. I ought to know. I'm one of the few members who wasn't born into the Kopolov family by blood. We've been friends since child-hood, long before his parents died and he became the guardian to his siblings before he was barely an adult himself.

When we were just kids, neither of us could've imagined the way we'd both face the kind of loss you never fully recover from.

I hit the button and call him.

"Where the *fuck* have you been?" he growls.

"Fell asleep. I didn't realize my phone was dead."

I hear him blow out a breath on the other side of the line. When he lowers his voice and gets calm, heads are about to roll. I grit my teeth.

"Vadka. We talked. I can't let this continue." I can almost imagine him shaking his head on the other side of the line. "I swear to god, brother, you fuck up like this again, and I'll demote you."

Demotion in the Bratva is a punishment worse than death. I'd rather die than face the embarrassment.

"It won't happen again, brother. I'm sorry."

He sighs. "Ruthie's at the house?"

"Yeah. She text you?"

"Yeah. Alright. Don't come to the house. Meet me at Black Line. We have shit to go over, and it'll be more fastidious that way."

"Got it."

I'm only a few minutes away.

I park my motorcycle in the *Owner* spot and tuck my helmet under my arm before I check my phone. Nothing from Ruthie.

Luka up yet?

I hate leaving him.

A few seconds later, I get a response. It's a picture of Luka sitting at the kitchen table, grinning, eating something topped with billows of whipped cream. I can't help but smile.

No juice until he ate first?

Ruthie
Yeah yeah

Little brat. I roll my eyes. I can still see her standing in the living room, eying my five o'clock shadow like she wanted to touch me.

My sister liked you clean-shaven.

It stuck with me for some reason, probably because I remember the way she and her sister used to bicker about it. Mariah hated beards, and Ruthie said she loved them and always teased me when she caught me first thing in the morning. Silly, pointless argument I thought I'd forgotten.

What the fuck's the matter with me? I can't think like this. *God.*

I move through the front of Black Line Security. My men nod. Some murmur greetings, but no one makes small talk. I get it. They don't know which version of me they're getting today. Hell, *I* don't know which version of myself I'm getting today.

My father was a useless asshole, but he loved his proverbs and spouted them with regularity. I still remember some of them.

Gore ne sprosit, kogda pridet.

Grief will not ask when it arrives.

And isn't that a bitch.

I swipe my badge at the entrance to the privacy room, the one with the maps, screens, and encrypted comms. This isn't any old security firm but a fortress and a front. And every man here knows which side of that line he stands.

Rafail is already waiting for me.

He doesn't look up when I enter but just points at the screen. The motherfucker can hold a grudge.

"They've moved."

Of course they fucking have.

I take in the red dots blinking on the map. "Any casualties?"

"None today, but it's only a matter of time, Vadka. And this was near a fucking *school.*"

"Jesus."

My jaw tightens.

"And the thumb drive?"

"Still encrypted. Even Matvei hasn't gotten shit."

I don't answer. Instead, I walk toward the screens, take the mouse, and pull up the files. I move fast. The Irish aren't stupid. They hit when we're weakest.

"You can't slip. Not now, Vadka," Rafail says softly.

I still. I hate that tone. It's worse than when he curses me out.

"I know."

"Your phone was off. You missed the alert last night. You didn't check until hours later, and only because Ruthie told you, didn't she?"

I don't answer. He's right.

"You used to be the first on-site. Now I have to send men to cover for you."

I turn to face him. "I'm sorry. Luka's had a few rough nights."

He raises a brow, cold and collected. "And you think the Irish give a shit about Luka's sleep schedule? You think they'll wait until you've had your morning coffee?" He leans forward, elbows resting on his knees. "Brother, I've been exactly where you are."

I know he has. I remember it vividly. It was the first night my father ever hit me, and I hit him back.

"I was eighteen when my parents died and left me with everything. I became a fucking father and *pakhan* overnight. I couldn't fall apart." He shakes his head. "The same day of their funeral, I buried my parents, then went straight to the butcher shop to slit the throat of a traitor who thought to make good on our temporary setback. Fucking asshole owed us and thought he'd run, thought grief made me soft."

I nod. I didn't know that. I wasn't in the Bratva, not yet.

"You want to feel something, Vadka? Do it *after* the war. *After* you know your son's safe. *After* you know you can wake up in the morning and depend on the sun to keep on rising."

Rafail's voice slices clean through the fog in my head, cutting deeper than a blade. I don't look at him. I stare at the red lips still pulsing on the screen, glowing like fresh wounds. Targets.

An odd one. My jaw is clenched so tight that I can feel the tension throbbing behind my ears. Or is that a headache? I've lost track.

"I won't ever tell you to stop grieving," Rafail says, his voice rough. I know he speaks from experience. "I don't know if that ever fully goes away. But I'm telling you to weaponize it before someone innocent gets caught in the crossfire. Be the fucking monster they're terrified of. Not reckless, not going off half-cocked on a shooting spree. Not the man who's burned himself the fuck out and is too tired to show up."

My eyes snap to his. He's not calling me any of those things, but he's telling me that's what could happen. We've both seen it happen before. We both know we could see it happen again.

I think of Matvei, how he watched his sister die, and his brother—killed by his own hand because of betrayal. He continued to show up, even after we found out his parents betrayed him, too, that his whole fucking family was useless. And yet—he's still here.

But now he's in love, and I wonder if it hits the same.

I bite down the instinct to snap back at Rafail, that old defense mechanism. I could tell him I'm doing my best, that I'm raising a son alone, that I'm walking through my dead wife's ghost every single fucking day.

But I know him, and I know myself. He doesn't want excuses. And I don't want to be weak. He wants results. So do I.

So I draw in a breath and let it out slowly. And I find myself wondering, oddly, what Ruthie is doing right now. Is Luka in her presence? Are they curled up on the couch watching TV? Did he help her load the dishes after breakfast? Is she sitting on the floor with him, pushing around his little race car that he loves so much?

She always had more patience with those things than I did —just like her sister—but Ruthie was crazier. Wilder. Mariah would be the one reminding Luka to brush his teeth, and Ruthie would be wondering how many more cookies they could have before bed.

Rafail clears his throat. I did it again—let my memory and focus wane. "What's the plan? What do you need from me?"

He lifts his chin toward the screen. "This school right here? It's not random. You know one of our shell companies owns the land behind it. What else can you tell me about this?"

I nod. I know one of our shell companies owns the land

behind it. That site is clean. Untouched for years, but now? Movement.

"They're using it as a base."

My stomach sinks, and my hands clench into fists. Right near the fucking school.

"We have to keep the kids safe."

"Yeah. It's a fine line... Right now, no one's said a word. Everyone's still going to class like nothing's wrong. Local police don't know a fucking thing." His voice is flat. Cold. "Fucking Irish scum using innocence like a shield."

They don't fucking care that the consequences for crime so close to school grounds carry a heavier weight.

I flex my hands, knuckles cracking under the pressure.

"We take them out."

Rafail nods once. "Quietly. No casualties. No mess. You lead."

Of course I fucking will. This is the price of coming back to life—of clawing my way out of the fucking bottle and putting my grief on hold. What did he say? *Weaponize it.*

I roll my shoulders, already calculating the angle of the approach. How many men. What time. What tools. "I'll handle it."

He studies me for a beat too long. "You sure I can trust you?"

There's a lot on the line.

I meet his gaze. "I'm done fucking up, Rafail."

He nods again, slower this time. He believes me—or at least he wants to. "You didn't fuck up, brother. You're grieving. There's a difference. Not once have you done anything I wouldn't have allowed. But you're on the verge of making decisions that you might regret, and I don't want that for you. Or for me."

I know. My throat burns.

"I'll have a file sent to your office. Clean team. Matvei will pull surveillance. Zoya's on inside recon as usual. You've got until Thursday."

"Thursday?"

He smirks, but it looks sad. "Luka's school has an orientation parent breakfast Friday morning. Thought you'd wanna make it. That's when they show him around, and he gets to meet his new teachers and all that shit. And..."

Fucker.

I blink, caught off guard. "You scheduled this around that?"

His smirk deepens. "I didn't say I was heartless. Just mean."

I'm already turning, my mind whirring. I can do this. Purpose. Rage—harnessed. I exit the ops room and move toward my office, my mind on Ruthie and Luka. Rafail's on the phone, calling a meeting. So I take a second to tap out a quick message to her.

> Don't let him eat all the whipped cream, he gets a tummy ache.

Ruthie
Did you just say… tummy ache?

SECONDS LATER, my screen lights up with a photo—Luka at the kitchen table, his bedhead wild, cheeks puffed out, whipped cream on his nose, his cheeks, and his chin, grinning like he didn't cry himself to sleep the night before. I can't help the smile that twitches at the corner of my mouth.

No juice yet, right?

Ruthie
What do you think, I'm new at this?

Fucking brat.

Ruthie
He said please. I bribed him with extra whipped cream and I regret nothing.

I have a quiet laugh. My thumb hovers over the screen longer than it should. What am I doing? I tap out a message before I can regret it.

He's lucky you're there. I mean it.

The typing bubbles appear. Disappear. Appear again. Like I've set her off-kilter. She's always quick with a response.

So I send another one.

I have shit to do. I'll be home late.

Ruthie
Oh no. Missing thrilling morning debates
about cartoons and existential dread over
coffee?

I groan.

You let him watch that stupid blue dog
cartoon again, didn't you?

Ruthie
Don't come for me. That stupid fucking
blue dog is holding this family together,
Vadka. !

I stare at the word longer than I should. Family. It shouldn't fit, but it does—too fucking well. Maybe that's the worst of it because when I close my eyes, I can still see her in my kitchen—barefoot, hair twisted up like a storm cloud, leaning over Luka with that half smile like the world isn't ending around us, and her heart isn't broken into pieces like mine.

Standing where she used to stand, where she used to sway her hips and hum when she made her coffee. Ruthie sings off-key. Mariah had the voice of an angel. It's... different.

And I miss her.

I miss her so fucking much.

Luka reminds me of Mariah. And Ruthie... in a way I didn't expect.

CHAPTER 5

RUTHIE

I DON'T REALIZE that I am still staring at my phone until Luka pulls at my arm. I blink, disoriented, and wonder what just happened. Vadka feels like a connection to my sister that no one else has. Not really.

Mom remembers the Mariah of my childhood—the one with braids and scraped knees, who danced barefoot in the yard—but she barely remembers me, not anymore. So a visit to her always leaves me hollower than before. More raw. More exposed. It makes everything more painful.

My only friends, other than Zoya, are a couple of locals, the ones who've stuck around, and a couple of bar regulars who can still look me in the eye. Even they talk to me now like I'm a walking time bomb, ticking slow, dangerous. That's nothing new. People have done that before. But not them. Not the ones who used to treat me like I was made of iron. Now I feel fragile, like I'm made of thin glass. And I hate it. God, I hate it so much.

But Vadka talks about Mariah like she's still here. And a part of me—one I don't say out loud—believes maybe she is.

One month after she died, Matvei's wife, Anissa, came to the bar. She didn't say much. Just ordered a drink and pushed a pretty purple crystal into my palm. "This is amethyst," she said gently, like her words might bruise. "It's for healing. Some believe it connects us to our loved ones."

I thanked her as politely as I could manage and slid the drink across the bar. Matvei calls her his little witch. She's always been into that stuff—tarot cards, crystals, essential oils, all of it. I never paid much attention to it before. Just smiled and nodded.

I tossed the rock into the back of the change drawer because I didn't want to look at it. But somehow, putting it there created the exact opposite effect. Now I have to look at it every time I open the drawer to give a customer change. Doesn't happen often, not these days. No one pays with cash anymore. But still. A couple of times a night is maybe too often.

I should move that. Do crystals need to be cleaned or something?

"Can I have more whipped cream, Mama?"

My heart leaps into my throat. My eyes blur with sudden, stinging tears. But he stops himself and quickly shakes his head.

"No. Not Mama. Sorry."

Hearing him say "sorry" in that small voice—so soft, so careful—would break anyone's heart. Mine cracks down the middle. So I crouch down in front of him, meet his eyes, and force a watery smile. "It's fine, baby. I do look a little like her, don't I?"

He nods, a small motion. Then he looks back down at his pancakes and doesn't say much more.

"Here. You can have a little more whipped cream."

"You give me more than Papa."

Of course I do. Vadka is such a scrooge. *Give him too much whipped cream, and he'll have a tummy ache...*

I roll my eyes at the thin air and turn back to the dishes, wiping at my face quickly before he sees.

"We have to go to the grocery store and buy some food. Do you want to come with Auntie?"

"Yes! I'll be your helper," he says, swinging his little legs with enthusiasm. I glance at him over my shoulder and smile, even as something in my chest tugs painfully. I know Vadka only sees Mariah when he looks at him—the same bright eyes, the same rosy cheeks, the same soft brown curls that frame his face just right.

But he looks a good bit like his daddy too. He has his mouth, that stern little curve, the strong jaw and a cleft chin. And even though his face is still round from childhood, I can already see it—that it's going to sharpen one day. Harden the same way Vadka's did. He's got those dark brows and that same quiet, serious expression.

I turn away. Why am I thinking that right now?

Some kids look just like their moms. Some look just like their dads. Then some, like Luka, are perfect blends of both.

My phone buzzes with a text, and my heart leaps into my throat again, stupidly hoping it's Vadka.

What the hell is wrong with me?

I can't help it though. These little exchanges—these short, awkward, strange texts—have been the most excitement I've had in months. The most... *feeling* I've had in months. I don't fully understand it, but somehow, our shared grief makes mine feel a little lighter. Like I was dragging it alongside me, and he wordlessly came up beside me and lifted it with me.

When I'm by myself, or worse, in front of other people, the effort of hiding it feels impossible. But I don't have to hide it with Vadka. And that makes it easier to carry.

"I'm starting school soon, Auntie," Luka says, swinging his feet at the table as he downs the last of his juice.

"More juice?"

I pour him a little more and can already imagine Vadka's stern look. The shake of his head. The quiet, parental disapproval.

He wouldn't let him have any more. Whatever.

"Are you excited?" I ask, forcing brightness into my voice like sunlight through a crack in the wall. "We should go get you some clothes and shoes and things. A backpack too."

He nods, face lighting up like I've just promised him the world. And maybe, for a little boy, I have.

He's starting preschool in the fall—something Mariah never wanted him to do. She liked being his teacher and had decided, with Vadka, that they would enroll Luka in school when he turned six years old, something quite common in these parts.

There was a waiting list though—a long one. The kind that takes years, not months. I remember when they first put his name down. Mr. I Plan Everything—Vadka—figured that if Luka could get in by the time he was five, he'd ease into childhood school a little more smoothly. I know Vadka wants him to have the routine though.

"Help me put the dishes in the dishwasher," I tell him with a smile. "We're gonna do some cleaning before we head to the supermarket."

He gets up from the table and eyes his plate. "I don't want to."

I lift a brow at him and wonder if he would have the audacity to tell *Vadka* he didn't want to.

I first met Vadka when I was only fourteen years old. He was my older sister's boyfriend, and I crushed on him at first, but then quickly squashed it. She was madly in love with him.

We all had shitty backgrounds. His dad was an abusive asshole, and my mom was almost a child herself. So he eased into our lives, and once he came, he never left.

I knew him before he was brought in, and I knew once Rafail became guardian of his siblings—and the *pakhan* of the Kopolov family Bratva, it was only a matter of time before Vadka would follow his best friend.

Vadka and Mariah made sure I went to school. They were serious about it, about schedules and clean clothes and grades and parent-teacher meetings. His dad was a member of the *Night Wolves*, kind of like Russia's version of Hell's Angels. He took his temper out on Vadka as a punching bag. I still remember the night Vadka said he would never raise his hand to his child, no matter what, and that he would be the dad he didn't have.

He and Mariah agreed. They were an excellent team. They were the kind of parents I wished I could've had. Sometimes, it just works out that way.

I stare at my nephew and wonder. We have a whole day together. They're letting him get away with being naughty now—that's going to make for a very long day. Is he trying to get attention, or what? I don't know anything about raising kids. So I tilt my head to the side and give him a look.

"You ate off that plate. I made you breakfast. The right thing to do is to put it in the dishwasher."

"No," Luka says, crossing his arms over his chest. He still has those little dimples in his arms that remind me of him as a toddler.

"Would you tell your papa no?" I ask, and it feels weirdly reminiscent of *Wait until your father gets home*, so I immediately regret it—but it has the desired effect. He opens his eyes wide, then shakes his head and hangs it a little.

"No."

"Why not?"

"Because I would get in trouble with Papa."

I cross my arms and muster up the sternest look I can manage. Why is it so easy for me to stand up to adults, but I'm learning a four-year-old can get the better of me?

"Do you think you won't get in trouble with your auntie?"

He's right—he won't. But maybe I can bluff?

He frowns and looks as if he's thinking it over.

"I told you we were going shopping, and I'm not going to buy you a treat if you're not going to behave yourself," I explain. "Don't you know that?"

I totally will.

He thinks this over, then picks up his plate and brings it over to me. I blow out a breath. Crisis averted.

Okay. So bribery. Bribery works.

"You help me get this laundry going, we'll whip through this house, and I'll let you watch a quick show before we go. Okay?"

My head hurts. Vadka was right—I didn't get much sleep last night. I didn't get home until two a.m., and then I couldn't sleep, thinking about my nephew and brother-in-law. Thinking about Mariah.

Some people let their lives come to a halt when they're grieving. They don't eat, don't sleep, don't work. And then some people keep on going, pretending that their lives haven't come to a screeching halt, pretending that the sun still rises, pretending that they are not carrying a boulder on their chest every minute of every day.

I guess not feeling anything would be worse than this.

I guess. I wouldn't know.

So I throw myself into cleaning the house. That's what I've always done, and it definitely does help. I put on some music and load the dishwasher. I gather up all the dirty laundry and put it in the laundry room, start a wash cycle, and fold wrinkled clothes in the dryer. I put away Luka's toys, take the recycling to the porch for Vadka, and make a note to myself to organize the pantry and refrigerator later.

Right now, we'll get things started. The freezer is nearly empty, but I find a few meals labeled. Looks like he threw some casseroles in the freezer when the old babushka came to visit. Old Russian women don't like to see Russian widowers go hungry. It's kind of a law. I pull out one of the casseroles and slide it onto the counter to thaw a little bit, then go to check on Luka. He's got a tattered blanket pulled up to his chest, and he's staring at the screen. He gives me a little wave.

"A few more minutes and then we're going to get ready to go."

My phone buzzes with another text, and I figure it's another ad, but this time, when I look, it's a phone call. Oh no. It's Mom's facility. I hit *answer* and pray for good news.

"This is Ruth."

"Hello, Ruth," a brisk voice says on the other line. "We've had an episode with your mother, and I'm hoping you can talk some sense into her."

Oh no. Why now?

I can hear screaming in the background. Shit.

I grit my teeth. "What's going on?"

"She's refusing to take her meds," a nurse says.

How the hell do they expect me to help her take her meds? That's their job, not mine.

"Yes, so? That's your job. I can't make her take her meds."

If it's possible to hear someone roll their eyes on the other end of a phone, I just did.

"You're her daughter. We tried her other daughter's number, but it went to voicemail, so we called you next."

I clench my teeth together. "This is at least the sixth time I've told you that her older daughter is not with us anymore. Please strike her phone number from your list."

"Okay, fine. No need to get snippy with me."

Lovely. Someone who's chosen to get defensive rather than recognize that they're rubbing salt in an open wound.

"Thank you. Put me on speaker, and I'll talk to my mother."

"Have to go potty," Luka says, his legs crossed.

"Go. Go use the potty. You're a big boy."

I hope? Does he need me to, like... wipe or something? What the hell?

"Hello? Are you still there?" the rude voice says on the other end of the line.

"I'm here. I'm just here with my nephew."

"Mariah, I am not taking these meds," my mother says. "They're poisoning me! You have no idea what they've done to me! They made me take medication the other night that made me loopy. I couldn't remember a damn thing."

I actually let out a little laugh. Mom not remembering a damn thing is definitely not the medication.

"Mom, the doctors know what kind of medication you need. You have to trust them, okay? Just take it this one time, and I'll talk to them when I come in to see you later today."

I pinch the bridge of my nose and check on Luka to see him doing his business unassisted. Good boy. Thank fuck.

The washing machine buzzes, and I look over to see a red light blinking. I narrow my eyes at it. Wait, is that an error code? Oh god, no. I don't have time for this.

I shake my head and wish that Vadka were here. How does he do all this on his own? He doesn't have Mom to deal with —often, anyway. But he has a son and a business and a house. And this all sorta feels like a two-person job.

Mom always loved him. He was the one who could reason with her. Her decline began shortly after he came into our lives... I know he goes to see her sometimes. Maybe that's the catch—that's what I need. I need him to go with me to see her.

Everybody loves him. He can be charming when he wants to be.

"If you don't take your medication, you're going to get sick," I say to my mom, wondering if that's actually true. "Tell her again which one this is," I ask the nurse.

"It's her anti-seizure medication," she snaps at me. I grit my teeth.

"Mom, if you take it, I'll bring you those cookies you like

from Anya's bakery," I say, like I do with Luka. Mom seems to be thinking this over.

"No."

Jesus.

I grit my teeth and shake my head. "If you don't take your medication, I'm shutting off your Wi-Fi!" Oh god, now I'm fucking parenting a teen.

"I don't use Wi-Fi!" she snaps back.

I shake my head. Of course she does; she just doesn't realize she does. *Great.*

"I don't know what to tell you," I tell the nurse. "I don't have any more control over her than you do."

"Can you bring in your husband? He always talks to her. He was the only one who was able to convince her to visit her therapist last week."

My husband? Why does the universe hate me?

Wait. He was?

"He's not my husband," I say quietly. "He's my brother-in-law."

"Whatever, can he come in?"

I blow out a breath and feel like I could either cry or break something. "Yeah, I can ask him to come in."

"Okay, bye." The line goes dead.

"Auntie, I need help wiping."

Literally, fuck my life.

An hour later, the house is clean, laundry is tumbling in the dryer, dinner is thawing, and Luka is happily swinging his feet in the back of the car in his car seat. We're heading for respite at the Kopolovs.

How do people do this full-time?

Vadka will probably be at work, but I know Zoya is on break.

We show up at lunchtime. As soon as the front door opens, my heart feels lighter. Zoya stands on the other side, her eyes twinkling. She gets to one knee and opens her arms up big for Luka.

"Oh my goodness, look how much taller you've gotten," she says, ruffling his hair. "Give Auntie Zoya a big hug."

They're not related by blood, but they're Vadka's family, so they might as well be.

"Auntie Zoya, Aunt Ruthie gave me *ten times* as much whipped cream as Papa does," Luka says, grinning like the cat that ate the fucking canary. I tell him to hush in case someone's going to rat me out.

"*And* my tummy hurts," Luka says.

Shit.

"I told you that would happen if you gave him too much," a deep voice comes from behind Zoya.

Well, great. Guess Vadka is not at the office.

"Hey, buddy." His eyes crinkle around the edges, and his face softens when he sees Luka.

"Papa!" Luka does a full run at Vadka and tackles him at the knees, but Vadka has the wherewithal to brace himself before impact. He catches him, swings him up into his arms, and kisses his cheek. Then he fixes me with a stern look.

"How much juice did he have?"

"Not too much," I lie, looking away. "You're out. We're just coming in for a quick visit before we go to the supermarket." And I give Vadka a sharp look. "And I don't need a lecture about not buying cookies and sweets." As if I'm going to get through this without chocolate?

He runs a hand through his hair and nods. "Thanks for doing that. Do you want me to grill tonight when I get home?" I shrug.

"Do you have to go to work? What time do you have to be in?"

"It's my night off."

It feels domestic and homey and... *wrong*.

Zoya takes Luka's hand and leads him to the kitchen, so I'm in the empty foyer with Vadka. My god, why does the man wear a suit like that? It's obscene. He looks so fucking hot all dressed up. He may have lost a little weight and looks a little gaunt around the eyes, but he definitely hasn't skipped his gym routine. If anything... it kinda looks like he's thrown himself into it harder, which tracks.

Fuck. I need to get laid. I *can't* look at my brother-in-law like this. I need to go to the bar, find a sweet young guy who's eager to please, and seduce the fuck out of him. I'd give him a good night to ease my conscience.

"How'd the morning go?" he asks, his hands in his pockets.

A lump rises in my throat. I want to tell him that Luka called me Mama. I want to tell him that I don't like being in the place where my sister's presence still lingers. I want to tell him my mother's getting worse, and she doesn't know me anymore.

I want to tell him everything and nothing.

"Fine. Luka's a good boy. Mostly."

Vadka grows stern, his brow coming together. "He's gotten more stubborn and defiant since Mariah's been gone. Did he give you a hard time?" he asks.

Why does he look at me like that? I don't like it when he looks at me like that.

No. Scratch that—I like it too much when he looks at me like that.

I swallow. "Eh, he likes to push boundaries, but we figured it out." I don't want to tattle on the little guy, but I'm not gonna lie either.

He nods. "It'll help him to have the structure of school. Hey —Zoya has a list of nannies, but we've got some shit I need to do. Do you think you could help her look over the list? Maybe interview some of them?"

He shoves his hands in his pockets and looks away. "I don't think anyone is as invested in who watches Luka as me—except you."

Do I nod too quickly? Am I too eager?

What is it about the two of us that makes me feel like a little girl crushing on her big sister's boyfriend all over again?

"Thanks."

He swallows, and his voice is a little husky. "I'll be home by five. We'll have an early dinner so we can get Luka to bed. You said no work tonight?"

I nod and swallow hard. "Yeah."

"Okay."

"I pulled a casserole out of the freezer."

The corner of his lips quirks up. How did I not know that he had a dimple there?

My heart turns over in my chest. I wish that it wouldn't.

"You did?"

"Yeah. There were a lot. Whatever it is—we can eat it as a side dish or something. Text me what you need from the grocery store, and I'll add it to my list."

He smiles—a flash of white teeth against those sinfully full lips.

God, he's so fucking hot, all raw, masculine brutality. The hint of a beard on his jaw, the coiled muscle under the black shirt that fits like a second skin, the tats inked across his skin. He was more awkward when he was younger—shoulders too big for his body. But now he's all man.

Fuck.

Rugged and broad, there's a reason heads snap around

wherever he goes. And when he turns those warm brown eyes on you, there's no escaping.

He hasn't dated yet. I know he hasn't. It's too soon. But I wonder if he will. I wonder if he'll remarry. I wonder who she'll be. I wonder if I'll like her.

I hate these kinds of thoughts, so I push them away. But when he starts to smile at me—

"Look at you, all grown up and mature." He shakes his head.

"Shut up," I tell him. But I can't help my smile, adding, "You still remember that night? You had to come get me because I ran out of gas on the highway?"

His mouth curves, slow and dangerous. He remembers.

"You didn't just run out of gas," he says, his voice low and rough. "You called us crying. Said someone was following you."

Us. I called Mariah and Vadka. My anchors.

Heat floods my face, but I still laugh. "I wasn't *crying*," I lie, even though we both know the truth.

His smile deepens, those gorgeous lips tilting in a way that makes my stomach knot. "You were terrified."

Not mocking. Not cruel. Just a bittersweet memory.

"You always came when I called you," I say, quieter.

"Of course I did," he adds, softer now. Serious. For a second, the air between us vibrates. "You were just a kid then."

Neither of us talks.

I'm not anymore.

"Do you actually change your car oil and check your tires now?" he asks, smirking.

I don't tell him that, no, I'm still absolute shit with my car.

"Well..."

He smiles and shakes his head. "I gotta get back to work."

"What's going on? Is everything okay?"

I hear things at the bar sometimes—before the Kopolovs do—but not always.

He looks away and blows out a breath. "We're not entirely sure yet."

"Is it the Irish?"

The Irish mob, Keenan McCarthy's Clan, were the ones who killed my sister. They're not welcome in the bar anymore. None of them. As soon as I hear the accent, I look for the tattoo that marks them as McCarthy—but no one's come in for months.

"Yeah."

But when he doesn't offer any more information, I don't push. "Tell me if you need me."

I can at least spy—though not from the bar.

"Of course."

Then he's gone—without a backward glance or a word. Just gone. And again, it feels like I pick up the weight of my grief.

But when I go to find Luka, Grandfather is in the kitchen

too. Savva Kopolov is everyone's grandpa. I'm happy to see him.

"Ruthie," he says with a bright smile that makes his eyes twinkle at the edges. "It's a *delight* to see you. How are you?"

God, he's so cute.

He asks in a way that isn't fake but shows genuine concern.

I smile at him. "I'm great," I lie. "Better since I spent a little time with this guy." I ruffle Luka's hair.

He nods softly. He understands.

"It's hard—seeing the people who remind you of the ones you've lost."

I answer quietly, "I know."

"But I heard you stayed at work, sweetheart. That's brave of you. I'm not sure I could've done that myself."

I shrug. I'm not sure how "brave" I am.

"Yeah, I did. But I have a home there. And, you know, I can do hard things and all that."

He lays a heavy, bony hand on top of mine.

"I know. I know you. And I'm proud of you."

Proud of you. There's a shortage of people in this world who have said, *I'm proud of you.* And it makes me feel damn good.

I lean in and kiss his papery cheek. "Thank you." He smells like mint toothpaste and aftershave.

"Zoya and I were just looking over these nannies who are applying to work with Luka," he says, frowning.

"Vadka asked me to take a look."

"We had four people," Zoya says, "but one canceled, so now we have three."

"You think they got the memo about what happened to the other nanny?" Grandfather asks.

"Yeah," I say softly.

"I wish *I* could..." Zoya begins.

"No." Grandfather shakes his head. "I know you care about them. I know you'd be excellent with Luka, but you have a future, and you can't always be the one who fills in the gaps when someone is needed, Zoya. You've been a little mother since you were a child, and you like taking care of people, but it's important to bring someone else in for this. And Rafail said no."

If Rafail said no, all bets are off. The *pakhan* makes the final call.

I shrug a shoulder. "Well, *I* like the idea of her working with Luka."

Zoya smiles. "That's just because you're a little territorial about who works with him."

I shrug again. So what if I am? He's my sister's child. Not everyone is capable of giving him what he needs.

Zoya looks at her screen. "Okay, here's the first. Older, retired schoolteacher. Gets excellent reviews, though people say she's very strict with the kids and kind of old-school."

She shows me a picture of a woman who looks like she could be retired military, not a retired schoolteacher. Short, severe gray hair. I shiver. She reminds me of a grade school teacher I had who used to make us stand in the corner if we sniffled too loudly.

"Next," I say.

Smirking, Zoya pulls up the second. "This one doesn't have a lot of experience, but she has three grown children, and her last nannying job ended because the child went to school. She seems nice enough, but I can't get the references to respond."

"Right," I murmur. "How long was she with the last family?"

Zoya glances over her notes. "Like three months."

"And that's the only experience she's ever had?"

Zoya nods. "Looks like it."

I frown. "Let's look at the third one, please."

She pulls up the next one. "Now, this one has four years of nannying experience. Her record checks out excellent. She studied early childhood education in college, and she has a perfectly clean background—not even so much as a speeding ticket. And she's available for all the hours he needs, unlike the other two who have limited availability."

"Sounds perfect," I say, leaning over. "Can I see her picture?"

Zoya flicks to the image on the computer screen, and an absolutely stunning bombshell of a woman pops up. Even dressed conservatively, she has huge, voluptuous breasts—breasts I would fucking kill for. Her long, thick hair is pulled into a braid, and her face is perfectly symmetrical, with delicately arched eyebrows, a small nose, warm golden-brown eyes, and full lips pulled back across perfectly straight, white teeth.

There's no fucking way I want that woman around my brother-in-law, flashing those huge tits in front of him.

I frown. "I think the retired schoolteacher sounds perfect."

"Really?" Zoya asks, tipping her head. "Are you sure you're not letting your own prejudices make the decision here? The last one sounds perfect."

That last one is going to saunter into his life while Vadka is desperate and vulnerable, and the next thing I know, he's going to be kissing her in the laundry room. No fucking way. I shake my head.

"She's temptation on a stick, Zoya."

Zoya's eyebrows rise, and she looks at me in silence for a full minute before she finally nods.

"What?"

"Oh, nothing," she says cryptically.

"There's a reason there are romance books about nannies and single dads, Zoya."

Grandfather sounds like he's either coughing or laughing, but I can't tell because he's buried his face in a cup of coffee.

"I'll call her for an interview," I say. "Thank you."

I feel a little guilty. Maybe brunette Barbie would be perfect for Luka, but would she be perfect for her boss? A beautiful woman like that on Vadka's arm—I blow out a breath and look away.

Am I jealous? Actually jealous?

It's not jealousy, is it?

...Or is it?

Why would I be *jealous*? I'm trying to protect him, just like Mariah would do.

We put away the paperwork, and I check in on little Luka, who is contentedly watching a TV show in the spacious, cozy family living room.

"Hey, we're gonna go pick up some cookies for Grandma, okay?"

Luka nods.

He's visited my mother before, but Mariah and Vadka made sure that it wasn't often—and when it was, it was always supervised. My mother is too unpredictable. And in recent years, now that she's declining, the visits are very brief.

"Can I get something to eat too?" he asks, smiling up at me.

"I'll think about it," I tease, ruffling his hair. "Of course you can get something to eat, sweetheart. I know you love the bakery."

I buckle him into his car seat, and we go for a little ride.

Anya's bakery isn't far from here, and when we arrive, her husband, Semyon, is there too.

"Hey, guys," he says with a smile. He's an interesting sort—quiet, aloof, loyal, and protective. "Heard there was a little commotion at work last night," he says.

"Is there anything you guys don't find out about?"

He shakes his head, always literal. "No."

"It's true," Anya says from the back. "You have to keep an eye out for this one. He misses nothing."

He gives me a shrug and goes back to his computer at a little table in the corner of the bakery. Semyon is one of the highest-ranking officials in the Kopolov family—friendly with Vadka, but not best friends like him and Rafail.

Anya comes out to the front, dusting her hands on her apron. "Ruthie! Luka," she says warmly. "What a welcome surprise. It's been a while since I've been able to give you a cookie." She smiles broadly at him. "What can I get you?"

He points to the biggest, chocolate-studded cookie on the top row—a chocolate chip one that Anya makes per her sister-in-law's request. Though she specializes in traditional Russian baked goods, she keeps one tray reserved for American favorites—chocolate chip cookies, cheesecake, and a few other notable treats. She wraps it in wax paper and slides it into a white paper bag.

"You can have this one," Anya says, "after you eat a good lunch." She's smiling.

"I told my mom I would bring her cookies," I say quietly, not meeting Anya's eyes. I can't stand the pitying look people give me. It makes me feel fragile for some crazy reason.

"How *is* your mother?" she asks gently while a few other customers come in. Semyon wordlessly takes his place at the counter, filling orders, pouring coffee, and making tea. It's homey and quiet, and it smells like cinnamon and sugar. I take a deep breath, inhaling the familiar scent before I meet Anya's eyes.

"Declining," I say in one word—one word that encapsulates an entire lifetime of agony. *Declining*, just like they said she would.

"I'm sorry to hear that," she says quietly. "If there's anything I can do, let me know. Any of us—you know that, Ruthie."

Though I'm not married into the Kopolov family, I'm still family by affiliation—just because my sister was.

"Thanks," I say with forced brightness. We make small talk, and then Luka starts getting antsy. Right before we leave, Semyon raises his voice.

"Ruthie, can I talk with you before you go?"

"Yeah," I tell him, looking at Luka, but Anya gestures for him to come behind the counter.

"I need a strong man to help me carry things from the back room," she says wistfully. "Do you know of anyone?"

"Me!" he says, as if he's just come up with the most brilliant idea. He trots back behind the counter with Anya, and the two of them disappear. Semyon rounds the counter toward me and quietly locks the door, ensuring we have privacy.

Uh-oh. My heart beats a little faster.

"Have you talked to Vadka about what we found out recently?"

I shake my head. "Not much. He made a couple of inferences but nothing in detail. Something I should know?"

"Not entirely sure you're safe at work," he says. "Vadka will tell you more, but I wanted to know if you've seen anything —heard anything—that could be suspicious."

I shake my head and think it over. "No, but what types of things?"

"New customers coming in. Illegal activity. People asking you questions or giving you a hard time."

I think back on the other night when that woman was almost drugged—how I had to call the bouncers. That was nothing truly out of the ordinary, though, since shit like that happens all the time...

"Nothing unusual," I tell him. "Nothing that really concerns me."

He nods. "If there is, I want you to let one of us know right away. Whoever you trust the most—it doesn't matter. We'll communicate."

"How long has Vadka known about this?" I ask curiously.

"We just found out," he says softly. Then he looks up at me, and his expression drops—almost angry.

"If your brother-in-law told you not to go to work, would you listen to him anyway?"

"It would depend on his reasoning," I answer, my voice hard. Just because I'm family by affiliation doesn't make me obedient to any of them. "If it was good enough, maybe. But I don't miss work, Semyon."

He blows out a breath.

"I figured as much. But in the past few years, you were the one who spied for us. You got information that was sensitive and passed it on. And nothing's come across at all?"

My heart races, and I'm getting nervous now. He's right. I haven't heard anything or seen anything. Haven't had anybody come to me.

If anything, that in itself is a warning sign.

I nod and tell him quietly," Not at all."

Semyon frowns. "The Irish killed your sister, Ruthie. Vadka has retaliated. It's been a fucking bloodbath. You're not safe."

God. Why haven't I stayed in touch with Vadka? Asked questions? Why has nobody told me?

Maybe they didn't know.

"Okay—what are you saying?"

Semyon blows out a breath and shoves his hands in his pockets.

"What I'm telling you is—I know you're just his sister-in-law, but whatever the hell he tells you to do, do it. Especially if you have anything to do with him or his son. They're ruthless, Ruthie. *Ruthless.* There's nothing they won't do."

I look back toward Anya and Luka, suddenly afraid for my nephew.

"Don't worry about them," Semyon says quietly. "We have three armed guards. They block and monitor each entrance

—quietly. We don't want to scare away the customers, but they're there."

I nod.

"Where are you going next?"

"We were going grocery shopping and then—"

He shakes his head. "No. That's not a good idea. Probably safest for you to stay here or go back to the family home."

Okay. All right. I can do this.

Why hasn't Vadka called me? Why does the warning have to come from Semyon?

And why does that make me feel so sad?

Luka comes trotting out, holding a bag of cookies, a smear of frosting on his lip.

"Looks like you had a taste," I say with a smile, trying to keep my tone light and airy.

I glance at my phone and realize I've missed five messages and phone calls from Vadka. My heart leaps into my throat. Even while I feel that leap, I also feel momentary relief. He did try to reach me. Us.

"Oh my god," I whisper. "I didn't realize..."

"What happened?" Semyon is immediately alert. His shoulders pull back, and his eyes snap to mine.

"Vadka *did* try to reach me, but my phone was on silent. Shit. I think I know what happened—Luka had my phone. He was watching a show back at your house, and he must've accidentally put it on silent."

Shit.

I shake my head. The kid is smarter than I think. Probably didn't want his show interrupted.

"That tracks," Semyon says. "Call Vadka back—and tell me what he wants you to do."

I nod, feeling like I'm almost in a sort of daze.

Okay, all right, I can do this. One step at a time.

I'm safe right now. Luka's safe right now.

I've got this.

"Auntie Ruthie? Are we going home?" Luka asks, and I can tell he's already tired.

"Soon, baby. But right now, you're gonna go back with Grandfather and Auntie Zoya, okay?"

"Can I go with you to bring Grandma her cookies?"

"Not this time. I'm sorry," I say quietly. "Grandma doesn't feel well. We have to wait until she's better, okay?"

He nods, thankfully oblivious to the lump in my throat and the way my voice wavers. Semyon may be too—but his wife isn't. She gives me a smile, warm and full of encouragement, and I realize then that I *can* handle sympathy. I can handle encouragement. But pity?

Pity makes me feel like I'm not capable of handling hard things.

And I am.

I'm still here, aren't I?

It doesn't take long to get back to the Kopolov family mansion. By the time we arrive, Rodion, the youngest Kopolov brother, and his wife Ember are there. He's got an adorable, fluffy puppy on a leash with him.

"The newest addition to the family," he says brightly, and Luka drops the cookies in the back seat of the car and runs to go see the puppy, who licks his face with so much excitement and enthusiasm—then promptly pees in the garden.

"Good boy!" Rodion says with a big grin. "See? I told you he'd train quickly."

Red-haired Ember gives him a smile.

"He peed because he was excited, not because he's trained, Rodion. But I think you're right. I'm pretty sure he is going to train really quickly. Aren't you, baby?" she says, scratching his ears.

"Uh, does Rafail know you're bringing a puppy into the house?" I ask.

Ember still talks in her baby voice to the dog, though she's answering my question.

"Would be bad if Rafail doesn't know, but it won't hurt him, will it?" she says, and I can't help but crack a smile.

I need to come here more often. It's so fucking good to be near family again. Even if it's found family, I'm welcome here.

There's always something happening, someone to talk to, someone to cry to.

I open my phone.

"I need to go see my mom," I tell Rodion, and his eyes cloud over.

"Did you run that by Rafail and Vadka first?"

I give him a noncommittal shrug.

I feel a little guilty because I'm not exactly trying to go against anything he told me, but I also know that if I call him right now, he's absolutely gonna tell me not to go see my mom. She needs me, though, and that matters.

I told him that I was bringing Luka here so that he could be safe, and Semyon said something about there being potential retaliation. If Rafail or Vadka tells me to come back, I will. But I'm worried about my mother. If I don't go see her, they could... A lump forms in my throat again. I am so overdue for a good cry. I think it'll do me some good.

I bring Luka inside the house, and then I head to Mom's before anyone can stop me. What if *she's* in danger?

I hate going to visit my mother. It takes energy I feel like I don't have, and then I hate myself for hating going. Who hates visiting their mother? She gave me birth. Life. I wouldn't be here without her—but here I am, wishing I could be anywhere except the place that smells like urine and desperation. I hate it so fucking much.

I park the car when my phone rings.

Vadka. Guiltily, I answer.

"Look, I brought Luka to the house. Semyon told me what's going on. I won't be long."

Maybe he'll listen. Maybe we can be reasonable. Maybe we can discuss this like reasonable adults.

Maybe not.

"Glad you took care of my son," Vadka says, and I swear I can hear him speaking through clenched teeth, even from here.

"This is not the time to be going to your mother's, Ruthie! Are you out of your mind?"

"Listen, all I know is that there's potential blowback. But you guys have been fighting the Irish for how long? Years?"

"It isn't like that," he says tightly. "You're in danger. I don't even want you to go back to work."

I straighten my spine.

"But you can't control that. That's up to me. You were married to my sister, not me, remember?"

Why does that make my heart ache? I can't speak for a minute.

"You don't have the right to tell me where I can go or who I can talk to—none of it, Vadka. You don't have that right."

"I promised your sister I would take care of you."

I stop. "Well, that's news to me. And when did you do that? You didn't know she was dying. It's not like you had some kind of deathbed conversation."

Okay, now that felt like a dick thing to say.

"When your mother was institutionalized, Ruth."

Ruth. Not Ruthie. He only calls me that when he's getting all big-brotherly and angry with me.

"I promised her that no matter what, I would take care of you. Who do you think paid that outstanding doctor bill when you wrecked your wrist?" His voice is like a blade, cutting through my defenses. "Who do you think made sure your eviction notice disappeared before you ever saw it? Who handled the cops when you got picked up for that damn bar brawl and kept your record clean?"

Each word slams into me. I can't reply.

"All those things," he growls. "All the things she would've worried herself sick over, you never knew because I handled them."

He handled them. Without permission. Without asking me.

"I never asked you for any of that," I say, aghast. "What the fuck? I had no idea you were doing all this behind my back."

"Of course you fucking didn't. You're too damn stubborn." He blows out a breath. "Hang up the phone. I'm right next to you."

I'm so surprised when I look out my window and see his huge, gleaming bike parked right next to me—still dressed, sexy as sin, in that white shirt with those charcoal-gray pants.

Only this time, his eyes are flashing at me, and he does not look too pleased.

I hang up the phone.

I hate coming here. I hate everything about it. Well, some of the staff are nice; some are not. It's expensive, my mother doesn't get the time or attention she needs, and it always smells like stale food and antiseptic.

So when I see the familiar chrome of Vadka's motorcycle, I feel like having a good cry. And I feel like that young girl again—at home, watching my older sister fall in love and share the burden of our mother's care with someone else. When Mariah was here, she spearheaded everything with our mother: getting her the help she needed and getting her into a group home. She was the one who took care of me when my mother couldn't, and she knew exactly when my mother needed to go in. Vadka helped her. Of course he did—it's what he always did.

I mean, I just found out he did more for me when I was a teen than my mom did her whole life. She needed a keeper herself.

"I thought you had an emergency?"

Why does my voice sound so sharp, so angry? Why do I always feel sharp and angry? I don't like feeling this way anymore. It makes me feel brittle.

"I do," he says quietly. "But Mariah would've wanted me to come."

So he didn't come here to help me, but out of some obligation to my dead sister. Somehow, that doesn't make me feel any better.

And then my phone rings, and I see it's the nurse again. "I'm here," I snap into the receiver.

"Second floor. Make it quick."

Jesus. I shove the phone into my pocket, and Vadka's eyebrows rise. "Nora?"

"Wait, you know her by name?"

"Yeah. She tried her bullshit with Mariah once."

"Once?"

He chuckles, and we are near enough now that I catch a whiff of his leather jacket. Why does he have to smell so fucking good?

"Yeah, I came with her the second time," he says.

I feel my jaw tighten. "Well, that's not fair. She treats my sister like shit, and a man comes on the scene, and all of a sudden she behaves herself?"

"Yeah, who said life was fair, Ruthie?"

Liars, that's who.

"And to be fair, I don't know if it had anything to do with me being a *man*," he adds pragmatically. "You'd be surprised what people do out of fear of the Bratva."

I roll my eyes, thankful that I'm wearing sunglasses so he doesn't see. He gets that strange look in his eyes, and his jaw clenches when I roll my eyes.

When we enter, they wave us past without having to show ID. We are regulars here. Josie, the head nurse on my mother's floor, sees us first.

"So glad you're here," she says with a sympathetic look. She was always kind. "How are you doing though?" she asks gently, and a lump forms in my throat. I don't like being so fragile that the smallest show of kindness makes me melt. I should be stronger.

"I'm good. How are you?" I manage to reply.

"Oh, good, good," she says quietly. "My dog had puppies, so I've been up all night taking care of the little rascals. Other than that, can't complain. They're adorable."

She smiles warmly, then turns her attention to Vadka.

"And you, Vadka?"

Vadka just nods, saying nothing else. Josie, undeterred, continues with a gentle smile.

"Bet your little boy's getting bigger," she says.

In my mother's room, there's a faded picture of Luka as a chubby, rosy-cheeked baby. It's the only thing she keeps—a tiny relic of the life she once had.

"He is," Vadka says, shoving his hands into his pockets. "Going to preschool in the fall."

We're all silent for a long moment, and I wonder if it's for the same reason. For me, it's because my mind can't help the mental gymnastics of imagining my sister's child getting older without her being here.

Will it always be like this? Will everything I do always be shadowed by the thought that Mariah isn't with us anymore?

An older man with sagging skin and wide, wild eyes screams obscenities from one corner of the hallway. Another woman wheels by us in her wheelchair, happily singing to herself—something about going to the zoo with her mother.

Someone pushes a tray with a squeaky wheel past us to the right, carrying bowls of soup and slices of bread. The smell makes me a little nauseous. I've never liked the food here.

Vadka clenches his jaw and stands up taller, bracing himself.

"She met with her physical therapist today?" he asks, voice steady.

Since when did my mother start meeting with a physical therapist? Why does *he* know that, and I don't?

And why does that unsettle me so much?

"Unfortunately, no," Josie says quietly. "She's too combative to meet with anybody today."

Vadka's phone buzzes with a text. He glances at it, his eyebrows knitting together before he taps something out quickly and shoves his phone back in his pocket.

"Did you move her?" I ask Josie. Mom's room used to be the first one on the right after the nurses' station, but we're walking even further down the hall now.

Josie looks at me almost apologetically. "Yeah, we had to bring her to a more secure location," she says gently.

Shit. This is worse than I feared. I'm glad we're here.

I'm glad *he's* here too.

I hear her screaming before we even reach the door. The closer we get, the louder and more desperate her voice becomes, hoarse with anger and confusion.

Inside, the room is smaller, more contained, and stripped of anything that could be used to hurt herself or others. I half expect padded walls and a straightjacket... and I'm not too far off. The curtains are heavy, and the windows are double-locked. A single bed, bolted to the floor, sits against the far wall. There's a chair in the corner and little else.

My heart twists painfully at the sight.

"Mary," Vadka greets in his calm way that always brings a flicker of peace to my mother's face.

"Vadka! Get me out of here! I hate it. They hurt me. I don't want to be here."

"You're safe here. We trust these people. They're here to help you," he says, voice gentle but firm, the way someone might speak to an overtired child.

She clenches her jaw and shakes her head, so thin and frail she reminds me of a scarecrow, her once-blonde hair now faded to gray, straggled and unbrushed.

"I won't." My mother's jaw clenches, and my stomach tightens. I hate when she does this. She's impossible to reason with and sometimes becomes volatile. I don't know what's worse—knowing I can't help her or when they have to restrain her.

I open my mouth to try to cajole her into behaving when Vadka's voice sharpens, taking on a sterner edge. He anchors his hands on his hips. "Alright. That's enough. You need to do what they say now. Do you understand me?"

My mother folds her arms across her chest, jutting her chin out stubbornly. For one brief, scary moment, she looks just like my sister used to. I look away quickly, swallowing the lump in my throat.

I can't think of Mariah now.

"She said she shut off my Wi-Fi," she says, stabbing a finger at me accusingly.

Vadka's eyebrows rise slightly, clearly amused.

"Snitching?" he says, almost teasing.

I shrug. "She has to take her medication. Do you want another seizure, Mom?"

"I don't have seizures. They made that up," she says petulantly, her voice small and furious. Her fingers fiddle with the frayed edge of a blanket. "And where are my cookies?"

I hold the white paper bag in front of me. "I told you, you would get them if you did what your nurse said."

She scowls, and Vadka gets the same kind of look he gets when he's dealing with a grumpy Luka. Patient but implacable. Immovable.

"Do what she says, Mary. There's no reason for you not to take your medicine." He squats down in front of her, his forearms resting on his knees so they're at eye level. "Why don't you want to do it?"

"I told her already. It makes me feel loopy."

"It makes you feel loopy because the last time you took it, you took it with your sleep pills," the nurse says patiently, just as heavy footsteps sound in the hallway. Someone shoves open the door.

"Well? Did she take them or not?"

Sigh. Nora. White-gray hair pulled into a severe bun, round glasses perched on the edge of her nose, lips pressed into a familiar thin line.

Then she sees Vadka and takes a step back. "Oh. I didn't know you were here."

He gives her a tight smile. "So nice to see you again." He turns back to Mom. "Yes, Mary's going to take her meds," he says, looking at her. "Aren't you? Just like the nurse explained to you. You didn't feel loopy because of this one—it was because of your sleep med. And if you need to take another sleep med, we can talk to your doctor about that. Right?"

My mom eyes the bag of cookies and frowns. She's softening. She's thinking about it.

"Okay, fine," she says, and the entire room breathes a sigh of relief.

I don't always like my job, but all of a sudden, serving drinks, dealing with predators, a demanding late-night schedule, being on my feet all day, and spying on various syndicates sounds like a fantastic idea.

My god, I'm tired. My eyes are all scratchy, and my throat hurts.

I watch my mother take the small paper cup and, with a scowl, drink her water with her medication.

Thank. *Fuck.*

I hand her the bag of cookies. "Anya said she put in a little something special for you too." I hand the second bag to Josie, hoping they aren't too crumbled after the ride.

"She said—"

The nurse peeks in. Her breath catches. "Oh. Are those the honey-walnut pirozhki? With the citrus glaze?"

She takes one out like it's sacred.

"Those are my favorite. She only makes them seasonally."

There's a beat of reverent silence.

"She said you looked tired last week," I say. "Wanted to make sure someone was looking after you too."

Josie sighs. "Tell her thank you. Tell her... that mattered. This is sometimes a thankless job, you know?" She smiles. "These are my favorite though."

"I bet," I say with a sigh, riddled with guilt that I'm not here more often.

My mom sits back in her chair and looks out the window, nibbling her cookie in silence.

"How's Luka?" Mom asks. "Is he walking yet?"

A shadow crosses Vadka's face. "Yes," Vadka says, glancing at me. My heart tumbles in my chest.

He's been walking for years. I wonder what Vadka's thinking. Is he immediately transported back to Luka's toddler days too?

Vadka actually stifles a chuckle. "He's gotten quite good at walking."

Glad one of us has a sense of humor about this.

"What a good boy," she says softly. "He has his mother's eyes, doesn't he?"

"Yeah," I say, and then, before I know what's happening, I'm blinking rapidly. And then I'm crying. I hate it. But the harder I try to stop, the faster the tears fall. Because he *does* have his mother's eyes, and I miss my sister, and it's *not fair*.

I swipe at my tears and try to turn away from Vadka, but it's too late—he knows I'm crying too. Quietly, wordlessly, he reaches for my hand. His larger, warm hand means more than any smile, and the lump in my throat dissolves. And then I'm crying harder, tears falling down my cheeks.

Quietly, he tugs me over to him and gives me a warm hug. I bury my head on his shoulder, even as my brain tells me this is wrong, that I'll regret it, and I shouldn't be doing this. But my fucking *god*, it feels good to be comforted by someone—especially by someone who loved my sister as much as I did.

The tears end quickly, almost abruptly, and I feel a little lighter. I sniffle and wipe my eyes, grateful that my mom is still looking out the window and oblivious to the fact that I just cried. I don't want to explain myself.

Vadka presses a hand to the back of my head, stroking once, down the length of my hair, before he pulls away.

"Bring him in to see me, will you?" my mother asks.

Vadka nods. Even though it's a lie. My mother only knows baby Luka. She doesn't understand that he's getting older. Every time she sees him, it sends her into another tailspin.

No, she won't be seeing him.

Then she gives me a watery smile. "You two always were the most beautiful couple," she says.

Now it's my turn to wince at Vadka.

"Are we? Thanks, Mom." My cheeks feel hot.

What is going on with me? I don't blush. I never used to cry. And now I've done both in the space of two minutes.

"We have to go," Vadka says, more serious now, not as amused by my mother's comment as I am.

Shit. Does he think that I'm hitting on him? I don't want to do anything that's going to make him pull away from me.

"Sorry," he says quietly. "The text I got when I came in here was from Rafail. We need to go. It's urgent."

My heart thumps faster.

"Okay. Bummer," I mutter. "I was hoping we could hang out here all day."

Why does it always make me feel like I won something when he smiles at me? But I feel better knowing that my mom has taken her medication, that she's getting ready for lunch. Her room looks clean and bright, and I'm glad they moved her. This one gets more sun.

I hate coming in here alone, but it's not so bad when I have somebody with me. And I feel better after the little cry. I needed to do that. I might need to do it again soon.

"What's going on?" I ask him. He mentioned something with the Irish.

"I'm not sure yet. I need to check in with Rafail."

"And Luka?"

"He's safe with Zoya."

As we get to my car, I feel a little guilty—until I remember that Luka is with the Kopolovs, and I'm confident that they are feeding him and entertaining him and taking care of him. We were supposed to go back to the house and grill food and have dinner. Like a family. But Mom's at peace now, she's taking her meds, and I need a little time to myself.

"See you back at the house?"

"Yeah," I tell him with a little nod. I do want to say goodbye to my nephew, and I'm starving. But I'm not gonna stay long because I need to get home. I need to veg out on my couch and maybe eat some ice cream and doomscroll for a little bit. "I'll see you there," I tell him.

I get in my car, and he gets on the back of his bike and starts it up. It rumbles beside me, and I pull up my phone, checking my messages.

Why hasn't he left yet? Is he making sure that I get home alright, or... He hasn't moved. I pretend I'm not looking at him in my peripheral vision and start my car.

Or *try* to. A strange little clicking sound happens when I turn the key. Disbelieving, I turn it again.

And again.

And again.

Fuck.

Vadka is watching me, his helmet on, his huge bike rumbling beneath him, but he doesn't move. Finally, he swings his leg off the side of the bike, walks over to me, and wraps a knuckle on my window. I roll it down.

"Won't start?"

"Yeah," I say with a sigh. "I have no idea what's wrong."

"Pop the hood," he rumbles. His eyes are narrowed on me because obviously, he thinks this has something to do with me neglecting the care of my car. With a sigh, I pop the hood. He pokes around, looks at things that I have no clue about because I'm not a car person, and he scowls and shakes his head.

"Hey, my service stuff is up-to-date, okay? Don't start judging me, buddy."

A brisk wind has kicked up, and I'm cold. I rub my bare arms. It was a warm day that's quickly faded to overcast and chilly, and I'm kicking myself for not bringing a sweatshirt or sweater or something.

He looks at me curiously. "Why did your mind go there? Why are you thinking that?"

"Because earlier, you were saying shit about me not taking care of my car," I say with a shrug. "I mean, obviously, right?"

He bends over the hood of my car, and a lock of hair falls across his forehead. I want to brush it off. I want to tell him he doesn't have to do this because I would feel shitty if he got grease on that perfectly white shirt. But I'm too mesmerized by the span of his large hands on each side of my car, the way his lips are pressed together in a thin line, and the memory of how he handled my mother with such perfect ease.

Oh, Vadka.

"I'm not checking in on how well you cared for your car, Ruthie. I'm checking to see if someone has fucked around with it."

For the past years since my sister was married into this family, I've only been tangentially related to them. And now this is the first time I'm realizing that the life Vadka—and even my sister—lead is so vastly different from mine.

Yes, I've given them information when I found it. Yes, I've befriended the family, but I can't ever remember wondering if someone *fucked around with my car.*

What does this mean? I remember going shopping with Mariah, and she would have bodyguards. I remember the little red light flashing on her phone, indicating that Vadka was tracking her location at all times. I thought it was a little much, a little over the top, and I never really understood what was going on.

But I'm starting to understand now.

I rub my arms again, and it does little to warm me up.

"Put my jacket on," he rumbles, jerking his head at a leather jacket strewn across his seat.

No. I don't want to put his jacket on. It will smell like him and be all warm and leathery, and it's so fucking intimate, and I'm not in a place where I welcome intimacy. Not now. So I shake my head.

"I'm fine."

His eyes flicker to mine, and I wonder if he's going to push the issue, but he only shakes his head and goes back to the car.

"Well?"

"I think it's your starter. I don't see any indication that anybody fucked around with it. *Yet.*"

"So we will call a tow truck or—"

"No. I'll have Matvei come pick it up. He'll take a closer look. You'll ride on the back of my bike, and I'll take you home."

What does "home" mean? Does he mean he'll take me back to his house, the Kopolov family house? Or back to my apartment?

Does it matter?

I need to get out of here.

"You're not driving this," he growls.

I open my mouth to argue.

"*Not* negotiable." His voice is steel. Final. Not just because he's in control but because he cares in that brutal, infuriating way that makes me want to both scream and melt all at once.

And goddammit, why does that make me feel safe?

So I do the only sensible thing. I nod my head and agree. Still... "But I've never ridden a motorcycle before."

His brows quirk up. "Really? It's easy. I'll help you."

I'm not even sure my sister ever rode on one either. She was terrified of motorcycles and hated that he drove one, but finally caved when she saw how much joy it brought him. He has one of those thick, sturdy ones, and it's so fucking beautiful, all shining black and silvery chrome. I run a finger over the black edge of a tire and don't realize he's watching till the corner of his lips quirks. He wipes his hand with a rag.

"Where did you get that?" I ask him.

"I keep them with me," he says, as if it's the most natural thing in the world.

I keep lip gloss in my purse, and he keeps rags on his motorcycle.

All right then. Fine.

Why is it so sexy watching him step back from the hood of the car and wipe grease off his big, manly hands? His shirt sleeves are rolled up to the elbow, his collar undone, revealing tanned skin and tats.

Okay. All right.

Time to pull myself together.

So Vadka is an *objectively* attractive male. *Fact.* I'd have to be a fucking *moron* not to see it.

Also fact: He was married *to my sister*. Should that gross me out? No idea.

Does it? Sigh. No.

Does it make me feel guilty? *Guilty as fuck.* Why?

Am I attracted to him? No question. I'm practically school-girl-crushing on the guy.

So the next question is... Is he attracted to *me?*

I saw him fall in love with my sister. I saw how much he adored her. I was with him the day she was shot, and *I watched* as she died in his arms. And I will never, ever, as long as I live, forget the sound of him screaming, trying to save her, begging for help—that sound that haunts me to this day.

I look away from him. I wish we could erase that night, not just because Mariah should be here with us, but because I don't want to relive that pain over and over and over again, just like I do every time I'm with him.

Then why does it feel like he's the only one who understands that there's a hole in my heart that will never be filled again—not by anyone?

He walks over and wordlessly takes his leather jacket off the back of the bike.

"You'll wear this, and that's not a suggestion. It's not safe for you to ride on a motorcycle without leather."

"What about you?"

He gives me a withering look and rolls his eyes, then holds the sleeves out for me to slide into. I blush and look away as I slide my arms in.

I was right. It's soft, buttery leather, still warm, and it smells like him. And I love it.

"But I don't have a—"

He slams a helmet on the back of my head before I can finish. Then he helps me adjust the strap.

"I guess you keep a spare helmet with your rags?" I ask.

"Yeah," he rumbles. "But this one was fitted for your sister."

My god.

I'm wearing a helmet that my sister was supposed to wear... on the back of her husband's motorcycle.

But then he adds quietly, "She never wore it. I just kept it with me in case she decided to change her mind and give it a go."

And my heart—oh god, my heart.

I am *not* okay. I think I need therapy or something.

"I don't know how to ride on the back of a motorcycle," I admit, and I feel like I want to pout like a child. I'm not crazy about admitting I don't know how to do something. I value my independence and autonomy.

But he doesn't tease me. Doesn't laugh. Just looks at me with that quiet, steady gaze and says, "You don't need to know much. Just get on and hold tight." He climbs on, turns slightly, and motions. "Put your left foot on the peg. Swing your right leg over. Then sit close—yeah, like that. Now wrap your arms around my waist." I do. I can feel how strong he is, how large and muscular. It's immediately intimate in a way I'm not prepared for.

"Just hold on," he says. "Keep your arms around my waist and don't let go. I know how to drive this. I'm not going to hurt us."

Then he kicks the ignition, and we start moving. And my crazy, self-deprecating, grief-riddled thoughts—cease.

Because *this. Is. Amazing.*

My heart soars, my brain clears, exhilaration floods my limbs. And we're not even going fast yet.

My arms are wrapped around the only person in my life I can depend on, on the back of his bike, my hair that escaped the helmet flying behind me as the wind whips past and cars blur by us.

I've never felt so free in my life.

"This is awesommmme!" I scream into the air, and my words are immediately swallowed by the wind. I don't even know if he hears me.

He rides with masterful skill, like he was built to ride it—with confidence and grace. I think he's maybe showing off a little, and that's fine with me.

I don't know how to explain it, except to say it's...beautiful. Like a horse galloping wild through a field. An eagle taking flight. A waterfall crashing on craggy rocks below.

There's something majestic, powerful, and intoxicating about watching him ride. I've never seen anything like it in my life.

I blink back tears. I didn't know how much I needed this.

I don't want to stop. *I want him to keep going forever.*

I want to stay right here, on the back of his bike, forgetting my pain, my fears, my worries.

Forgetting that my sister died in a way she never should have.

Forgetting that I couldn't hold the pieces of my family together, no matter how hard I tried.

Forgetting everything except this—right here, right now—*freedom.*

I don't know where we're going or how we're getting there.

I see him tap the side of his helmet, and it looks like he's speaking into it.

And then his voice sounds in my ear. "How are you doing back there?"

Oh my gosh.

There are *intercoms* in the helmets? *That is so cool.*

I'm sitting directly behind him, and now I can hear him like he's whispering right into my ear.

Of course we couldn't hear each other over the wind and the engine's growl. But then his voice crackles in my ear— low, rough, unmistakably close. *"Press the button on your left side. You'll hear a click. That means I can hear you."*

I fumble along the side of the helmet, fingers shaking slightly, find the small raised circle, and press. *Click.*

"*Good,*" he says, voice sliding right into my head like he's inside me now. *"There's a mic near your chin. Don't shout. Just talk. I'll hear everything."*

The way he says it—*I'll hear everything*—sends a shiver down my spine.

"*Even if I curse you out?*" I test, the tease automatic—armor against how exposed I suddenly feel with his voice in my ear and my arms locked around his body.

"*Especially then, you little brat,*" he growls. "*Now hold on. We're not cruising. We're running.*"

And just like that, the engine roars, and we're gone—my

breath caught somewhere between fear and the brutal comfort of his control.

"Can we keep going?" I say, unable to squelch the excitement in my voice. "This is the most amazing fucking thing I've ever done in my life. I don't ever want to stop. I want you to keep going and going. Oh my god, I can't believe this feels so good."

His chuckle skates down my spine, and I'm grinning—no, I'm fucking smiling—and I think it might be the first time I've smiled since my sister's funeral.

Nothing makes me this happy anymore. Fucking nothing.

"It's amazing, isn't it? I wish Mariah could've experienced this."

I nod because I agree. And it feels right, talking about my sister like this. Like she just went on a little trip, and not like we're collectively breaking into pieces remembering her.

"I don't really think she would've liked it," I tell him. "She didn't like roller coasters. Or even riding a bike. And she hated heights."

"That's true," he says, and I realize that somehow, not having to look at him—even with my arms wrapped around his solid midsection and his voice in my ear—is intimate, but it makes it easier to talk to him this way.

And I want to tell him everything. I want to tell him that I'm sorry for yelling at him for not taking care of my nephew when he's done his very best. I want to tell him that I'm sorry it was my fault Mariah came into the bar that night— that if I hadn't asked her to come talk about my latest drama, she would've been home with Luka.

I want to tell him that he was the very best husband he could've been to my sister and that even though she died too soon, she lived the life she deserved—being worshipped by her husband. Surrounded by people who loved her. Loved by the sweetest little boy in the world.

I want to tell him all of these things, and I say nothing. I lose myself to the ride once more.

And it feels so goddamn good. I let out a sigh at the same time he does, and I want to hug him. I want to tell him I love him—but not in the way a woman in love with a man would. I love him like a brother.

Do I?

And then he taps something on his helmet and starts talking into it again, but this time, I don't hear what he says. I can feel the tension shift in his body before he even speaks—the way his back straightens a little, even on the bike.

Something happened. Something's changed.

His voice is in my ear again.

"Change of plans, Ruthie."

CHAPTER 6

VADKA

THE FIRST THING I do is call Zoya. "How's Luka?"

"He's fine," she says, her voice laced with steel. The Kopolov women don't fuck around—and she's seen more than one tense situation.

Rafail raised them right. Zoya was just a child when Rafail became the legal guardian of her and her siblings. He taught them to be strong, loyal, and fastidious. And to this day, I'm not sure there's anything the Kopolov family can't handle. They know how to use weapons, how to navigate tense situations. They've seen people they love hurt and killed. And when shit hits the fan, the Kopolov family stands strong.

"Luka's packing a bag right now," she says more quietly. "I told him we're going on a trip and that he'll see his Auntie Ruthie and his Papa soon."

"Thank you."

I used to like to think that even the Irish weren't so cold they'd go after a child. But I don't have the luxury of thinking that anymore. Not after they killed my innocent wife.

A little voice in the back of my mind reminds me that her death was an accident—that they didn't come straight for her—she just got caught in the line of fire when the Irish were on a rampage. But it doesn't soothe anything.

The Irish are my mortal enemies. The most dangerous fuckers I've ever met, and I've been swimming with sharks since I was a kid.

"We're twenty minutes out," I say. "We're on my bike now. Ruthie's car broke down, and I can't tell if it was mechanical or if it was intentional."

"Let me check with Matvei, see if we have surveillance outside the area you're in. You were with her mother, yes?"

Brilliant. Why didn't I think of that?

"Yes. Good idea. Thank you."

"It's filling up here fast. Everyone was at the house when Rafail hit the alarm. I'll make sure I save space for you."

She has to. She has my son. "Thank you."

"Are you two hungry?"

"Yeah."

She's so cute. Literal lives are on the line, and Zoya's worried about feeding us. Always the little mother hen— even when she was little. I remember the first time she saw a bruise on my shoulder, back when my father had decked me, the fucking asshole. I remember when she started realizing the bruises on my arms and cheeks weren't from falling or walking into walls, like I told everyone. That I wasn't just clumsy.

She reached out and touched a black eye with a small, trembling hand. "No one's perfect, Vadka. But no one deserves this either."

I slept on the Kopolov couch that night. And I never went home.

"I'll have some food prepared for you," she says. "Luka is tired. We had a busy day. He might be asleep when you get back."

"I know. I just want what's best for the little guy. Thank you."

I decide to tell Ruthie what's going on, so I fill her in on the comm and tell her she should come with me.

I realize then that I like the feel of her behind me. It makes me a little sad, honestly. I could never convince Mariah to sit on the back of the bike with me.

Ruthie reminds me of her sister—but only the best parts of Mariah. She probably fears that when I look at her, I see a smaller, younger version of her sister. Hell, *I* feared that.

But I don't.

I see *Ruthie.* Brilliant, headstrong, somewhat chaotic Ruthie. The most loyal woman I know. The strongest.

The one who clutches her vulnerability with a death grip, unlike anyone else I've ever seen.

Dusk has fallen by the time we pull down a long, quiet street. I check behind us carefully, making sure we're not being followed.

No shadows. No headlights tailing us. Just the steady rumble of the engine beneath us and the way Ruthie exhales—slow, uncertain—as I ease the bike down a narrow back alley.

We don't pull up to the front of anything. That's suicide. I cut the engine behind an abandoned auto shop with rusted signage and boarded windows. The back lot is gravel and overgrown. Only the locals know the garage door still works.

It groans as it lifts.

We roll in silently. No interior lights. Just a single, motion-activated bulb that flickers when we pass under it. I kill the ignition.

Ruthie slides off behind me. She looks around, frowning.

"This can't be the safe house," she says.

"No." I take her hand before she can wander. "It's the entrance."

We walk. Around the side of the garage, across a broken alley. The kind of place you don't look too long at if you want to stay alive.

I stop outside the side door of a grimy dive bar—"Crescent," the faded lettering above the awning reads. It used to be a jazz bar back in the '6os. Now, it's mostly forgotten.

But not by us.

We step inside. The place is nearly empty—just an old bartender cleaning a glass and a silent man in the corner who doesn't glance up. No music. Just the hum of an old fridge and the tick of a slow ceiling fan.

Ruthie gives me a sidelong look. "This where we drink or die?"

I almost smile. "Both, maybe. Come on. Let's get a table."

"I mean, I could definitely use a cheap beer," she mutters.

God, me too.

I look at my phone and see a message from Rafail.

Rafail
Zoya is trying to get Luka to sleep. He's almost there. If you come in now he'll get all wound up, so can you kill some time?

I show Ruthie. "Bingo."

We get drinks and sit alone in the back. She regales me with stories from her work at the bar—A fight that broke out over a spilled drink when some suit in a linen blazer shoved the wrong man and got his teeth kissed by a barstool. A guy who tried to flirt with her by sliding her a poetry book—dog-eared and underlined, as if his annotated Pablo Neruda was supposed to win her over.

And then there was the wannabe playboy who ordered a "non-alcoholic vodka" and declared he was "sober but fun," to which she replied, "Then why are you trying so hard?"

She makes me laugh. *Really* laugh. The kind that slips past my ribs before I can cage it. I forget for a moment that the fucking Irish are on the move, that we're about to lock down in a safe house so nobody gets hurt. That I'm supposed to be dead inside.

And somehow, here I am—I'm drinking cheap beer and laughing with my sister-in-law, hiding out like fugitives in a place no one knows exists.

Feels a little rebellious. But Rafail told me to take my time.

"I love shitty bars," I mutter, leaning back as she finishes telling me a story.

She smiles. "Me too. No pretense. Drown your sorrows at a discount."

I tilt my head. "So people hit on you at the bar?"

She snorts. "Not really. I'm not pretty enough for that."

I stare at her. Blink. She means it. She actually believes that.

"Are you fucking kidding me?" I say, leaning forward. "Is this some kind of self-deprecating bullshit?"

"What? No."

The words slip out before I can stop them. "Ruthie, *Jesus*. You're beautiful." She is.

She gets shy, eyes darting away. Then she clears her throat and straightens up. "We should go."

Of course. We should. But all I can think about is how wrong she is about herself—and how dangerously right she feels *beside me*.

"Yeah," I tell her. "We should."

But we don't.

Instead, we order another round.

"I know your dad was an asshole," she says. "But I was too young... or maybe too self-focused to understand." She sips her drink. There's a little froth on her lip, and it's adorable. "Tell me about your dad?"

So we're going there.

"My dad was a biker," I say. "I don't mean the weekend bikers with leather vests and toy drives. I mean the kind who ran meth across state lines. People thought he was all chill because he never raised his voice, but the real reason was because his fists did the talking." I shake my head. "And I was his fucking punching bag. He said I had to be 'toughened up.' That the world doesn't spare weak boys. By the time I was ten, I could stitch my own eyebrow and lie to the ER nurse without flinching. By fourteen, I stopped crying when he broke something in me—because I knew it wouldn't be the last time."

I said too much. I've barely scratched the surface. I look away.

"He died when I was nineteen. Bike wreck. Drunk and fast and finally out of luck."

I didn't cry. I didn't go to the funeral. I just stood in the kitchen, blood still drying on my cheek from the night before and thought: *You finally did one good thing. You left.*

"I'm sorry he wasn't good to you."

I shrug and bury myself in my drink. I've almost made my peace with it. "I used to tell myself he had a hard life, that he didn't know how to deal with his anger. But now that I have a kid of my own, it's harder for me to reconcile the way he treated me. Kids are innocent. They trust easily and love so hard." I shake my head. "They deserve to be treated with love and respect."

I pause.

The memory surfaces unbidden, like something half-drowned. The beer's made me talk more than normal.

"I remember when I was seven. I dropped a glass of milk—barely touched it, and it slipped right out of my hands. He didn't say a word. Just grabbed the broken pieces and threw them in the trash. Then he made me kneel on the kitchen floor until my legs fell asleep. One of them was cut on the broken glass. Said I needed to learn consequences."

"Are you fucking kidding me?" Ruthie glares.

My voice goes quiet. "I remember how cold the tile was. I remember the sound of the clock ticking while I tried not to cry. That sound stuck with me longer than the pain. I mean, I got the damn milk because I was thirsty."

There's a silence between us now—thick but not empty.

She reaches her small hand out to mine and rubs her thumb gently across the top of it. Her nails are short, unpainted, and shaped in soft ovals.

"I'm sorry," she says, and I know she means it.

Mariah was the one who helped me when I struggled with my own anger. When I was frustrated that Luka wouldn't sleep, when he had his first tantrums—throwing things, shouting "No!" She would lay her hand on my arm and say, "Walk away. I've got this."

She stayed calm. Always calm. She learned that early—she had to. She was the one who took care of her mom and her sister. I learned patience from her.

"Mariah was so patient," I say, my voice shaking. "I hated that my first impulse was toward anger. I had to walk away. But Mariah explained that when you're raised like that, it's harder to break the cycle. It becomes second nature. You have to willfully break the chain. Learn. Do better." I shrug. "And she was right."

I blow out a breath. "I pride myself on the fact that, to this day, I've never raised my hand to my son. Not once. I'd rather be too lenient than someone who takes his anger out on a child."

"I agree," she says. "He's not spoiled. He's a small child. You've given him guidelines and discipline. Discipline doesn't have to involve pain or shame." She shakes her head. "It's almost like we had the opposite childhoods," she says. "You already know what *I* grew up with."

I do. Her mother was too sick to care for the kids. There were nights they didn't eat—food insecurity was constant. They lived in a dilapidated apartment they could barely afford, not until Mariah started working to help keep them afloat. I would've married her when we were barely twenty. She wouldn't marry me until Ruthie was old enough to stand on her own and we could get her mother the help she needed.

That was who she was—always carrying someone. Always putting herself last.

I hated it, sometimes. Just the way the world never gave her a break, and she never asked for one. Like she believed suffering was something noble if it kept the people she loved breathing.

I feel Ruthie watching me. Her silence isn't passive but deliberate—a weight pressing into my chest.

When I finally look up, she's staring at me like she sees all of it. The guilt I try to bury. The man I used to be. The one who couldn't save her sister.

She doesn't speak right away.

She reaches across again, this time gripping my hand—not gentle, but grounding.

"And you're not the only one who lost her," she adds, barely above a whisper.

I nod. Because if I speak now, I might say the wrong thing. Or worse—say everything I've never let myself feel.

Ruthie lifts her glass again, but her hand wobbles. Is she drunk? I look in surprise at the tray of empties beside us.

She stares at me for a beat too long.

"You wear your grief well, Vadka."

The words fall out soft. She swallows hard and sets the glass down. "I do the same thing. And it's not a compliment. It's... armor. You wear it so no one can touch what's underneath."

I don't respond. She keeps going like she can't stop herself. "Sometimes I think you *like* being broken. Like it gives you permission to not feel." Her voice falters. "Makes it easier to push everyone away."

Is she talking about me?

Or herself?

My stare sharpens. My grip on my drink tightens. But she doesn't flinch. She leans back in her chair, her eyes glossy and defiant. "I get it. I do. But it's not really any way to live, is it?"

Her mouth opens like she wants to take it all back... but she doesn't.

It's too late anyway.

She sighs. "People mistake it for strength though."

My voice is quiet. Dangerous. "You think I want anyone's pity?"

"I think you don't want anything." She sways a little, then steadies herself. "That's the problem."

I lean forward. Just a little.

She falters for a second. Then her mouth twists into a smile. Defiant. Reckless. "I shouldn't have said that."

Regret? From Ruthie?

I shrug. "You never held back from saying the truth, did you?"

Something flickers in her expression. A crack in the bravado.

"I don't pity you, Vadka," she murmurs. "I just... I see you. And sometimes I think, maybe that's worse."

 I get a text from Zoya at the same time as I get one from Rafail.

Zoya
Luka's asleep.

Rafail
We need you now.

I place my phone down and stifle a sigh. Duty calls.

For one small sliver of time, I felt relief—from the grief I carry, from the responsibilities that hang over my head like a noose. For one little moment, I felt like myself again. And I want that back.

"We have to go," I say quietly, and I imagine the look on her face tells me she felt the same. I don't know if that's a good thing.

We head to the back. Past the bathroom doors, past a locked supply closet. There's an unmarked hallway where the floor changes from warped wood to new linoleum.

At the end—an unlit door behind a row of industrial trash bins. No handle. Just a black panel on the wall.

I punch in the code.

Click.

The door hisses open just an inch.

"Wow," Ruthie mutters, stepping past me, eyes darting. "This is some next-level James Bond shit, huh?"

But I see it in her shoulders.

The tension.

The fight-or-flight instinct flaring under the sarcasm.

Because she knows now: This isn't just hiding.

It's *war*.

"Yeah," I say with a short laugh. "Remember a couple of years ago, when Rafail married Polina, and we had to borrow a safe house?"

She shakes her head. I guess those weren't the kinds of things we talked about publicly. I forget she's not technically Bratva.

"Well, after that, Rafail decided we needed our own. The larger the safe house, the easier it is to find—and then we're fucked. So instead of one big one, we have multiple small ones scattered throughout the city and on the outskirts of Moscow."

"Oh. That makes sense. Except... it's a large family, so..."

"Rafail figured that a lot of people were often not home." As his brothers have gotten older and married, started families of their own, and his sister Yana relocated to South Africa with her husband, the number of people at the Kopolov compound at any given moment was smaller than it used to be.

She looks up at me, her eyes luminous, her gaze just enough unfocused to make me look away. I have to protect her right now.

"What happens next, Vadka?" she asks quietly.

I swallow and hold my head up high. "Next, I keep you and my boy safe."

CHAPTER 7

RUTHIE

"I LITERALLY FEEL like I'm on a TV show. This is fucking *awesome*," I tell him.

He gives me a mock serious look, but even mocking, Vadka all stern makes my heart beat faster. "It is not *awesome*. We are on the run from people who want to kill you."

"Wait, I thought they wanted to kill *you*? Why do they give two shits about me?"

"They know that killing you is the best way to get to me, so that's their plan."

I give him a sidelong look and don't reply because I need a minute. He just freely admitted that it would hurt him to lose me. Of course it would—because I'm like his sister, right?

But I'm not his sister. And he's not my brother.

We had a relationship that was different when my sister was here. But she isn't anymore.

No. I can't think like that.

"You're going to have to lock your phone in a safe box." And then he turns to look at me, as serious as I've ever seen him.

I stand up straighter.

"What?" I kind of snap, trying to protect myself. It doesn't work.

"You have to follow the rules here. No fucking around. If Rafail tells you to hide, you hide. If he tells you to run, you run. If he tells you to put on a clown wig and go into Central Square and pretend you're entertaining a group of kids at a birthday party, you do it. Got it?"

"Or what?" I ask. "Put on a clown wig? Really? Remember that I'm not in the Bratva. Remember that I'm not your *wife*, Vadka." My voice wobbles. "Remember that I'm not obedient to Rafail."

I'm not someone who hands over my autonomy so easily. Hell, I gave up my virginity easier than that.

He takes a step closer. Our toes touch. He anchors his hands on his hips and does something that makes my brain short-circuit—he reaches for my chin and holds my gaze with his.

I can't look away, not now, not for anything. I'm mesmerized, engulfed in his gaze, unable to do anything but stare back.

"I lost my wife," he says, and I don't know how he keeps his voice steady because I don't even trust myself to speak right now. He pauses, then says softly, "Do you really need to let your stubbornness threaten us losing each other now?"

I expected him to lecture. I expected him to get all stern and bossy, which is how he normally is—but this plea undoes me in a way that sternness wouldn't.

I shake my head, and when I blink, hot, fat tears roll down my cheeks.

"No, of course not."

"Do it for Luka," he says quietly, and I nod. But I'm not sure what I'm doing for Luka or what I'm agreeing to.

"So I need to know, Ruthie... Are you going to behave, or are we going to have a problem here?"

My heart. Goddammit, I think I might be ovulating because I am suddenly, *instantly* turned on.

I scoff. "Whatever. I'm not a *good girl*, Vadka. Not like Mariah was." She played by the rules.

He's leaning in too close. He smells too good. His eyes flash with something I don't understand, and the corner of his lips quirks.

"Don't I know it."

Something hangs in the air between us—something neither of us wants to name.

And then he pulls away, and I turn my head.

The worst possible solution to losing my sister is flirting with a man who doesn't want me, who *I can't have.*

What's left of my broken heart would be shattered.

I can't allow that to happen.

"Be a good girl, Ruthie, just this once," he says softly and hooks his pinky finger with mine.

I don't know if this is supposed to feel big-brotherly, but it absolutely doesn't.

"You say that to all the girls, don't you," I whisper, not trusting my voice.

Oh my *god*.

I squirm uncomfortably and nod.

"Tell me, Ruthie," he says, in that same tone he uses when Luka refuses to go to bed, the tone that brooks no argument. "Tell me you'll be a good girl this time."

I nod and swallow hard.

"Fine. I'll behave." But I tack on at the end, "For now. If I give Rafail shit, will it reflect poorly on you? Are they going to expect you to... keep me in line, or whatever?"

His lips press together, and his jaw ticks. "Absolutely."

All right, all right, *fine*. I'll do whatever the fuck they tell me.

I don't say that out loud though. I nod and shrug one shoulder. "Fine."

He draws in a breath and releases it through his nostrils, then jerks his head toward the door.

Two uniformed men appear almost out of thin air. They nod and almost bow toward Vadka in a gesture of respect.

I forget how high-ranking he is. How powerful.

To me, he's just... Vadka. The guy I've always looked up to. The only one I ever trusted to take care of my sister.

Fuck. My eyes are getting watery again.

One of the men takes a tiny device out of his pocket, scans Vadka's eyes, and then shows him something to imprint his fingers. I do the same, following suit.

Then we're in a steel cage that might look like an elevator shaft if it wasn't so small and so tight. The walls around us are made of cement.

If I were claustrophobic, I'd be having a fucking heart attack right now.

We're going down. Down.

My belly plunges to my toes, and suddenly I realize... maybe I *am* claustrophobic. I just never challenged it before.

I've never been in something that resembled a tomb encased in concrete, sinking down into the center of the earth.

Dramatic, maybe, but that's what it fucking feels like.

Jesus.

I keep going, and then I realize I'm holding my breath. My vision's a little dizzy.

Vadka is talking with the men, then he turns to me, and it seems he knows right away I'm not okay.

"Hey. Ruthie," he says, his voice laced with concern, gentle, as if he might be coaxing a child to bed. "Are you okay?"

I open my mouth to tell him yes, to lie through my fear, but instead, I shake my head. I close my eyes and try to remember how to get air in my lungs.

"Breathe," he says in my ear.

But it does nothing.

He might as well tell me to stop anything—stop my heart, stop existing—because I can't breathe, and it scares the life out of me. I'm drowning, and there's no water in sight.

And then... his forehead presses to mine.

He smells so fucking good. He's so warm. His hand laces with mine, palm to palm, finger to finger, and right then, I forget how to breathe in *a totally different way*. I wish I could hit the pause button because I've never felt so safe in my life.

"Breathe with me, sweetheart," he says quietly.

Maybe?

"Sorry," he whispers. "I didn't mean that."

That breaks my heart a little. I don't want him to take it back.

"No," I whisper. "I liked that. I like it a lot."

"Deep breath," he says again, this time a little firmer. "Together. Breathe with me, Ruthie. Just like this."

He takes a big, dramatic breath. His chest expands, and his shoulders pull back. I mimic him, and the dizzy feeling dulls just a little. It still feels like there's a weight sitting on my chest, but his fingers are tight around mine, grounding.

"You can do this," he murmurs. "Just like that. Good girl. Breathe."

Maybe I should pretend I'm panicking more often...

"And exhale..."

We come to a stop, and the two uniformed men, still staring straight ahead, push a button. Vadka is still holding my hands. Whoever's on the other side of the door is going to see us like this—forehead to forehead, palm to palm.

He doesn't seem to care.

Of course he doesn't.

He's never changed anything about himself for anyone.

"You made it," he says finally. "We're here."

"We need a minute," he says to someone. His voice is steady but low, and I can hear the strain in it.

I blink, and it feels like waking up.

"Understood. Ruthie, are you okay?"

I take a breath. I let it out again and give Rafail a watery smile.

"Yeah. Turns out I have claustrophobia when I'm in a small enclosed space that resembles a tomb."

"Understood," he says again. My cheeks heat, and I half expect someone else to be in the room with us, but it looks like we're in a small, enclosed entryway. Shoes and coats are stacked neatly along the wall. There's a cabinet for hats. It's quiet.

"Phone goes in here." Rafail gestures to a safe. "You'll have to clean up here. We're doing our best to keep the place sanitized. It's tight quarters."

"Understood." Everything feels surreal.

"Who else is here?" Vadka asks.

"Rodion and Ember. You. Luka. Everyone else is at the secondary house. The kids are with Polina's mom."

Polina's mom is none other than Ekaterina Romanova. They're safe.

"I wouldn't know what we'd do with them in a place like this," Rafail admits.

Vadka smiles, the warmth coming off him like the glow of a dying fire that still has heat.

"I need to see Luka," Vadka says. "Can we see him without waking him up?"

"Of course," Rafail replies. He leads us down the short corridor, tapping on a door. A few seconds later, we hear rustling on the other side.

The house is surprisingly homey, given the starkness of the situation. The walls are painted soft neutral tones, the lighting warm and low. There's a lived-in feel—blankets draped over the couch, half-empty cups on a shelf, books stacked on the end table. It's tight quarters but not cold.

Zoya opens the door and puts a finger to her lips. She wiggles her fingers in greeting, then gestures toward the bed where Luka is fast asleep.

My heart melts.

"How was he?" Vadka asks softly.

"Great," she replies just as quietly. "I made him some warm milk and got him good and sleepy, but Rodion wore him out playing outside today, so he was exhausted. He fell asleep at dinner."

I love this. I love them. I love that Luka doesn't just have Vadka and me, both half human from our own grief, but others too. A whole little village helping raise him.

"I read him stories until he was dead asleep," Zoya adds, her voice warm. "He was so cute; his head was on my shoulder."

Vadka smiles and says softly, almost to himself, "He loves when we read to him."

Then he crosses the room, lowering himself to his knees beside the bed. His face softens as he runs one large, calloused hand over his boy's head. Gently, he strokes the damp hair back from Luka's forehead.

He says something in Russian, something I don't quite catch. Something about sweet dreams.

Zoya's eyes are shining. Mine are too. Good. It's not just me, then.

I kneel on the other side of the bed, looking down at the small, angelic form of my little nephew. There's something about sleeping children that pulls on the heartstrings like nothing else. His cheeks are flushed rosy red. He's wearing Superman pajamas that are already a little too tight, stretched over that still-round little belly.

Vadka and I both bend to kiss his forehead at the same time —and freeze, noses nearly touching.

I pull back first and lift Luka's little hand and kiss each sweet knuckle. Then I arrange the blanket around him and push to my feet. Something about seeing him safe, breathing easy, at rest... it makes my heart rest too.

Then he stirs and rolls over. One sleepy eye opens.

"Papa," he says quietly and then looks at me. His eyes flutter shut again, and he snuggles deeper beneath the blanket with a sleepy smile.

When Vadka gets to his feet, his eyes are shining too.

Why did we ever teach men that it's wrong to cry?

If I ever have a son, I will make sure he knows that emotions are strength. That good men cry. That everyone cries.

Everyone.

When we leave the room, Vadka sighs heavily. I stifle a yawn. I'm so damn ready for bed.

Rafail meets us on the other side.

"So... there's only one problem," Rafail says, clearing his throat. He tucks his hands into his pockets, and I think this may very well be the first time I've ever seen Rafail look *sheepish.*

"These bunkers were built for couples. Rodion and Ember are in one room. Polina and I are in another. Luka's with Zoya, and there's only one room left."

He looks away.

Oh god.

Oh no.

I know exactly what he's going to say before he says it.

"That means you have this room, and it's kind of tight quarters," he says apologetically. "And there's only one bed."

CHAPTER 8

VADKA

I BLOW OUT A BREATH. In my head, I'm groaning, but we have to make this work. I'm an adult, not a horny fucking teenager.

So I nod. "Alright, we'll make it work."

If it weren't for the apologetic look on Rafail's face, I'd almost think they were trying to set us the fuck up. But I know they're not. They're just trying to keep people alive.

Ruthie's eyes are wide, but she doesn't say anything out loud.

Fine. I'll take the floor. Or the couch. Or whatever.

But the second I open the door, I realize what Rafail meant when he said tight quarters.

There's no fucking way I'll get a decent night's sleep on that floor. I'd have to curl into the fetal position just to fit between the edge of the bed and the wall.

I'll survive.

"I'll take the floor," I grunt.

Ruthie snorts. "Yeah, no fucking way, babe. You really think I'm gonna risk my sister coming back from the grave to strangle me in my sleep because I made her husband sleep on a *cement floor*? Are you fucking kidding me?"

Babe? I like that.

Fuck.

She gives me a sharp nod.

"What are we, in seventh grade? We're gonna share the damn bed, and we're gonna keep our hands off each other."

Then she quickly looks away, and her cheeks flush pink. I almost laugh.

She's so fucking beautiful. And a man has needs. My fist in the shower is nothing like a hot, sweet cunt.

What if I lose control with all this sleep deprivation? What if I get hard? How can I *not* get hard?

Because I'm a fucking grown-up, that's how. Of course I can do this.

She plants her hands on her hips and stares at me. "What are our options? I could go sleep on the toddler bed in Zoya's room, and we could wake up Luka and make him sleep in bed with you."

I roll my eyes. "You're being ridiculous."

"*I'm* the one being ridiculous? You just suggested sleeping on cement."

"Fine. All right then. There's a duffel bag of clothes—generic leggings, shorts, a tee, and such—in our bathroom there."

I point to the bathroom. "Go get ready," I grumble at her.

"Go get ready," she throws over her shoulder like a dare, all sass.

And I swear to god, it takes every ounce of control I have not to drag her back by that smart little mouth and put her over my knee. She's always been a brat. When she wasn't mine, I let it slide.

But now?

Now I can't stop picturing how she'd look with my handprint on her ass.

And she's still not mine.

I fucking hate that I love brats.

She's in front of the mirror, twisting her hair up, spine arched like she knows exactly what she's doing to me.

I grab the clothes just to have something to hold that isn't her. Just to keep my hands from acting on instinct.

Is she baiting me? Of all the women in my life, I'd never say Ruthie was a flirt. She's too snarky, too independent.

But I was married to her sister, a little voice in the back of my head reminds me...

She turns, catches my stare, and smirks. "Oh, relax. I know you're picturing me naked, but I'll make sure the lights are off. For your... *comfort*." She sways a bit, wobbly on her feet.

Jesus.

Ruthie's still tipsy.

"You're drunk, Ruthie. Drink some water and get your ass in bed."

"I'm not drunk." She rolls her eyes at me, and I'm losing a grip on my self-control.

"You're one more bratty word from getting thrown over my knee," I threaten her. "Drunk or not, I'll fucking sober you up."

That gets her attention. Her mouth parts, and she doesn't move. Doesn't speak. But her eyes flare, and her voice drops.

"Getting kinky on me, Vadka?" she asks. And then she grins. Fucking grins.

"Ruthie," I growl and flex my hand. I can already feel the sting on my palm.

Mariah wasn't into any of that, and I—

I can't think about Mariah.

I turn away as Ruthie grabs her stuff and heads for the bathroom, mouthing off at me under her breath as she goes. I grit my teeth and take a step toward her.

What the hell am I doing?

She's not mine. She might deserve a good spanking, but I can't go there. She'd either slice my throat or kiss me—and neither of those are viable options.

Jesus.

I hear her fumbling around in the bathroom when my exhaustion hits me like a two-by-four. I've barely slept today. My eyes are sandpaper-dry, my throat aches, and my head is pounding from lack of sleep. I need to sleep so fucking bad. I'm gonna sleep like the dead when I hit the bed, whether she's beside me or not.

I grab a pair of boxers—don't sleep in anything more than that—strip out of my clothes and fold them on top of the dresser.

The first couple of weeks after Mariah died, I couldn't eat. Couldn't sleep. I threw myself into the gym, the one thing I could still control. The burn made my own pain easier to bear, if only for a little while.

And the results? Not bad. I'd gotten soft with marriage and parenthood. It feels good to get stronger.

I strip off my shirt. Step out of my pants. I figure I've got a few seconds to get dressed while Ruthie's still in the bathroom.

Just as I'm stepping into my boxers, the door swings open.

"Hey, do you have—"

I spin around so she doesn't see my dick, and instead, flash her my ass. Great.

"Nice ass," she says. "Tell your trainer that whatever he's doing with your glutes, it's working." She giggles, and it's so fucking adorable, I smile.

"Just wondering if you had something that resembles a comb or a hairbrush," she says, running her fingers through her tangled hair. "*Look* at this mess."

She's beautiful. Disheveled. Windswept. Her eyes are bright. And there's something about her—always *something* —that makes me want to wrap her in my arms and kiss her until she forgets every damn thing that ever hurt.

I need another fucking drink.

"I'll find one," I say. "I'm getting another drink too. Do you want anything?"

"I had enough," she says. "And wait, there's a brush in the bottom of this bag."

I decide bed will be a better option than another drink. So I peel back the covers to what is, thankfully, a very large bed, and I lie down. God, it feels good to lie down. Every muscle in my body is tense and aching, and my whole body needs rest. I'm suddenly aware of my lack of clothing.

I glance over at the sweaty, folded T-shirt on the dresser. I don't want to wear it.

Ruthie notices where my focus is. "You don't have to wear that. I'm not interested in sleeping in bed with you and your body odor."

Brat. She's so getting it for that.

"I bet you usually sleep naked or something," she adds.

I grunt.

Her cheeks flush, and she rolls her eyes. "Listen, just sleep in your boxers. I'm immune to you guys by now." She waves a hand in the air.

"Spends two hours at the gym for weeks on end only to hear

she's fucking *immune* to me," I mutter. "You really know how to build a guy up."

But I'm not dumb. And I don't miss the way her nipples peak through her T-shirt.

She snorts. "Well, if you think I'm wearing a bra to bed again—fucking torture devices. I hardly wear one during the day as it is."

I did not need to know that.

I did *not* need to know that.

"How long do you think we'll be here?" she asks.

"Couple days," I tell her. "These places aren't meant for long-term. Just enough time so we can secure the safety of everybody here. Know where we stand."

Right now, everything feels tense—on edge. Our rivals are circling, waiting for us to slip. Trying to squeeze us out of the port, threaten the docks, poison our routes. We've lost two runners already. Another went missing.

This safe house is a band-aid on a bullet wound, but it's all we've got while Matvei figures out what comes next.

"I'll have to get in touch with my boss," she says with a frown.

"If I know Rafail, he already did."

I watch as she swipes at her face with a round cotton pad, tosses it in the trash, and then runs the brush she found through her hair. She brushes her teeth and secures her hair in a tiny little braid. I didn't even know it was long enough to do that.

She puts lotion on her hands and lifts her foot onto the tub to moisturize her legs. She has beautiful legs—long and strong—the legs of a dancer. She took ballet when she was younger but stopped because her mother couldn't afford it anymore. I wonder if she still likes it.

"Vadka. Why are you watching me?" she asks softly, without a trace of judgment in her voice.

I am. I am watching her.

It feels intimate and, somehow, soothing. I didn't realize until right now how much I miss watching Mariah get ready for bed. There was something about her habits, her rituals, her routines—it would signal to me that it was time to sleep. And I feel the same about Ruthie now.

"I don't know," I say quietly. "It's soothing."

She's looking down at her legs, and I watch her swallow once, then twice. "Why do you keep saying things that make me wanna cry?" she says, and her voice breaks.

"I don't know," I tell her honestly. I sigh. "Why do you?"

And then she crosses the room to me, and she's crying. Tears stream down her face, and my heart aches.

"Oh, Vadka," she says, her voice cracking. "I miss her so much."

And then she's sobbing.

And fuck it all to hell—so am I.

I tug her to me, wrap my arms around her, bury my face in her hair, and cry along with her. Both of us hold onto each other like it's the only way to stay grounded, the only way to keep each other safe. I cry like I haven't in weeks.

"I miss her too, Ruthie. I do too."

"Feels like a piece of me died right along with her," she says through her tears, her voice wobbly.

"I know exactly what you mean," I whisper, sniffling. Just when I think I'm getting better—that I'm stronger, that I can go on missing her and still be human again—part of me breaks all over again. I look at Luka, and I see Mariah. And I remember she's not going to watch him get older.

It's messy and heartbreaking as we both cry, but we need it. Both of us.

And then, after a few minutes, she stills. And so do I. She's lying in my arms with her head on my shoulder, and it feels so fucking good to have someone to hold again.

A part of me wants to say I'm sorry. I wish I could've been stronger for her. But another part of me knows—I can only give her what I have. I can't pretend to be whole when I'm broken. When I'm aching. When sometimes it feels too hard to breathe.

I reach for the bedside table and find a small square box of tissues and hand her some. She blows her nose. I grab a couple and blow mine.

"Fuck it," I tell her. "I'm sorry—" I start to say, but she puts a hand on my shoulder.

"For loving my sister?" she says. "Don't you ever fucking apologize for that again."

"No," I say quietly. "I just... I want to stay strong for you. That's what Mariah would've wanted."

She rests her hand on my cheek and holds my gaze with hers. Her voice is strong now. Certain.

"And at what point," she whispers, "have you ever stopped being strong for me?"

"God, Ruthie."

I tug her to my chest and hold her in a hug, one hand on the back of her head, my other arm wrapped around her—because I never wanna let go. *Never*.

"Oh look, there's a little fridge in here," she whispers.

And I finally release her.

"Maybe there's water?"

She opens it and finds two bottles of water. "Almost as if somebody knew we'd either be crying or drunk or both," she says and hands me a bottle. I twist off the top and quietly drink the water. Funny how a cold bottle of water actually does help.

"Come on," I say quietly, patting the bed next to me. "Get in bed. I won't touch you."

"What if I want you to?" she says with a giggle. And this time, she doesn't meet my eyes. "I mean, you don't have to feel me up or anything, but... might be nice to fall asleep next to each other? And..."

I roll her over and give her ass a good, hard swat. My hand is big, so it covers a lot of real estate. "Behave, woman."

"My fucking god, your hand is like a paddle!" Her cheeks are flushed as she rolls over.

"I said behave and go to sleep," I growl.

"Fine," she says, and I don't miss the little smile she gives me.

She nestles down beside me, chasing sleep. And right now, sex is the furthest thing from my mind—because my arm is around her, and she's tucked up against my chest, and I realize just how much I fucking miss this. Holding someone. Protecting them. It fulfills something primal in me.

It doesn't take long for her breathing to slow.

And it doesn't take long for me to get turned on. I can't help it—it's just life. I pull back a little, just to give her space, but I keep my arm around her. My eyes feel so heavy.

I WAKE up the next morning, my arm still draped over Ruthie. It's the first night I've slept through since Mariah died.

I tell myself it's because we're in the safe house, my brothers are here, and there's no fucking way anybody's getting to the people I love—not while we're here. But I know, deep down, it's due in some part to the beautiful woman beside me.

She's snoring, and there's a line of drool stretching from her lip to the pillow. I can't help it—I laugh out loud, which jolts her.

"What?" she says, blinking, startled. "Rude."

She sees me grinning. "Whatever. That's what happens when people sleep. Forgive me if I was fucking exhausted."

"Not judging," I tell her. I roll over and stretch my arms above my head, adjusting the sheets around me so she doesn't see the raging fucking wood I woke up with. Natural biological thing, sure—but something tells me it would complicate things. I'm a big guy, and I'm pretty sure she notices.

She stretches, too, arms over her head, and yawns like a cat. "Did you sleep?"

"Like a fucking baby. You?"

"Yeah. You know, it's so strange that people say, 'slept like a baby.' Babies sleep like shit," she says, shaking her head.

I laugh. "Luka did. You remember that?"

"Do I remember that? I thought we were gonna have to commit my sister." She shakes her head again. "I've never seen a human being so sleep-deprived in my life."

I smile, staring up at the flat white ceiling, one arm above my head, the other folded across my chest. "She was so insistent on breastfeeding him. She'd barely let me touch him. All night, I swear to fuck, she was up every hour with that kid."

"But she pulled through, didn't she?" Ruthie says.

"She did," I agree. "It's the one thing you can say about you girls. You don't give up easily."

"*You* definitely didn't," she says, shaking her head.

The smell of coffee and bacon wafts through the air. My stomach rumbles.

"I'm gonna go see if Luka is up."

"I'll see too," she says, pushing out of bed.

The loose T-shirt she's wearing has ridden up during the night, exposing her back—and I realize for the first time, it's covered in ink.

"Wait a minute," I say, voice going stern. "When the fuck did you get a back tattoo?"

She starts tugging her shirt down.

"Ruthie!"

"What?"

"Did Mariah know about this?"

"She did not. Why would she have to know about my tattoos? I'm an adult."

I lower my voice dangerously. "Were you an adult when you *got* them?"

"Does that matter?" she snaps back, answering her own question.

"It fucking does. Your sister would've killed you. Let me see."

It's not the tats, but we would've wanted to make sure her tattoo artist was legit.

She rolls her eyes. "Fine."

Then she turns, slow and unbothered, and lifts her shirt again—baring her back like she doesn't know what she's doing to me. Or maybe she does.

Hell, maybe that's the point.

And I freeze.

The gentle curve of her lower back catches the light—subtle muscle, smooth skin. The slope of her spine disappears into the waistband of those too-tight shorts, and I swear I can see her pulse flickering beneath the surface.

But it's the ink that kills me.

I reach for her without thinking. My fingertips barely graze her, tracing the black lines carved into her skin.

The tattoos are fucking stunning.

Delicate, fierce, feminine—like her.

Wings unfurling from her shoulder blades, a dagger entwined in roses down her spine, thorns curling around words I can't fully read from here.

"Jesus Christ," I breathe out. "They're fucking gorgeous."

She hums, smug. "You gonna kiss them or just stare like a creep?"

I don't answer. Because now all I can think about is where the ink ends.

"Do you have any others?" I ask, my voice rough.

"Wouldn't you like to know." She glances over her shoulder, her grin lazy and lethal.

"Yes, *sir*. In places *you're* not allowed to see," she says coyly.

And I want to kiss her.

I'm *consumed* with the desire to kiss her. I want to gather her in my arms, bury my fingers in her hair, and taste her lips. Quiet the fire. Every step I take brings me closer to her, and I want to take that next step more than anything.

But I don't. I can't. It's wrong.

What the hell is wrong with me?

She speaks softly, her voice barely above a whisper. "Go check on Luka. I'll get dressed. It would be kind of awkward if we left the room at the same time, anyway, wouldn't it?"

"I don't give a fuck. Those are my brothers."

"I think... I'd feel better not planting suggestions."

Fair enough.

I push out of bed and pull on a pair of gray sweats.

"Did someone put those there as a prank?" she says from the bed, eyeing them with a raised brow.

I glance at her, confused. "What?"

"Nothing," she says, rolling her eyes and heading to the bathroom. "Gray sweats are just the male equivalent of lingerie."

What the fuck is she talking about?

She disappears into the bathroom, taking care of whatever she needs to, and I head out to the main room.

Luka is sitting at the table with Polina—Rafail's wife—and Zoya. I can hear Rafail's voice coming from the other room, probably in the middle of a call.

"Papa!" Luka leaps up from his seat, promptly knocking his juice to the floor. It splashes across the tile. He looks horrified, frozen in the moment, but Polina and Zoya are on their feet in seconds.

"Hey, it's okay," Polina says gently. "Accidents happen. Come help me clean this up, Luka."

He clumsily helps them mop up the mess while I walk over to the table, crouching down in front of him. I reach for him.

"She's right," I say softly. "Accidents happen. Come here, buddy. I missed you."

He jumps into my arms, and I scoop him up. His little legs wrap around my waist, arms loop around my neck, and he rests his head against my shoulder.

"I missed you too. I had fun with Auntie Zoya, but I like my bed at home better. When can we go home, Papa?"

"Soon," I promise him. "We'll have some more fun today, okay?"

He lifts his head. "Is Auntie Ruthie coming?"

I freeze for half a second. I wish he hadn't asked. I'd rather not bring attention to the fact that Ruthie and I are sharing a bed.

"She's here, buddy."

He grins. "I like it when she visits."

"Morning."

Ruthie steps out just then.

Luka shimmies down my chest and launches himself at her.

"Hey!" I call out. "Don't knock your auntie down."

"Sorry," he says, hugging her tightly. "I'm just excited to see you."

She ruffles his hair. "Thank you. I'm not as sturdy as your daddy, and I think I'd fall over a lot easier than he would."

"Let's not test that theory," I mutter.

She's changed clothes—simple, clean—but she looks... stunning. She always wears black, nothing fitted or curvy. But now? She's in a pair of jeans that hug her hips and a little white tank top. Beautiful.

I can't believe I almost kissed her. What the fuck is wrong with me?

"Alright, we need to make some plans," Rafail says, coming around the corner.

It's unusual to see him all casual. He's in jeans and a Henley—uncommon for him. "Let's talk details. Turns out, it was a false alarm. We intercepted data about the Irish, but it didn't pan out. The threats didn't come to fruition, and no one was hurt. Just a whole lot of noise and nothing real behind it. So after I get clearance today, we should be free to go home."

Free to go home.

Why does that make me feel so disappointed?

CHAPTER 9

RUTHIE

I DON'T SEE either of them for two days, and it aches.

But once I'm sober, once the fog in my head starts to lift, it's like I need a sign—something, anything—to prove everything's okay.

A few days have passed since the safe house, and I'm lying in bed, staring up at the ceiling. No news from the Irish side of things, which I'm taking as a good sign. No news is good news in our world.

I grab my phone, scrolling through old messages until my eyes land on one I know by heart. From my sister.

I've read her last text to me more times than I can count. I can hear her voice when I see the words.

Mariah
On my way, beautiful. I saw the cutest little
top for you and picked it up the other day.
Luka is with Ekaterina and Polina, and
they're going on a day trip. Girl night
tonight?

She was excited. Sweet. So her.

I called her after that and said I needed to talk about breaking up with my ex. She came. No hesitation, just met me at the bar.

That was the last text she ever sent me. The last time she ever came to the bar.

Because that was the night she was shot. Killed. Her light and life just snuffed from the world like a candle with a gust of wind. Just like that.

And I can't stop carrying the guilt of it—because she was only there for me. She wasn't even supposed to be at the damn bar.

I stare at the phone, and I wonder... is Vadka still paying her phone bill? Does he want the line to stay active? A little thread that keeps her in this world?

I check the time. He's at work. Knowing him, he probably has her phone with him. Luka is with Zoya today, and the new nanny's supposed to be starting her trial run.

I tap her name. Swallowing hard, I ignore the brutal flash of pain in my chest and hit call.

My nose tingles, my eyes well up. As the phone rings, I wish for the impossible. I wish she'd pick up, just like she always did. *"Hey, beautiful."*

We didn't grow up with a lot of love or praise. Affirmation was scarce and rationed. But Mariah? She made sure I knew I was loved. She called me beautiful every single time.

Of course she doesn't answer.

Then it goes to voicemail. Her voice. Still there. Strong and sweet and somehow so alive.

"Hey, sorry I missed your call. You know what to do. Hope you have a great day."

Some people might call it generic. I don't. I knew she meant every damn word.

I pinch the bridge of my nose and let the pain roll over me. I don't know what else to do.

Beep.

Time to leave a message.

"Hey," I say softly. "I guess part of me wants to believe you'll get this. Maybe heaven has voicemail. I don't know. I don't even know if I believe in places like that... but if it exists, you're definitely there. If anyone is, you will be."

I pause. Swallow.

There's so much I want to tell her.

That Luka's getting taller. His eyes are starting to look more like hers than ever.

That I haven't bought a single new thing for *myself* since she died—not clothes, not shoes, nothing. I can't even step into the stores we used to shop at.

That I got a stupid infection because I'm constantly dehydrated. It's crazy, but I refuse to use the bathroom at work—that's where she died.

That I want to quit that job, but doing so feels like giving up on her. Like walking away from the last place she was.

That I'm drawn to her husband in a way that scares me. That I think he feels it too.

But I don't say any of that.

Because maybe I am talking into a void. Maybe someone will hear.

"I miss you. I miss you so much," I whisper. "And I'm sorry. I'm sorry I asked you to come to that bar. I'm sorry for all of it."

What I don't say out loud—the secret lodged in my chest—is what I feel the most shame over: I'm sorry I'm falling in love with your husband. And now I know why you did.

"I love you." I breathe. "So much."

Then I hang up.

I can at least shower. Wash the day off. Wash the grief off—at least for a few minutes.

I hop in the shower. Wash my hair. Condition. Exfoliate my face with that little bottle Mariah gave me forever ago that I never even opened. Brush my teeth. Shave my legs. And, of course, I nick my ankle so bad I have to slap a Band-Aid on it and hiss through my teeth. Hurts like a motherfucker.

When I towel off, my phone buzzes on the sink.

And just like always, I glance at it with that same irrational hope—that it might be from her. Even though I know it won't be.

They say it's normal. That grief does that to you.

But I'm so tired of this part.

I swipe.

It's Vadka.

My heart flinches.

I miss her.

> **Vadka**
> Hey, where have you been? We miss you.
> Are you all right?

We.

They miss me.

Not just Luka.

Vadka does.

Of course he does. I'm the living thread to his dead wife. The only connection left.

I don't resent him for it, but I do wish he missed me, not just who I represent and the comfort that might bring.

I type back:

> Hey, I'm good. Just working a lot, getting some things done. Need to get a haircut.

Vadka
And an oil change.

I can practically hear his voice. That low, rich sound that's starting to haunt my dreams. We're talking about haircuts and oil changes. The next thing up, we'll talk about the weather or maybe the price of milk. *God.*

An oil change.

I smirk.

Yeah, I guess I should probably do that too.

Vadka
Luka has been asking for you every day.
When are you free again?

My heart thumps. I hesitate. Then type:

I'm free now. How's the new nanny working out?

Vadka
I don't know yet. Trying not to judge too
fast. But she seems… strict.

Why didn't it dawn on me? That Vadka wouldn't be into hiring someone from the district. That's not his style. He grew up, and he's changed. Lately, he doesn't want anyone like that around Luka. He wants someone different. Someone better. He wants someone who will love Luka the way his mother did. Full stop.

I'm gonna give her more time though. She just started. Luka doesn't like her.

Great. Did I let my own selfish, tangled-up feelings cloud my ability to be fair? Was I judging her too quickly? Was I making it about me instead of about what Luka needed?

I really fucking did.

Well, that sucks. Yeah… give it a couple days and see what happens. Maybe she'll soften up a bit. Um. How are things with the Irish?

Vadka
That's something we should talk about in person. But the short answer is… quiet.

Is that a good thing?

Vadka
In person, Ruthie.

My heart skips a beat and flips over in my chest like it's trying to get free. I stick my tongue out at the phone like a teenager with a crush. I remember the way he slapped my ass that night we shared a bed, the way my whole body lit up like a fuse was lit under my skin. The way I tumbled straight out of my head and into pure sensation.

Vadka
Early dinner today?

Yes. Please. I'd like that.

Vadka
I'll pick you up. See you in an hour?

Perfect.

Vadka
See you then.

I set my phone down and stare at myself in the mirror. My hair's in a messy bun. I'm in a T-shirt with no bra underneath. I haven't touched my eyebrows in… I don't even know how long. And—oh my god—is that a white hair on my chin? What the actual fuck? When did that happen?

My clothes are cold and a little stiff—they're old and don't fit like they used to. Not surprising, honestly. I wear things until they fall apart. I hate shopping for clothes. Always have. There are maybe two things on earth I'd rather do less than shop, and that's saying something. I only ever enjoyed it with Mariah because she made it feel like a game, like something we could laugh through. She made it bearable, even fun. She was taller and curvier than me, so we never shared clothes. But God, I wish we could have. I'd give anything to have a piece of her that I could wrap around me and pull close like armor. Like comfort. Anything.

I throw on a pair of black leggings and a black shirt. And I already hear my sister's voice in my head, scolding me with love.

"You need color, beautiful. It's like you're in mourning every day."

I am now.

That voice... might be the only thing that could convince me to try something other than this all-black armor I live in. I don't want to stay here anymore. I don't want to be frozen in time. What is this? Old-school Italy? I'll mourn the death of my sister—my best friend—until the day I die. But mourning doesn't mean I stop living. Mourning doesn't mean I pull the blinds closed on my entire life.

Still... I don't know how to dress myself anymore.

Talking to her voicemail helped. So I decide to text her.

Will Vadka see it? Would he read her texts? I don't know why he would... Who's texting a dead woman, right?

> I need new clothes. I don't know how to shop for myself. You once told me that when I wear all black, it makes me look like I'm in mourning. And there's never been a time when that mattered more than now. I don't want to look like mourning anymore, Mariah. Because maybe... if I don't look like mourning... it won't feel like I am.

I wipe my eyes. The message says delivered. I pick my phone back up, not ready to stop. Not ready to let it go.

I'm not going to send it, but I can type it. I can say it somewhere. Even if it's just for me.

Maybe I'll feel better.

> Forgive me, please forgive me, but I think I'm falling in love with your husband.

There. I said it. And now that I have, I have more to say.

> I see now why you loved him, Mariah. I was always a good sister to you. I never let myself look at him as anything but a brother. But god, he's hot. He's funny. He's sweet. He's hardworking as hell. And he makes me feel safe. I like who I am when I'm with him. I like how I feel.

My finger hovers over the X. Just delete it. Just delete it.

But when I try, my phone freezes. The screen locks, and it gets hot in my hand. Overheating again. I forgot this has been happening.

Oh shit. Oh fuck.

Now I can't delete it.

Panic rises like fire in my chest.

"You stupid motherfucking—"

So I go nuclear. I press the power button and hold it down until the screen goes black. Power off. Power down.

I'm breathing like I just ran a marathon. My hands are shaking. Okay. Okay. Let's be rational.

First—even if it sent, what are the chances he sees it immediately?

Second—if you shut off the phone, doesn't that stop the message from going through?

Third—what's the worst that could happen?

Worst case? He reads it. He realizes I'm crushing on him. And he doesn't feel the same way.

Fuck. My. Actual. Life.

I power the phone back on. My stomach flips over itself. I open messages.

And scream. Out loud.

"No! Oh my god."

The message sent. The fucking message sent. Shit, shit, fuck, shit.

I dial Vadka. Fast. I have to get to the house. I have to find her phone. I have to delete the message. I try to delete it on my end, but all it says is:

"This message may not be deleted by all parties."

Perfect. Fucking useless.

He answers, all calm and casual.

"Hey, what's up? We haven't left yet. Are you okay?"

God, of course that's his first thought.

Are you okay?

Yeah. I'm fine.

No. I'm not.

"Why don't I just come to your house? You don't have to pick me up for dinner. We can do something else."

There.

"Well," he says slowly. "I already promised Luka I'd take him to the place with the french fries and the animal-shaped milk cups."

"...There's a place that has animal-shaped milk cups?"

I want one.

Shit. Focus.

"That's cool. But we can head back to the house after, if you want. Hang out for a bit, maybe watch a movie. Put him to bed, you know? Let it feel like dinner time, not just some rushed afternoon."

So I send Zoya a quick SOS message and tell her as much as I can.

> **Zoya**
> Oh god. I'm on it. I know he still has her phone and I might be able to locate it because Rafail tracks all of them and she was on our family plan. Stay calm.

Okay, this might work out. I can do this.

I'm staring out my window, nerves coiled tight, when I finally see them. Vadka's just pulling up, and before I can even get to the door, I see him already out of the car, unbuckling Luka from his seat. And—wait. Is Luka holding flowers?

Oh my god. He is. That little boy is actually holding flowers.

I open the door, and there he is, standing with a proud little grin, a colorful bouquet in his tiny hands, and Vadka just behind him, looking... a little *sheepish*. Which, honestly, might be the most shocking part. I've never seen him with such boyish charm.

"Vadka," I say, smiling even as my heart does this slow, weightless somersault. "I would've come out to the car. You didn't have to unbuckle him and all that."

Vadka shrugs, serious. His brow creases as he ruffles Luka's hair, that quiet, protective energy radiating off him naturally. My throat tightens. Somehow, seeing the way he is with this little boy makes my own need to be protected, cared for, and cherished heighten.

"I need to teach him how to be a man," he says, like it's the most obvious thing in the world. "A real man doesn't wait curbside for his woman. He goes to the door. Luka—open the door for your auntie. Let her have a seat."

My heart does a full-on collapse.

"That's right," Luka says, nodding solemnly, like he's practiced the line a dozen times. "And brings her flowers. You look so pretty, Auntie. So, so pretty."

He hands me the bouquet, beaming, that one dimple of his popping like a secret weapon he absolutely knows how to use. I crouch down, kiss his sweet cheek, and wrap him in a hug that I never want to let go.

"You picked these out for me?"

"No," he says honestly, like kids do. "Papa did. But he told me to bring them to you."

I try to bite back my smile, but it still breaks through. I glance up at Vadka and swear—*swear*—he's *blushing*.

This massive, tattooed, leather-jacket-wearing, motorcycle-riding badass enforcer is blushing on my front stoop because his son just outed him as soft and sweet.

My damn heart.

"Well, please tell your papa they're beautiful," I say, winking at Luka.

"She says they're beautiful!" Luka yells up to Vadka, bouncing like a pogo stick.

"I heard her," Vadka replies, voice low and smooth but laced with warmth only Luka can bring out. He winks at me, and the flutter it ignites low in my stomach is immediate and dangerous. "Let's get these in some water. I'll put them in a vase and be right back—then we can grab dinner. I heard this place has animal-shaped cups?"

Luka lights up. "Animal cups!"

Seriously, are kids this easy to please?

"We'll go with you," Vadka says, trailing after us.

I don't want them to come in though. I haven't tidied up.

Mariah used to rag on me for being messy—always immaculate, always put-together, like a living Pinterest board—but I'm not a total disaster. There's a laundry basket I haven't folded, a couple of glasses in the sink, a leaning tower of unopened mail, and, yeah, some shopping bags I haven't gone through. It's... lived-in. Not gross or even chaos.

While I'm fussing with the flowers, I catch Vadka staring at my front door like it personally offended him. He touches the lock and glances at the windows, assesses the doorframe with that stern look that tells me he's not happy.

"This is your lock?" he asks, like I just told him I leave my door open at night.

"What?"

"I could get through this with one of Luka's plastic hammers. This is not okay."

I roll my eyes, exhaling hard. "Didn't you say the threat from the Irish wasn't real?"

"No," he snaps, eyes going dark and stormy. "I said that particular lead is a red herring. But you are absolutely in danger, Ruthie. We've had guards on you."

I freeze. "When were you planning on telling me that?"

"Today," he says, shaking his head like he's already tired of the conversation. "They started last night. But this lock? No. This isn't amateur hour. I'm gonna talk to your landlord."

"*I* can talk to my landlord."

"You can. But I'll get it done faster. And before you hit me with that 'strong woman' argument, remember—"

"This is the biggest bed I've ever seen!" Luka shouts from the bedroom, suddenly airborne on my mattress, bouncing like he has springs in his feet. I gasp.

"Oh my god, Luka—don't do that! You could fall!" I start toward him.

"Luka!" Vadka's *dad* voice cuts through the room, sharp and commanding. "Get down. *Now.*"

Luka flops onto his butt, wide-eyed, lower lip already trembling. "I just wanted to jump," he says in a small voice.

Vadka strides over, kneels, and wraps his arms around him in one swift, protective move.

"I know, bud. But you could get hurt. Badly. I had a cousin fall off a bed and break his collarbone."

"His what?" Luka asks, eyes wide.

"This bone." Vadka touches Luka's shoulder gently. "It's not fun. You'd be in pain and stuck in a sling for weeks."

Luka's lip starts to wobble again. "But I wanna." He scowls. "You can't make me not jump on the bed!"

Oh no. Here it comes.

"It's my bed," I say firmly, stepping in. "And if your papa says you can't jump, then you can't jump. Even if he said yes, *I'd* still say no. That's not what beds are for."

He launches into a mini tantrum, limbs flailing, noises dramatic and relentless. Vadka scoops him up again, holding him close, his jaw tight and eyes clouded. I see it— the razor's edge of his restraint. I remember Mariah telling me how she'd sit with Luka during moments like this, helping Vadka soften the sharp edges and unlearn the violence passed down like a curse.

He's come so far. People love to villainize men who lose control, even for a second, but I understand the pressure. Parenting is brutal. Constant. Unrelenting. And sometimes it feels like your very sanity is splintering.

"You alright?" I ask gently, remembering what Mariah said about standing beside him in these moments.

"I'm fine," he says, too quietly.

I know better.

We'll talk about it later. We need to. I think it might help both of us.

"I've had a lot of practice by now," he says eventually, his voice low. "And honestly? It's unrealistic to expect kids to control their emotions when the adults raising them can't even control their own." He smirks. "I'm not bothered by a little ball of unrestrained emotional energy."

Hmm. I'll keep that in mind.

He settles Luka on his knee, meeting his gaze evenly. "But listen. If you don't behave, we're not going to that restaurant. We'll go home. You'll eat, and then it's straight to bed. *No* animal cups. No shows. No dessert."

Oof. He's playing hardball.

"But I—"

"Luka." Vadka interrupts, his tone unrelenting. "You heard me."

Luka pouts, but he nods. The tantrum dissolves, and the storm passes.

And me? I'm just standing there, watching the man I might be falling for turn into the kind of father his son can rely on.

And I think it's kind of absurd—no, it *is* absurd—that some parents expect their kids to have this airtight control over their emotions when they can't even regulate their own for five damn minutes. Like, really? You're throwing tantrums in traffic, but your kid's not allowed to cry about being told "no"? Come on. Meanwhile, I'm over here like, I can schedule my emotions. Compartmentalize like a pro. Lock them up, put them in a box, label it with a smile, and keep moving.

Vadka continues in that deep, composed voice of his, "But if you don't behave yourself at that restaurant, you know what happens."

He gives Luka a look—one of those silent, steady ones that cuts right through any argument before it's even formed—and Luka doesn't say a word. Not one. Just nods with a little pout.

Vadka doesn't trust the moratorium on Luka's fit. Something tells me this comes from personal experience.

And I can't explain it—god, I wish I could—but seeing a man in control like that? That balance of stern and soft, of authority laced with love? It melts me. Completely. It unravels something inside me that I didn't even know was tightly wound.

Maybe it's because I never had that. Maybe it's because that was the kind of love I craved as a kid—unshakable, certain, strong. I didn't have so much as a father figure or mother who was actively involved in my life. I was either flying solo or under Mariah's care until Vadka came around.

It's why I decided a long time ago that I wasn't meant to be a mother. I'm not wired for it. I'm not soft in the ways children need, and I don't want to do more harm than good. I've always believed I wouldn't make a suitable mom.

"I disagree," Mariah once told me. "You already know how to love unconditionally, and that's the important part. Maybe the most important."

I wanted to believe her. I did. But I'm not sure she was right.

I watch Vadka take little Luka to the bathroom before we go, and I take a minute to breathe deeply and think.

Lately, I've been keeping my distance from Vadka. Things were starting to feel... too familiar. Too comfortable. Too flirty. And that's not safe. Not for him. Not for me. That night in the safe house—if he had touched me, *really* touched me, not a chaste hug or brotherly kiss on the cheek —would I have stopped him?

Would I have wanted to?

No. Dammit, I wouldn't have.

Every time I'm near him, it's like my skin's on fire. My heart kicks up, and this strange, almost teenage version of me takes over—cool, flirty, reckless. I've never looked at him this way before. Not until recently. But the cruel truth is this: He's not married anymore. And how do you not fall in love with someone who so effortlessly loves the people you care about most?

I love seeing Luka. I do. But I know it's better—safer—if I keep my distance from his father.

"I want to have french fries," Luka says, walking back in the room and sticking out his lower lip like a little duckbill, all pout and stubborn charm.

"Then are you going to behave?" I ask, raising an eyebrow at him. "Or do you need to go home and sit in your bed instead?"

Luka squirms in place, shifting from one foot to the other like a tiny ball of restless energy. But there's no possible way I could win an argument with Vadka if I tried—never mind this little boy. Luka's good. A bit wild sometimes, sure, but good. He's got that strong will but a soft heart.

"Fine," he says finally, exhaling like it's costing him something enormous. "I'll be good. Can I jump just one more time, please?"

Vadka's lips twitch with the ghost of a smile. He shakes his head slowly, then releases his boy's tiny hand. "One more jump," he agrees, pointing at the bed. "But jump toward me, okay? So I can catch you if you fall."

"All right, Auntie Ruthie?" Luka asks, wide-eyed.

Why is that the most adorable thing I've ever seen?

He runs and jumps in the middle of the bed, arms flying out, aiming straight for Vadka. And like it's the most natural thing in the world, Vadka catches him in mid-air and cradles him against his chest. He presses a kiss to the top of Luka's hair.

It's one of those stupidly soft moments that hits hard. So goddamn cute it hurts a little.

And then I remember the text. And the voicemail.

"Hey... do you ever check Mariah's phone anymore?" I ask him quietly.

He shakes his head. "Nah. I don't check it. But I still listen to her voicemail sometimes." There's a pause, then, "She doesn't get anything anymore. No messages, no voicemails. Even when she was still here, it was always just you."

"Okay. Well, I may have left her a voicemail. I miss her, and I—" My throat tightens.

"It's alright," he says softly. "I won't listen."

I try to breathe a sigh of relief, but it doesn't come easy.

I don't tell him about the text. I can't.

I don't know if I'm actually relieved. And then my phone buzzes with a message from Zoya.

Zoya
Located Mariah's phone.

And the follow-up comes fast:

Zoya
It's in his pocket.

Fuck my life.

CHAPTER 10

I LOVE SEEING Ruthie with Luka. There's something grounding about it, something whole. Knowing your kid doesn't have what they need—whether it's food, shelter, love, security—it breaks something fundamental in you. A good parent bleeds for their child. We empty our wallets and sacrifice sleep, comfort, even sanity, just to make sure they're okay. And since Mariah's been gone, there's this one thing—this massive, gaping need in Luka—that I can't fill, no matter how hard I try.

Because I'm not her.

She was soft where I'm hard. She nurtured where I protect. She was gentle in the spaces I don't even know how to reach.

And Ruthie... damn. I know I'm falling in love with her. It's impossible not to. Watching her love my son, knowing how deeply she loved my wife—it's overwhelming. And terrifying.

Because what we have, Ruthie and I, matters. It's this delicate flicker of warmth in a world that's been mostly cold and dark since Mariah died. And I'm so afraid that if I move too fast or make the wrong move, I'll snuff it out. I'll lose her. And I can't afford that. I can't lose Ruthie.

We get to the restaurant, and Ruthie's a fucking wonder. Luka's bouncing around, restless, and she just rolls with it. She pulls a crayon out from the table setup and starts drawing on the paper placemat—tic-tac-toe and little stick figures. Then she starts making up this ridiculous story about "King Luka," brave and bold, ruling over his magical kingdom with his sword forged from dragon bones and his crown made of sunlight.

I sit back in my chair and just watch them.

"Papa," Luka says, glancing over at me with that grin of his. "Do the voices."

"Luka... not here. We're in a restaurant. You're playing with your aunt—"

"Papa, please. Do the voices, Papa."

Ruthie's eyes sparkle with mischief. She smirks. "Yeah, Papa. Do the voices."

Jesus Christ. I roll my eyes dramatically, grab a napkin, and wrap it around my finger like a makeshift puppet. And then I'm off—doing this whole ridiculous act with finger puppets and over-the-top voices. Ruthie's laughing so hard she's crying, and Luka's clapping like he's at a Broadway show.

And you know what?

It feels... nice. It feels like not solo parenting for once. And not because Ruthie's like Mariah—she's not. She's nothing like Mariah. And I have to stop comparing them. Ruthie is Ruthie. And I love her just as she is.

It's not a new realization. I've loved her for a long time... in different ways. I loved her when she was that awkward, gangly teenager who needed someone—anyone—to love her back. Back then, I was her sister's boyfriend. I was her protector, her pseudo-big brother. I fought off her bullies, taught her how to drive, and helped her learn how to budget. With Mariah's help, we made sure she had everything she needed.

But this? What I feel now? It's not the same.

And I keep asking myself—do I love her because I'm vulnerable?

The waitress finally brings out our food—burgers and fries stacked high, trays of ketchup on the side. Luka dives in like he hasn't eaten in days.

"Boy, this guy's going through a growth spurt," she says with a grin.

"Tell me about it," I mutter. "I'm fucked when he's older."

She chuckles. "Mariah would've *killed* you for swearing in front of him."

It's the first time her name's been said aloud tonight, and I don't feel like curling into myself and crying. Progress, I guess.

"Sorry, Luka," I say, rubbing the back of my neck. "Don't repeat that word."

"I know," he says, chomping on a fry. "I'm not supposed to say *fuck*."

Ruthie snorts. Little brat. Pretty sure she swears more than I do.

We're halfway through dessert when the hairs on the back of my neck lift. That electric, crawling sense that something's wrong. That someone's here.

No fucking *way*. Not now. Not when I'm out with my son and my sister-in-law.

But the Irish—they don't stop. They don't quit. And I know that. I know it too damn well. They've been too quiet, and I don't trust it.

I tap the table twice to get Ruthie's attention. Luka's happily eating his ice cream. She looks over at me, questioning.

"Stay here a minute? I'll be right back."

She tilts her head, brows raised, but I just shake mine once. No. I'm not going to scare her over something that might be nothing. We don't chase shadows. We don't breathe life into ghosts.

I take the scenic route to the bathroom, a slow loop around the place. Everything seems fine—until it's not.

There's a table in the corner. Four men. Their eyes are locked on me.

I don't look back. Don't engage. Just slide my hand to the butt of my pistol, and feel the cool, hard reassurance there. Then I walk straight back to the table, grab my wallet, and throw down some cash.

"We need to go," I say quietly but firmly. "Right now."

"Papa—" Luka starts.

"*Now*, Luka," I say, my voice low and sharp.

His lip trembles, but Ruthie doesn't hesitate. She picks him up like she's done it a thousand times.

"Listen to your papa," she says, steady and calm. "Right now."

The three of us move like a nuclear unit, tight and contained, toward the exit. Behind us—chairs scrape. Shit.

I could take them. Every one of them. But I've got Ruthie and Luka with me.

Shit.

I scan the parking garage and spot our car—an SUV, parked next to a van. I did that on purpose. Cover. Options.

"Go to the car," I say to Ruthie, low and fast. "Immediately. Buckle him in."

I'm done playing defense. I'm going to be proactive this time.

She starts moving fast, dragging Luka along and holding him tight. He's a big kid for his age, and she's so small—it looks like she's about to fold under his weight. I turn, and just like that, I'm face-to-face with two men. I know instantly: Irish. I can feel it in their stance, see it in their eyes. Their weapons are already out. I don't wait. I don't hesitate.

"Run, Ruthie!" I shout.

Ice in my veins, I pull the trigger.

First one—straight between the eyes. The second—I hit his shoulder. He drops, screaming, and I finish the job. Another shot. Right between the eyes. I walk toward them, pumping lead into their bodies. One after the other. I make sure they stay down. No second chances. No mercy.

They didn't even have their guns fully drawn. *Amateurs.* Or maybe they just underestimated me.

The back parking lot's empty, no witnesses—except one old man sitting in his car, eyes wide, frozen. He stares at me like he's seen death walking. And maybe he has. I rip open my shirt and show him the sign of the Bratva burned into my skin. Brotherhood. "Fucking leave," I tell him, voice low and calm. He nods, peeling off like a scared dog. Good.

No one's gonna fuck with the Bratva. And even if they do—Rafail has the chief of police tucked in his fucking pocket.

I call Rafail immediately, scanning the area for movement, making sure no one else is stupid enough to come after us.

I fill him in.

"Where are you headed?" he asks.

"Back to my house."

I don't see any sign we were followed. It doesn't feel like a safe-house call, not yet. But I have a bag packed, ready to go, just in case.

Fucking shit.

I holster my gun and head to the car. Ruthie and Luka are safe... for now. But *fuck* these people.

I open the driver's side door—and she's sitting there. In my seat. "I'll drive," she says.

"The fuck you will," I snap. "Get in the passenger seat."

She glares. "Are you kidding me? You've got adrenaline pumping through your veins like a junkie coming down off a high. It's not safe for you to drive right now. I'll drive."

I exhale hard. She's right. I hate it, but she's right. I circle the car, but before I climb in, I lean down. I don't fucking care anymore. She crossed the line. She needs to know who she's dealing with.

I pause, then smirk.

"I'll let you drive for now, little Ruthie. But you're going over my knee for this. I swear to fuck. This is not how I operate, and—"

"Threatening me with a good time," she cuts in with a grin, not missing a beat. But her cheeks are flushed pink.

Fuck my life.

She's into this.

Damn.

I shut the door behind me and slide into the passenger seat. She's right—my body's still humming with adrenaline. I need to cool down. And I need to check in with Rafail again.

"You okay?" I ask her.

"I'm fine," she says, eyes on the road. "Are you?"

I glance into the back. Luka's got his headphones on, watching a show on her phone, totally unbothered. Oblivious.

"He didn't see anything," she whispers, like she's trying to believe it herself.

"Fuck."

"Vadka," she mutters under her breath. "You really need to stop swearing."

"I know, I know…"

I check my texts with Rafail. There's no evidence the Irish are still close, but those two? They felt personal. Too personal. Like they had a vendetta or maybe tied to someone I've already put six feet under. Figures. I've hosed down half of fucking Ireland at this point. I'm a walking target.

We pull into the driveway. Luka's head is bobbing. He's barely awake.

"Stay here tonight," I say to Ruthie, and I know how it sounds. Like I'm hitting on her by asking her to stay. But it's not that. Not this time. "Just tonight. I wanna make sure your place is more secure before you go back, okay?"

"Fine. But if you think we're snuggling in your bed again, think again."

There's a flicker of a smile on her lips.

"Of course not. You'll be in the guest room. It's a nice one."

"I know. Mariah made it that way. She always hoped Mom would come visit."

But she never did. Not once.

We go inside, and she gets Luka ready for bed while I head to the kitchen.

"You need to check in with Rafail?" she asks, returning, her voice tight, like she's bracing for something.

"Yeah. Why?"

"I'm gonna get ready for bed."

I glance down. Luka's already clean, teeth brushed, dressed in his little pajamas and clutching his favorite stuffed animal. She did all of it. Quietly. Efficiently. It's like having another adult around shifted something heavy off my shoulders I didn't even know I was carrying.

"Yeah. I'm almost done."

"Okay," she says softly. "I'm gonna change into something. I probably have clothes here, don't I?"

Maybe she does.

She used to be here all the time—when Mariah was here.

I sink onto the couch, and she looks back at me.

"You should change into something more comfortable too," she says.

She's right. We put Luka to bed and walk to the guest room together, pretending it's not intimate. Pretending we're not thinking about what it feels like to be close. To touch.

"Luka's asleep," I tell her quietly. "And you... you're in trouble."

"We don't have that kind of relationship," she says, but the look in her eyes betrays her. She wants to. God, she wants to. "You think you can tell me what to do?"

"All right," I say, low and deliberate, as I cross the room. "You get dressed. I'll go change too. Then you're going to lay yourself over my lap and take what's been coming to you."

She just stands there.

Challenging. Smiling that wicked little smile that says she's not scared of me—no, she wants me to lose control. Wants to see how far I'll go.

Dangerous little thing.

"Ruthie," I warn.

She turns, slow as sin, and bends over the dresser. On purpose. Her ass tilts up—taunting me. Daring me.

That's when I see it. The way her breath catches. The way her thighs part just slightly. The way her hands tighten around the edge of the wood like she's bracing.

She's not resisting. She's *offering* herself.

The warning slap I meant to give her turns into something else the moment my palm lands. The sound cracks loud—flesh to flesh. She gasps, then moans.

Fuck.

I'm hard instantly.

I watch the ripple of heat across her skin, the way her spine arches, pushing back for more. So I give her more. Another smack. Then another.

By the fourth, she's panting. Her legs spread wider, shameless now, her hips rocking forward like she needs the friction. My restraint slips. I can't stop.

"You think this is a game?" I rasp, my voice rough against her ear as I lean in close. I breathe her in—heat, sweat, need. "You like pushing me, baby?"

She nods, breathless, shameless. "Yeah," she whispers. "I want you to."

Fucking hell.

My hand comes down again, harder this time, angled to the crease where her ass meets her thigh. Her whole body jolts —then melts into it. She moans again, and it sounds like a prayer.

"Now tell me," I murmur, lips against her jaw, "are you going to behave yourself?"

"For now," she says. Still defiant. Still smiling.

I grin. Dark. Dangerous. "Little brat."

"If I don't... will you do that again?" she asks, her voice a tease but trembling at the edges.

I grip her hip, fingers digging in. "You do that again," I growl, "and I'll take my belt to your ass."

She shudders—visibly. Not in fear.

In *want.*

She scrambles to gather her clothes, but her hands are shaking.

"I'm gonna get dressed in the bathroom," she says, her voice tight. Then, with a glance over her shoulder, soft and serious, "We need to be careful, Vadka."

I don't need her to explain. She's not talking about the Irish. Or any threat outside this door.

She's talking about *us*. This. The edge we're dancing on.

I strip, shirt first. Then pants, the rush still buzzing in my blood like lightning. Mariah's phone falls from the pocket—thudding against the floor like a verdict.

Guilt flashes through me, sharp and fast.

I pick it up and set it on the dresser.

Then I stare at the ceiling.

What the fuck are we doing?

And why does it feel so good to lose control—only with her?

There's one new voicemail.

Who even sends those anymore?

Then I remember Ruthie said she left one, and I told her I wouldn't listen.

But then I see a text too.

So I sit on the bed, thumbing through it. My eyes go wide. My heart beats faster.

Well, damn.

CHAPTER 11

RUTHIE

I DON'T THINK I've ever been this turned on in my entire life.

Not once. Not even close.

I've never even thought about getting spanked by a guy, not seriously. But with Vadka? The way he looked at me. The authority in his voice. The rough slap of his palm against my skin? It sent me straight into overdrive. I'm soaked. Drenched. So fucking wet, I'm two seconds away from crawling into that bed, yanking off these clothes, and rubbing one out just to take the edge off.

And the worst part? He knew. That smug bastard knew exactly what he was doing to me. Every time he gets bossy. Every time I push back. Every time he calls me "little brat," a thrill zips through me like a live wire. My whole body hums with it. I shiver just thinking about it.

I want him. Desperately.

Would it be so terrible if it was just casual? Just... comfort. Skin against skin. Who could blame us? We've both been through so much.

What the fuck am I even thinking?

Oh my god.

But here I am, in his house. In his space. More turned on than I've ever been with any man who's ever touched me. And I've never—never—had sex with someone I actually cared about. Not once. I don't even know what that feels like.

And I want to.

God, I want to.

But I have to be here for Luka. I have to be his auntie. His anchor. I can't blur the lines and become his daddy's girlfriend.

...Right?

I shake my head, forcing the fantasy away. I check my messages. One from Zoya.

> **Zoya**
> Are you in the house? I heard there was
> drama at the restaurant.

So that's what we're calling it now? Drama? Oh, I'm definitely going to give him shit for that.

> I'm fine. He's getting dressed, so I'm gonna
> sneak in and delete the message from her
> phone.

Zoya
Good. He hasn't seen it yet?

I don't think so…?

Do I really know? No. Fuck it.

I have to plot a way to get into his room. He had her phone —in his hand, in his pockets—and I know exactly what has to happen next. It's essential that I get that phone because if he sees that stupid fucking text I sent…

God. But why am I in such denial? Would it really be the end of the world if he saw it? If anything, the way he touched me in that room just now made me wonder… Maybe it's not just me. Maybe I'm not the only one feeling this. Maybe he feels it too. Does he?

But what if he does want me? What if something starts—anything, even just a moment—and then… what if he realizes he doesn't? I'm not Mariah. I never was, and I never will be.

I make my way to the living room. Every corner of the space holds a memory of my sister—echoes of her life still lingering here—and maybe that's it. Maybe that's the thread I need to hold onto. Vadka and Luka, the reminders that even when someone we love is gone, the world keeps spinning. Life doesn't stop. And maybe, just maybe, I have to remember that there's always—always—something to be grateful for.

This is a small house. My sister and Vadka made sure Luka was always nearby. His little room is right off the kitchen, so he could play close, walk out to help her cook, or just be around. It was cozy, intimate, thoughtful. My sister loved decorating—obsessed over her space—and she made it beautiful. A soft white and beige aesthetic, clean lines, and gentle textures. And Luka's room? That was the one place she let chaos bloom. She let him make a mess, let his imagination spill everywhere.

I peek in and see his artwork on the dresser. Pink smudges. A crooked jug. Portraits taped to the walls, messy, bold, and full of life.

It's my fault he has a bitch for a nanny, and I need to fix this. He deserves better—so much better—than this. Of course he does.

I strain to hear Vadka in the other room. Maybe he's gone to his office or the kitchen. But of course—he's in his bedroom. What if he's looking at her phone right now? Shit.

I move quietly down the hall toward his room, every sound amplified. My heart beats like a warning in my chest. Then —I see it. A thin sliver of light glowing from under the office door. He's not in the bedroom. My heart stalls and then pounds harder. I need to move—now.

I push open the bedroom door fast. The scent hits me first. No trace of my sister anymore. None of her perfume, her lotion, her presence. Just Vadka. The quiet weight of his cologne. The clean scent of his body wash. The steam still clinging faintly to the room from his shower.

Even the bed's different. Dark navy sheets, a blue coverlet— neutral, masculine. Housekeepers come a few times a month, and it looks like they've made small changes. The room doesn't feel like Vadka and Mariah's anymore. It's just his now.

I scan the room quickly. The phone's not on the dresser. My gaze flicks to the nightstand—and there it is. A small black phone, plugged in, charging. He touched it. He's charging it. Shit. The chances he saw that text... I rush over, grab it, unlock the screen, and delete the message.

"What are you doing in my room?"

I scream. The phone slips from my hand and hits the floor with a sharp crack. No. No. I drop to my knees, hands trembling, and stare at the screen. A long, jagged crack splits the glass. A sob catches in my throat.

"I'm so sorry. I didn't mean to—"

"It's fine," he says, his voice low. "It's just a crack. We can fix it."

"I was just trying—" I'm out of breath, the words caught somewhere between shame and panic.

And then he's there. Right in front of me. His forehead touches mine, and his hands come up, framing my face.

"It's okay, Ruthie."

And I wonder why he's saying it's okay—what exactly he thinks I need comfort for. His voice is relaxed, almost soothing, and he leans in, kissing my temple gently like I'm something precious. Then I realize—he's only wearing a pair of boxers. And those boxers? They're doing absolutely nothing to hide his erection. He's hard as fuck. Bare-chested, sexy as sin. Tattoos trail along his arms, crawl up his neck, and stretch across the broad, solid plane of his chest—ink on muscle, power in every inch of him.

I reach out with a tentative hand, not even sure why, only that I have to. Like I don't have a choice. I press my palm flat to the front of his stomach—the lower part of his belly—and he feels like everything I imagined—warm, solid, strong. Masculine in a way that shakes something loose inside me. A sound rises from my throat, low and raw, escaping before I can stop it. I'm aware—painfully aware—of my own heart-beat. Of the throbbing ache building between my legs. Of how my emotions are flipping, swinging wildly—from grief to loneliness to burning, undeniable need.

Then he's pulling me toward him, his hands shifting from cradling my face to tangling into my hair. He tilts my head back, bending my mouth to his without a single word. And when his lips press to mine, something electric explodes in me. Every nerve lights up. I drop out of my head and straight into my body—fully, completely—like I never have before. His mouth takes mine, and his tongue? It slants over mine, commanding and hot. I lick him back, needing the taste of him, and he makes this low, masculine noise—half growl, half groan—that floods me with want. His arm traces down the length of my back, smooth and sure, then cups my ass in one big, possessive hand. Awareness fires through my body again, thick and sharp.

He kisses me like a man starving—and I'm the only thing that can save him. There's pain in it, yes. But underneath that pain, a glimmer of hope. Like this could mean some-thing. Like maybe we both still can.

"My sister died," I whisper, my voice catching. "But we didn't die with her. We're still here. We're still alive. Don't we deserve to live?"

I'm crying—just a little—and I know I am because my chest feels cracked open and raw, and our kiss, the intimacy of it, blends with something deeper, something breaking inside me. He pulls back, only barely, burying his face in my hair. His voice is rough, a sound like shattered glass.

"Ruthie. God, Ruthie. I read your texts to your sister. I thought it was just me. I thought I was the only one. I didn't know. I didn't know you felt it too. I thought you—"

His voice cuts off as if it's physically painful to say more. He just shakes his head, then suddenly he's lifting me—his hands under my ass, his mouth grazing mine again. He walks toward the bed like he can't wait another second. And honestly? Neither can I. I can't think beyond this moment, beyond what I need—what I want. And I know it now. I want him.

He lays me on the bed. "You're so beautiful," he whispers. "So fucking beautiful."

"Take the shirt off, Ruthie," he rasps, voice thick. "I want to see you."

I hesitate, the fabric balled in my fist. But then he cups my face, holding my gaze with something so sincere, so reverent, it undoes me.

"Beautiful girl," he whispers. "Can you trust me?"

I nod. I just know.

"Then let's give this to each other," he says quietly. "No one can touch me like you do. I don't want anyone else. I can't trust anyone else but you, Ruthie."

I slip my T-shirt over my head. My breasts spill free, and his eyes darken. His mouth closes over my nipple, and heat explodes low in my belly. Need twists inside me, and I whimper. I brace myself against the bed as he licks, his tongue flattening against my nipple until it's tight and aching. Then he grazes it with his teeth while sliding his hand between my thighs, pressing the heel of his palm into the wet, swollen center of me.

One hand rolls a nipple while his mouth works the other, switching back and forth until I feel like I might scream.

"You're so fucking beautiful," he growls. "And I want you."

I run my hands along his arms—those powerful, inked arms —and for the first time, I don't see the man who once loved my sister. I see the man who loves me. And somehow, impossibly, that makes all the difference.

He presses his face to my belly, breathing me in deep, then spreads my legs with his broad hands.

And when he licks me—fuck—I've never felt anything so good, so perfectly made to unravel me. I moan, my hand reaching instinctively for him—only for his palm to slam down on my thigh in warning.

"Put your hands by your sides," he says in that same low, commanding tone. "There's something you're gonna learn, woman. I let you get away with your mouth. I let you be a little brat. But in here? Behind these doors? I am king. Do you understand that?"

"What if I say no?"

His eyes darken, lips curling into a slow smirk as he shakes his head with a low, dangerous chuckle. "Then I'll have to teach you how to obey."

"Is that what you need, little brat?" he asks, mouth brushing my belly, inhaling deeply as he parts my legs. "You need a lesson?"

He ends the sentence with a long, lazy lick to my clit, and my hips arch instinctively. I can't help it. I whisper, "No, of course not. I'm a good girl."

He licks me again, slower this time. "Then show me how good girls come," he murmurs—a challenge, a dare. "Go ahead, angel. Come on my tongue. Let yourself go, baby."

And then he's devouring me, two fingers sliding into my slick heat, curling just right as his tongue torments my clit. I moan, reaching out before I even realize I've moved.

His hand smacks down hard across my thigh, his voice a dark warning between my legs. "I told you not to move those hands," he growls. "If you want to come, you'll do what I say. Understand me?"

"Yes," I breathe out. My hands fall obediently back to my sides. I've never played a game like this before. But god—it's making me burn.

He licks me again, his fingers pressing deeper, firmer. It's perfect—so perfectly placed I could scream. I feel it building, that sweet, devastating pressure.

"Are you close, beautiful?" he murmurs, voice low and reverent. "Come on my tongue. I want to feel it. I want to taste you. Come for me."

I fall over the edge, crashing into the kind of orgasm that rewrites reality. My pussy clenches and pulses around nothing and everything, shaking with the force of it. Earth-shattering. Bone-melting. The best of my life. It's so much I can't breathe. I'm wrecked and weightless—and yet all I want is more of him. A primal, feral need coils inside me.

"I want you inside me," I say, desperate now. "I'm on birth control. I trust you. I know you haven't been with anyone. I need you."

He shoves his boxers down and slides into me, thick and perfect, filling me to the brim. Stretching me until I'm trembling, gasping, mindless. Every thrust is a promise, every drag of his cock inside me a possession. He moves like he owns me. Because in that moment—he does. He fucks me until we're both coming, and it's everything. Raw and real and emotional. The kind of sex that changes something inside you.

I wait for the guilt. I expect it. But it never comes.

I love him. I wanted to comfort him. And it felt right. It still does.

"Stay there," he says again in that low, growling voice. "I'll clean you up, baby."

His hand is warm again, comforting. I'm half-asleep when he returns with the washcloth and carefully slides it between my thighs, wiping me down. I make it to the bathroom, freshen up, but I'm still dazed, still spinning. I feel high. Victorious. I'm not alone in this feeling. He feels it too. But I need to get out of here—before the weight of what just happened hits. Before consequences catch up with us. Still, I don't regret a thing. Not a single thing.

He climbs into bed with me, so sexy it should be illegal, and murmurs, "Don't say a word about regretting this." His voice is rough, raw. "I don't. And I don't want to be a regret for you."

But then, in a quieter moment, he says it differently: "I never slept so well as I did that night with you. You can stay, Ruthie. You don't need to go to the guest room. Stay here with me. Let's get some rest."

And I know what he means. Not just physical rest but the kind of rest that seeps into your bones. The letting go of everything—worry, grief, the gnawing fear about what's coming next.

"Yeah," I whisper, "let's get some rest."

Even as I say it, my mind refuses to still, already bubbling with questions. What did we just do? Where do we go from here? What does this even mean? But the feel of his heavy arm draped across my waist settles me more than anything else could. It makes my muscles soften, making me sink deeper into the mattress. He falls asleep long before I do, his breathing heavy and even, his body a warm, solid line at my back. And I find myself hoping—aching—that somewhere, somehow, Mariah will forgive me.

CHAPTER 12

RUTHIE

I WAKE up the next morning tangled in sheets heavy with the scent of *him*.

The warmth of last night still lingers, and I roll over instinctively to find him—but he's not there. The space beside me is cool. Empty.

And for one second, I fear it all—I stepped too far. He doesn't want me. I was only a temporary replacement for the loneliness he felt, and I—

Then I hear it, the running water in the bathroom. He's in the shower.

Oh god.

Way to catastrophize things again, Ruthie.

I sit up quickly the moment I hear little footsteps padding down the hallway and then—the sound of Luka's door opening. My heart jumps into my throat.

Oh my god. Is he old enough to understand what it means if I come out of Vadka's bedroom like this?

I scramble, tugging on a sweatshirt, my hair wild, my heart pounding, and bolt out of the room just in time—ducking into the guest room a second before Luka rounds the corner.

I throw the door open casually, stretching like I've been there all along, arms overhead, pretending I haven't just staged a hasty escape from his father's bed.

"Good morning," I say brightly, forcing a calm smile.

He looks adorable, cheeks rosy, his hair an unruly mop of sleep-tangled curls.

"Good morning." He grins, all teeth and innocence. "I'm hungry."

"Of course you are. Let's get you something to eat, buddy." I glance toward Vadka's room, but he's still in the bathroom. A flicker of uncertainty passes through me. Are we going to talk about what happened last night? Do I even want to?

I know Luka's routine now; I've been around long enough. I get him settled at the kitchen table with some toast, a sliced banana, and a cup of milk. His feet swing happily under the chair, his little face full of quiet contentment.

"Can you stay here today?" he asks, almost shyly. "I don't want to talk to the mean lady."

I know who he means. His nanny. And the guilt hits me harder than it did over anything I did with Vadka last night.

"Yeah, honey, I can stay today. I'm not sure what Papa has planned, but..."

"She'll be here soon though," he says.

"She's mean. She says mean things about Papa."

I sit up straighter, narrowing my eyes at him. "What do you mean, she says mean things about Papa?"

"Who does?" Vadka's voice cuts in from the hallway. And when he walks into the room, god help me, my ovaries combust.

He's freshly showered, his dark hair still damp and slicked back. His skin is flushed from the heat, and he looks like he just stepped out of some sultry, forbidden dream. He's in a charcoal-gray button-down, open at the collar—no tie, just confidence. His slacks are a shade darker, perfectly tailored, hugging every muscle like they were sewn onto him. He's devastating. And standing next to his son, with that intense gaze fixed on me, he looks even more dangerous, even more magnetic.

I can't breathe. I can't think. All I can do is feel.

He moves toward me, braces his hands on either side of my chair, and kisses my cheek—slow, intentional, soft. It's not just affection. It's a message. A declaration. He doesn't regret a single damn thing we did last night.

I smile, my eyes flicking to his.

Neither do I.

And for the first time in a long time, I feel free.

Even if my hair's a wreck, my clothes rumpled, thighs still sticky from the night before. It all feels deliciously dirty—wrong in a way that makes my breath catch. The power dynamic, the imbalance, it makes me pause. It makes me wonder what comes next.

"Good boy, Luka," Vadka says, ruffling his son's hair. "Your mama would be proud of you for drinking your milk."

My chest tightens. I remember when Luka was two or three, how Mariah used to beam every time he finished a cup. That ache is always there. But it softens in moments like this.

A car pulls up outside. Vadka glances toward the window, then back at me.

"It's the nanny," I tell him.

"Oh. Right," he says, his tone a little too heavy. Did he forget?

"You going into the office?" I ask.

"No," he says, jaw tensing. "I'm not. Rafail wanted me to go to London—there's something urgent over there—but I'm not leaving you and Luka. Not with the Irish still out there. I don't trust they won't show up again."

I nod. "Makes sense." Then I realize what I look like—bedhead, yesterday's clothes, last night's sin still clinging to my skin. I'm not presentable to meet this nanny. Especially not if she's the judgmental, old-school type.

I mutter, "I look like a mess."

His eyes spark, and he kisses my forehead. "You're beautiful."

I walk toward the room like I'm floating. I'm still grieving, still wrecked by guilt—but part of me feels seen. Desired. I need to talk to someone. Someone older. Someone who won't crumble under the weight of it.

I wash up as best I can and throw on my clothes.

Then I hear the nanny's voice. Sharp. Cold. She's snapping at Luka, and I pull in a breath. This is not going to last.

I walk into the kitchen just as she barks, "Put your plate in the sink." She's dressed head to toe in black, arms crossed like a judge ready to deliver a sentence.

"It does no good to coddle him," she says, stiff. "I've taught children his age for forty-five years. The sooner they learn independence, the sooner they stop relying on you."

Vadka winks behind her back. "Yes. I think you're right. That's exactly what independence means."

She continues, unfazed. "I understand young mothers these days like to baby their children. And I know your wife is no longer here, but she didn't do your son any favors by cleaning up after him." She rolls her eyes. "I wouldn't be surprised if she still wiped his bottom."

A muscle jumps in Vadka's jaw. My fists clench at my sides.

"My sister was an excellent mother," I snap, my voice cold steel.

The woman spins around, eyes raking me down without even a pretense of subtlety. She's assessing me—my messy hair, my crumpled clothes, the way I don't match the polished facade she and Vadka both wear.

I smile sweetly. "I'm Ruthie." I extend my hand. She doesn't take it.

"Heard about you," she mutters.

My eyebrows lift. "Oh, did you? Did Luka tell you about me?"

She shakes her head. "No."

Charming.

"I've got a few things to do around the house today," I say lightly, "but I'll be in and out, running errands. Let me know if you need anything."

I move to the fridge and start taking stock of what we've got. Groceries, chores, the usual. But underneath all that, there's a spark. A slow-burning fire that I know is only just getting started.

I don't want to leave my nephew here—not with this battle-axe of a nanny *I'm* apparently responsible for hiring.

"You working tonight?" Vadka asks, his voice low and quiet, the kind of tone he only uses when something's gnawing at him. His lips are pressed into a flat, unreadable line, and there's a furrow between his brows that tells me he's deep in thought—probably spiraling with all the ways things can go wrong.

I know that look too well, even as I write out a simple grocery list. I write down just the basics—things to cook and grill.

Something to feel normal again.

"Yeah," I tell him, not looking up. "I have to work, Vadka. I'm almost out of sick time."

His jaw tightens like he wants to argue, but we both glance at the nanny, who's watching us with that cold, flat look I hate. The kind of look that makes you feel like a problem she's been paid to tolerate.

Luka's little lower lip sticks out.

Oh no.

"Don't go, Papa," Luka pleads, his tiny arms wrapping tightly around Vadka's legs like he can physically anchor him to the ground. My heart aches. I hated this when Mariah was still alive—how Luka would sob and beg her not to leave, how she'd cry after closing the door. It hasn't changed. It's still gutting, and I know it's just part of having a small child.

Still, no one said I have to like it.

I don't miss the shadow that crosses Vadka's face, the way he holds his little boy as if he doesn't ever want to let him go. I guess parting from each other holds a different kind of weight these days.

"I'll be back soon, buddy." Vadka kneels and kisses Luka's forehead, but his voice falters. He doesn't want to go either.

We finally peel Luka off, and of course, Vadka does the rounds—checks in with the security team, glances at the surveillance feeds, and reads the angles like a general prepping for siege. He finally exhales, long and hard, shaking his head.

We both have jobs to do. We can't just sit here like targets.

And I can't take him with me. Not to the bar. It's not a place for a child. Today's the worst of the week—the only day we open early for "specials"—cheap drinks and sketchy charac-ters. I'll take a half-empty bar of regulars any day.

Shit.

"It's gonna be all right," Vadka murmurs, placing his hand on the small of my back. His touch is grounding and electric at the same time. It feels like it belongs there, even as my skin prickles like I'm on fire. The memory of last night burns in the corners of my mind and refuses to leave me. I keep reliving it—again and again and again—wanting to freeze it, to hold onto every inch of that memory.

For so long, I've been stumbling through darkness. Alone. The future seemed murky and scary, but now... now it's like I can actually see into a future that brings me hope.

Maybe... *maybe*... with a man I actually care about.

And I don't know how to feel about that.

Correction—*Sigh.* I *do.* I know exactly how I feel, and I'm absolutely fucking riddled with guilt.

It feels like hell.

Guilt clings to me like a second skin. I feel inadequate, tainted.

But if I'm being honest... I didn't feel worthy of love even when Mariah was alive.

The drive back to my place is quiet. When we get to my car, Vadka opens the door for me like always. I slide into the seat as he mindlessly reaches across to buckle me in. He checks it, pulls on it as if to make sure it's secure, and then stands with a satisfied nod.

He's always been like this—a caretaker. Not hard like Rafail, cold like Semyon, or a little unhinged like Matvei. No. Vadka's a protector.

And maybe... just maybe, I need to let someone take care of me. Something warm and unfamiliar unfurls in my chest.

"Heading into the office?" I ask, my voice strangely husky.

He nods, eyes flicking away. "Yeah. Eventually. I've got a few things to deal with. Need to talk to Rafail. Matvei intercepted communication. We've got to review it."

I nod and shrug. "Sounds good."

I shove my hands deep into my coat pockets—one of those futile gestures that hides too much, even from myself.

"Drive safe," he says, voice quiet again. "You coming by tonight?"

He catches himself. "No, wait—you're working." His eyes flicker with something like disappointment. Hope? I can't tell.

"Maybe after work," I say, but it comes out more like a question than an answer.

He leans in, bracing his arm on the car door, his warm brown eyes searching mine. "You'd be safer with me."

Would I? Physically, yes. Emotionally, I'm not so sure.

"I'll think about it," I murmur.

"Ruthie, if you—"

"Vadka," I cut him off gently. "Please. I know you want me

safe. But this... this is new. I've never gone home to a man in my life. Not like this."

Especially one who was married to my sister. *God.*

"It's not about that," he says, shaking his head slowly. "God, I don't mean it like that."

I look away, startled at the sharp sting of rejection.

"Ruthie," he says, softer this time. "Listen. The closer we stay, the easier it is for me to protect you."

"You've got guards at the bar, yes?" I ask.

He sighs through clenched teeth. "Yes."

"I've got location sharing on. You can track me."

"I know, Ruthie, but—"

"I'm not one of the Kopolovs, Vadka," I tell him gently. I'm not one of their wives, a Bratva princess, or even someone who works for them.

"Well aware, Ruth Marie." My heart does a little flip in my chest even as I narrow my eyes. "Oh, so we're pulling out middle names now? Getting all big brotherly now?"

We both know there's nothing big brotherly about it.

"You're so fucking stubborn," he growls.

I flash him a grin. "And you love it."

"Listen," he says, exhaling hard. "You can sleep in the guest room. Or I will. Whatever you want. This isn't about sex, Ruthie."

Did he just say that out loud? He did, right there in the open, for anyone to hear. For *me* to hear.

My cheeks flame. All it takes is that one sentence and my body betrays me.

I remember what it felt like being in his bed. I want it again—now, later, always.

"Shame," I mutter before I can stop myself. "That's a damn shame."

He doesn't answer. Just looks at me like he wants to say everything and nothing at once.

"Alright," I say, voice breaking just a little. Why is this whole exchange so emotionally charged? What the hell?

"I need to go. Please, Vadka. Let me go."

He breathes out like he's been holding it in for too long. But he lets me go. Finally. Reluctantly.

And I love that. He doesn't want me to go.

I find myself driving—aimless for a while until instinct takes the wheel. It leads me to the old church, but that's not where I'm going either.

I veer off the road and follow the gravel path to the ancient cemetery that clings to the edge of the forest. It's old, weather-worn. Familiar. My heart aches.

Buried here are pieces of the past. The Kopolov family's parents. My mother's parents. A friend from school who died too young, my favorite teacher. The old woman who sat outside the bakery feeding bread crumbs to the birds.

Mariah.

But I'm not thinking about her yet as I catalog everyone else.

The sky is heavy with dark clouds. I look over my shoulder more than once, convinced someone's following me. I'm not important enough for a guard this close, right? I mean, they'll go to my work, but...

Vadka might have a few things to say about that, and I'm not sure how that makes me feel.

I kill the engine and stare at my reflection in the rearview mirror. My hair's a mess, there are dark shadows under my eyes, and I need a good brow job. But somehow, I look... radiant. Flushed. Glowing like a woman in love.

I drop my head back against the seat, overwhelmed.

I *am*.

I am a woman in love, whether I want to be or not.

Maybe I've always loved him. I think I have. It was easier when it was quiet love—muted, safe. Platonic. But now it's changed. It's grown teeth.

And I don't know how to make sense of it.

I'd give anything to talk to Mariah. But even if Vadka were another man and Mariah were right here in front of me, I don't know if I could confess this.

But he isn't another man, and she isn't here.

I'm in love with your husband.

"Oh, Mariah," I whisper to the sky. With a sigh, I open the door and step into the wind.

I walk the worn path toward her grave. I know she's not here —not really. Just her body and bones, a decaying shell that once held life. But maybe... maybe there's something else. A presence. A spirit. A whisper of what she was.

I'm not religious. I can't bring myself to believe in heaven. But the idea that we go from bright, vivid people to nothing... to worm food... it feels wrong. There has to be something more.

Maybe she's reincarnated. Maybe she's part of the earth. Maybe she's finally at peace.

God, I hope she's at peace.

I walk amongst graves that are cracked, crooked, and forgotten. There are wooden crosses, black iron railings, and Orthodox icons bolted into stone. Rosaries, candles in glass, names in Cyrillic etched into crumbling marble.

Russian graveyards are different from others—more like sanctuaries than places of mourning. You find portraits carved into the headstones, domes on family mausoleums, and candles left behind that still flicker against the chill. They're private places for grief and memory and reverence.

I sigh and pinch the bridge of my nose. It does nothing to stop the tears threatening. My chest aches. My heart's a drumbeat of pain, and my head feels too full.

Mariah's grave is perched on a small hill, surrounded by white lilies—her favorite. The grass is a vivid green despite the clouds overhead. Forget-me-nots bloom in clusters nearby.

I haven't been here in two weeks, and guilt tears through

me. Is this how it goes? Weeks bleed into months, and then years?

But it's hard to come here. It's always hard.

I cry when I'm here.

I don't want to cry anymore.

But I need to talk to my sister.

I walk quickly, aware of my limited time and need to get to work.

It isn't until I round the corner that I see it—the gleaming, familiar chrome wheels.

I freeze, and my heart turns over in my chest as my brain catches up.

Oh my god. No. No, it can't be.

I'm not the only one who came to visit her grave. Was his visit prompted by guilt too?

I thought I could handle this, thought I was just barely holding myself together before I came, but seeing him here? God, no.

He's kneeling in front of her headstone, leather jacket clinging to his broad shoulders like a second skin. His head is bowed, hands limp in his lap, and I swear he looks like he's carrying the weight of the world. He misses her; of course he does. Even though I'm not religious, the old *and the two shall become one* somehow rings true.

Vadka needs to talk to her, just like I do.

"I'm sorry," he whispers, the words sharp and raw in the air. His back's to me, unaware of my presence. I feel like I'm snooping, but it's too late now to turn back.

"I'm sorry," he whispers again. "I shouldn't— I know I shouldn't— I never even looked at her that way before. But I miss you. God, I miss you. And she loved you." His voice cracks—splinters, really, like a snapped bone. "She misses you so much. And I... I *love* her. I'm sorry." He shakes his head, and I can see the desperation in the way his shoulders tremble. "I'm so fucking sorry. But this—this is the right choice. It makes sense. She loves Luka, Mariah. No one loves him the way I do. Except Ruthie. And you know she's safer with me than with anyone else on earth. You know that."

I shouldn't be hearing this. I know I shouldn't. I'm the last person who should be here, the absolute last. Guilt is already eating away at me like acid, but I can't move. I *won't* move. He's baring his soul to his dead wife, and all I can do is listen, frozen in place, while my heart shatters in my chest.

If I slip away now, will he even notice? Does he know I'm here? God, I hate this—I feel like I'm spying, like I'm trespassing on something sacred, something private. But I didn't mean to. I didn't know. I just came here to see her.

I try to back away quietly, carefully. But when I turn to go, my toe catches on a damn tree root, and I stumble, yelping as I go down hard on both knees. My hands slam against the earth in front of me to catch my fall, dirt grinding into my palms. Damp dirt presses into my skin. For a heartbeat, all I can hear is my own harsh breathing and stifled groan.

"*Shit.*"

"Ruthie?" His voice cuts through the air, startled. Too close.

"I'm sorry," I mutter, trying to push myself up. Sorry for what? Goddamn *everything*. For being here. For falling. For the sheer gravity of all of this.

I feel him before I see him, the familiar pull in my chest like the impending roll of thunder before a storm. The air shifts. Heavier. Charged.

The moment I try to shift my weight, pain slices up through my leg, bright and vicious. I stifle a cry. *Fuck.*

"Shit! What happened, Ruthie?"

Footsteps, a rustle of fabric, and then he's there, kneeling next to me like he was always going to end up here, beside me, holding space for memories and ghosts and pain.

I don't want to look up... I don't want to see his face right now. Not when I'm like this, weak. Caught, like I was trespassing when visiting my own sister's grave.

But the second I put weight on my ankle, pain lances through it like a blade. I lose my footing and stumble toward the ground again when his steady hand catches my elbow.

"I tripped. On the stupid tree root," I whisper, ashamed and hurting, words tumbling from my lips. "I didn't know you were going to be here."

"Did you follow me?" Even though his tone is curious and not accusatory, I feel the need to defend myself.

"*No!*"

I shake my head so hard it makes me dizzy. "No, I just— I just came to see my sister. I wanted to... talk to her."

It's funny how different things trigger grief. A smell, a memory, the realization that she won't pick up when you dial her number.

Knowing you're in pain and you don't have your big sister to make it better like you used to.

My voice wobbles. I try to hold back, try to hold on, but I can't.

I break. I shatter. The tears come fast, unrelenting, as I buckle under the weight of everything I'm not saying out loud.

I can't talk to her. I can't see her. Neither can he. The tears fall with no warning. Fast. Hot. Angry.

I hate this.

I *hate* that she's gone.

I *hate* that I feel so bereft and alone, like I'm flailing in a world of unknowns, and my only anchor has vanished.

And I hate that the only solid, real thing in a world of uncertainty is... *him.*

"I'm sorry," I sob, clutching my side. "I just needed to talk to her."

At first, he doesn't reach for me. His breath is steady as I shudder, sobbing. But I can feel his restraint, the way it's coiled like a leash pulled taut.

He's near me, his eyes searching mine, his hand hovering as if ready to catch me if I stumble. His voice is warm and compassionate, making my tears fall harder. I'm gulping for air, swiping at my eyes, when he leans in and cups my face.

"And what would you tell her, baby? What do you need to talk about that was so urgent you came here? Tell me."

I sniff and swallow, unable to look away. "You know exactly what I need to tell her."

His eyes search mine, hopeful and pained. "I want to hear you say it."

I blow out a breath. My voice wobbles. "I want to tell her that I'm falling in love with her husband. And I'm terrified he doesn't feel the same way I do. I want to tell her that I'm sorry, that I—"

And then his mouth is on mine—urgent, desperate. And we're both crying, tears mixing with the kiss, his hands tangled in my hair. "I know," he murmurs against my lips, his voice cracked open like mine. "I know, baby."

No one's ever called me that before him, and I love it. I love it so much.

The kiss is brief, healing, as we both pull away and meet each other's eyes.

"You don't have to explain anything, Ruthie," he whispers.

I'll never forget seeing him so strong, so powerful, brought to his knees by grief. It's beautiful in the most devastating way. I reach up to wipe his tears, and he brushes my hair gently from my face. "Let me see your ankle," he says softly.

It's something tangible. Something real. He bends down, careful, his touch gentle as he cradles my ankle in his hands. I wince—god, it hurts like a motherfucker.

"Bruised. Sprained at least," he mutters, examining it closely. "I don't think it's broken, but you definitely pulled something. You won't be able to walk on this."

I sigh. "Great. How am I supposed to work?"

"We'll get you a boot, maybe crutches. Honestly, it'd be better if you didn't work at all."

"It'd be better if I hadn't sprained my ankle," I say, sighing.

He sighs too. "Yeah. I know. Shit, baby."

God, I love the way he says that. Love the sound of his voice. Love everything about him.

"You sure you didn't come here to spy on me?" he asks, brow raised.

I shake my head, a ghost of a smile on my lips. "We just had the same brilliant, tragic idea at the same time."

Neither of us says what we're both thinking—that last night's mess, the tangle of grief and comfort and need, pushed us here. Maybe grief does that. Maybe it drives you into the arms of the only person who understands.

I wonder if I can trust Zoya with this. That woman's a vault, steel-reinforced.

"It looks beautiful," I whisper, my voice catching as I look at the grave. "You've done a great job keeping it up."

"Thanks," he murmurs. "All right. Let's figure this out. How did you get here?"

"I drove."

"I've got my bike," he says, frowning. "That's not a good idea for you. You won't be able to brace yourself with that ankle. You should have it elevated. I'll drive your car, and I'll have one of my guys come pick up the bike."

"I thought you didn't trust anyone to ride your bike."

He hesitates. "I don't. But your safety's more important."

I press my hand to my chest, feeling the flutter there. "Aw. Are you being *sweet* right now? Vadka, is that you?"

"Don't be a brat," he growls, and it's that voice—the one that guarantees I'll absolutely keep being a brat, just to make him say it again.

Truth be told, I don't like needing help. I hate being dependent. I pride myself on my strength. This whole thing sucks.

"Let's get you in the car. Get you looked at."

"I hate going to the doctor," I whine, fully aware that I sound like a child. I pout. "Doesn't Rafail have someone?"

"Yeah," he says with a smirk, eyebrows lifting. "But you're not one of the Bratva, remember? I believe you were the one who reminded me of that."

Oh, *fuck* my life. "I think I'm fine," I try to argue, attempting to get up.

"Ruthie."

He doesn't even let me. He just lifts me—bodily—and starts carrying me. "We'll let the doctor decide whether or not you're fine."

"Who asked you?" I grumble.

He leans in, his voice a whisper against my ear. "I know you hate being told what to do, Ruthie," he says, low and lethal. "But you do like getting your ass spanked. And you, little brat, are pushing every one of my goddamn buttons. Keep going. See what happens."

I would turn away from him, but where the hell would I even go? One way, I'm staring into those beautiful eyes. The other, I'm pressed against that absolutely sinful chest. Not exactly a bad place to be.

At least we're not talking about my dead sister anymore, I think bitterly. Which—yeah, I know—is a fucked-up thing to think. So sue me.

"Where'd you park?" he asks, not even winded. How? How is he not even breathing hard? He's carrying an entire human. I get winded carrying a gallon of milk.

"Around the corner."

We walk in silence, and now that my foot is dangling freely, the pain intensifies. It burns. Tears well in my eyes, and I don't think it's just the ankle anymore. Everything hurts. This *whole thing* hurts.

"You all right?" he asks, his voice so gentle it makes my throat ache. When we were younger, I didn't know this softer side of him, but being a dad has changed things.

"It hurts a lot," I whisper, swallowing hard. "I'm sorry."

"We talked about this, Ruthie," he says, his tone chiding.

"About what?"

"About apologizing for things that don't even deserve an apology. You don't get to say sorry for being sad, for visiting your sister's grave. Or for twisting your ankle while doing it. You should know by now—I'm not ashamed of crying. And you shouldn't be either. People cry. It's natural. It's survival. It's release."

"Is that what your brothers think?"

He scoffs, lips curling like the thought itself is offensive. "Who gives a fuck what my brothers think?" He might, but he won't admit that to me. And I don't ask again. I just nod because even if it's a little contradictory, there's truth buried in it.

And for one breathless, fragile moment, his forehead presses to mine. The kind of moment that would dissolve if we spoke too loudly, too fast. I feel his pulse fluttering beneath my fingers—racing, alive, real. It's steady and wild, like a storm that's chosen me as its eye.

"Tell me what's going on in that head of yours," he says low, his voice like gravel and velvet. "I'm taking you back to the Kopolovs. We'll get your ankle looked at. But right now, it's just me and you, Ruthie. No distractions. What are you thinking?"

I pause, then whisper, "I heard what you said to Mariah."

His body stills.

"Do you regret what we did?" My voice shakes a little. "Because I already feel like a regret. I was an accident. My mother didn't want me. And now..."

His grip tightens around me, and his eyes bore into mine.

"I have no regrets, Ruthie. Not one. I'd do it all again. Over. And over. And over. Every single damn night."

It has got to be wrong to be turned on in a cemetery. People fear getting struck by lightning if they're heathens in a church, but I'm practically looking over my shoulder for how desperately I want him.

I believe him. I don't need to ask if he loves me—I *know* he does. And I love him too. Recklessly. Messily. Desperately.

But still... there's a piece of me that needs to be sure I'm not just reacting to grief. That he's not just some kind of twisted solace. He deserves more than being a rebound. And I deserve more than being a mistake.

We make it to my car, and he slides me into the passenger seat. I don't even protest when he does my buckle and closes the door.

The drive to the Kopolov house is quiet, suspended in a strange kind of peace. At some point, his large hand finds my leg—resting, not roaming—and he strokes my kneecap with slow, steady fingers. It's not sexual, not this time. It doesn't spark lust. But something warm coils in my chest anyway. I like his hand there. It makes me feel... safe. Like I belong.

The house comes into view. It's quiet. Not many cars are outside, and I'm relieved. The fewer the witnesses, the less scrutiny. The less I have to lie or explain what even I haven't fully made peace with. I couldn't defend what we did if someone asked. Not now. Not yet.

But who decides the timeline for mourning anyway? Who writes the rules on how long you have to stay in the dark before you're allowed to find some sliver of light again?

Is there ever a "right time" to fall in love with your dead sister's husband?

Or maybe… maybe the only timeline that matters is ours.

The house is still.

"Zoya's not home," I say, a little disappointed. I could've used a good, old-fashioned girl talk. I need someone to tell me I'm not crazy. That this is okay. That love in the aftermath of death isn't betrayal. That I'm still allowed to want.

"Who's here?" I ask, glancing at the empty driveway. "Based on the cars."

He snorts, amused. "What is this, the eighties? We don't go by cars anymore."

He pulls up an app on his phone, and I see glowing little dots dancing across the screen.

"Wait. Is that me?" I ask, eyes narrowing.

"Of course it is."

"Who's tracking me?"

"Anyone under protection gets tracked," he says like it's obvious.

I don't know how I feel about that.

I watch him read the app.

"Rafail's home. Matvei, Anissa."

He squints at the screen. "No, wait. Zoya's home too. Her car's not here because someone probably borrowed it. Or maybe it's in the shop."

I exhale. "Weird."

"What?"

"Her location hasn't updated in three hours. You don't think that's strange?"

He shrugs. "She could be cooking. You know how she is. Sometimes, she preps for days."

"Yeah, but there's no holiday coming up."

And when we step into the house—Zoya is nowhere. Not in the kitchen. Not anywhere. But Vadka doesn't pause. He carries me straight into the living room.

The Cottage.

The place is cozy in a way that always surprises me. You'd expect something cold and severe—especially with all these stone-faced men storming through it—but no. The Cottage breathes warmth. The kind that seeps into your bones. Deep leather couches, worn from use. A fire that smells faintly like cedar. Quilts that look like someone's grandmother made them decades ago. It feels like home.

From the other room, I hear voices. Then the heavy, unmistakable footsteps of Rafail. His shadow crosses the doorway, and whatever he thinks about seeing Vadka carrying me, he doesn't say out loud.

"What happened?"

My cheeks flush pink. Accidents happen, but I don't like the immediate feeling that I did something wrong. "I think I sprained my ankle. Or did something equally *stupid*."

"It's not stupid," Vadka says, lowering his voice. "Don't say that about yourself, Ruthie. Injuries happen. You're human."

Rafail snorts as Vadka slides me down onto the couch. "God, you should've seen what Rodion put me through when he was a kid. The boy lived in a walking cast for years." He shakes his head. "We knew almost every nurse at the hospital on a first-name basis."

I smile at the image.

"I'll make a call. Get you looked at." He looks up at Vadka. "Good timing, anyway. Matvei's in the office." They look soberly at each other but don't offer details.

"Sir?" A tall, young man in a suit appears in the doorway, earpiece glinting under the light. "There's someone here to see you."

"Who?"

"Moroff," the man responds, waiting.

Rafail checks his watch and curses. "Shit. I forgot I scheduled him today."

"Should I bring him to your office?"

Rafail scowls. "No. Matvei's got his whole setup in there. Bring him here for now. If we need privacy, we'll move."

A man walks into the room; he's maybe twenty. There's something about him that reminds me of a jackrabbit ready to bolt. His smile is practiced, stretched too tight. He offers his hand to both Vadka and Rafail, his lips stretched over his teeth like a predator. I watch his eyes shift from me to

Vadka, then Rafail, before looking at the door. Yeah, that's not creepy at all.

Vadka stands beside my chair like a goddamned sentinel, immovable, unreadable, lethal in stillness. His presence coils around me, and I sit up straighter without meaning to, my ankle throbbing.

Across from us, Rafail doesn't even pretend to be impressed.

"Mr. Kopolov," the kid starts, trying to sound respectful, like that'll save him. "Thank you for your time. Good to see you."

He starts prattling, nervous energy leaking through his fake charm. Small talk drips from his lips, pointless and trite. Rafail isn't having it. He shakes his head, cuts through the bullshit. I watch, mesmerized. I haven't really seen these guys in action before.

"Get to the point of why you're here," he snaps, voice like a blade across stone.

The kid blinks, surprised by the sharpness. And instead of adjusting his tone, he gets defensive—makes the mistake of raising his voice.

"I'm getting there," he snaps. "If you hadn't invaded the southern border and taken my family's property—"

Oops. Wrong move.

Vadka rises.

Slowly. Deliberately.

And when he does, the entire room shifts. It's like gravity

bends around him. And my stern but gentle giant is suddenly terrifying.

I love it.

"Did you just raise your voice to Mr. Kopolov?" His tone is quiet, deadly calm, and all the more menacing because of it. "You come into his house and speak to him like that? Do you have any fucking idea who you're talking to?"

He never needs to yell. That calm fury of his is more effective than any screaming threat. A shiver runs down my spine.

Shit. My sexy enforcer just made my thighs clench. Vadka leans in closer to the man, towering over him.

"You ever raise your fucking voice to Mr. Kopolov again," he says, each word deliberate, "and that'll be the last time you ever speak. Do you understand me?"

The kid goes pale and throws his hands up in the universal sign of surrender. "I meant no disrespect. I didn't mean—"

"What you meant and what you did are two very different things," Vadka cuts in. He looks like a goddamn avenging angel. Dangerous, divine. I could listen to that tone of voice for hours... as long as it's never directed at me.

"We heard you," Rafail says, cool and composed. He tilts his head in my direction. "There's a witness."

"Ruthie?" he says. "Did you hear a tone of disrespect?"

I raise my eyebrows, surprised he's asking me. *Me.* But he wants my opinion, and I'm not gonna sugarcoat it.

"I think a third grader would've caught that tone," I say with a shrug. "So yeah. Loud and clear."

The corner of Rafail's mouth quirks up. He sits back in his chair, completely capable of defending himself but clearly comfortable letting Vadka do it for him. This side of Vadka —protector, weapon, sharp-edged and unyielding—it's not one I've seen often. But I need to. Because it's part of who he is. Just like me working the bar and tending to my mother is part of who I am. It's all different pieces of the same puzzle.

"Stay out of this," the guy snaps at me.

Vadka's eyes grow deadly, his voice just above a growl. "And did you just speak disrespectfully to my woman?"

My woman.

His woman.

Oh god.

"There's a nurse practitioner here to see you," Rafail says quietly. "Friend of Polina's. She'll assess the damage."

Vadka cracks his knuckles and takes the guy by the collar. "And anything else to say, Moroff?" he adds, tone final.

Moroff shakes his head quickly. "No. We'll consider our options. Thank you for the visit."

Rafail stands and opens the door while Vadka escorts him out.

I stare at Vadka's retreating back just as a woman steps in. She's tall, broad-shouldered, big-boned, with a presence that commands respect. But her voice is soft, almost gentle.

"Hello," she says. "And what have we here?"

She doesn't waste time with niceties. This woman's been doing this a long time—straightforward, no bullshit, but with kindness beneath the efficiency.

"Definitely bruised and a mild sprain," she says after examining me. "No signs of a break. I'm going to recommend you stay off your feet, ice, and elevate. Follow that, and you'll be back to normal in a few days."

She gives me a professional smile and starts packing up.

The door opens again, and Zoya hurries in—cheeks pink, slightly out of breath, like she ran the whole way.

"Hey, babe. Look at you— What happened?"

"You're safe here," Rafail tells me before he and Vadka leave the room.

Zoya settles in beside me as I tell her what happened, leaving out the details. All I say is that I tripped on a tree root.

"Oh, Ruthie." She winces. "That sucks. Okay, do you have meds? Have you eaten anything?"

I shake my head. "Not since breakfast."

It makes me think of Luka and the nanny... and the uneasy feeling in my chest returns. He didn't seem troubled, but I am. It doesn't feel right, leaving him like that.

"Something you wanna talk about, babe?" Zoya asks gently.

My throat tightens. I open my mouth, but I don't know what to say. I'm not the type to get all emotional, but here I am.

"I think I'm in love," I whisper.

CHAPTER 13

VADKA

"THIS IS NOT GOOD," Matvei mutters. His jaw's tight, the muscles twitching.

Matvei, Rafail's cousin, is one of the coldest, most brilliant minds in our crew. If you need someone to decode a message, hack a system, or find patterns in chaos—he's your man.

"Take a look at this."

He turns the screen toward us.

"Motherfucker." My voice is low. My hands curl into fists. "They want my son? Over my fucking dead body."

"I know," Rafail says, slow and measured. "But we have to be careful. No rash moves."

"You've got bodyguards at your house, right?"

"Of course. Luka's safe."

Still, for my own peace of mind, I pull up the app on my phone. The nanny's washing dishes, and Luka's at the kitchen table, coloring happily. I see guards stationed at every entry point, cameras everywhere. Nothing's getting through that perimeter.

Still... that sinking feeling doesn't leave me. Because only a monster would target a child. And monsters do exist.

"What about Ruthie?" I ask, voice tight. "Do they have anything on her?"

Matvei scrolls. "No. Nothing yet."

"How do we know this isn't a setup? Or misinformation?"

"We don't," Rafail says. "Which is why we keep it business as usual. Until we know more."

He blows out a breath, then shows me the message on his encrypted channel.

Sever the bloodline. The letters are crimson, bold.

"Sever the bloodline," I echo.

Rafail nods. "They mean us. The Kopolov bloodline. That includes our children. Our wives. All of them are targets now."

I let out a bitter laugh. "What the fuck, Rafail?"

"How many of them did you kill?" he asks, tone sharp.

I shake my head slowly.

"You don't know... because you stopped counting."

I check the Wi-Fi—encrypted and locked. GPS jammers in

place. Cameras. Patrols. Motion detectors. Nothing's getting through, not unless we let it.

Still.

"Nothing," I say. "But I need to speak with Rafail. Privately."

Matvei gets up and steps out of the office.

Rafail glances at me. "Something I need to know between you and Ruthie?"

I scowl. "You judging?"

"Of course fucking not," he says. "You think I'd judge you? After everything? You think I'm a heartless bastard?"

I shrug.

He punches my arm, light but firm. "Don't answer that."

Then he softens. "Seriously though, Vadka. What's going on between you two?"

He has a right to know. He's my brother in every way that counts.

So I tell him. Not everything, but enough.

"I love her," I say. Quietly. Like the words might shatter if I speak them too loud.

"I feel so fucking guilty."

He leans forward, hands steepled beneath his chin, studying me.

"That's why most people avoid falling in love, Vadka. It

makes you vulnerable. I can kill a man, but I can't kill the ache that comes with losing someone who matters."

"I know."

"What's the problem, then?"

"She's my wife's sister."

Rafail nods slowly. Then leans in, his voice deliberate.

"Correction, brother. She's your dead wife's sister. There's a difference."

I flinch. I knew he'd say it. Still hurts.

"I think she thinks I'm only interested because she reminds me of Mariah."

He leans back. Ever the pragmatist. "Well. Are you?"

"No. God, no. She's night and day from Mariah."

"They didn't even look alike," he agrees. "You could tell they were related, sure. But they were nothing alike."

"Exactly."

"There's a simple solution to this," he says flatly, the kind of pragmatism that grates when you're barely holding yourself together. "You want to test how she feels? How you feel? Make sure you're not leaping in with both feet before you've had a damn second to breathe, to process? Is that what this is?"

I shrug, but my throat feels like it's caving in on itself.

"I don't know. Is it?" A hollow laugh, humorless. "Who the hell knows anymore?"

"Then give it time," he says, always the rational one. "Stay out of her pants." His eyes cut to me hard. "Don't even look. As tempting as it might be to bury your grief, it's only going to cloud your judgment, brother."

He's right. Of course he's right. But fuck, I hate that he's right.

"You're worried about Luka," he adds, voice gentling. "She's good with him. Makes sense. If my wife weren't here anymore, I'd be worried about my kids too." He pauses, lets the weight of it settle before he adds, "But I'm more concerned about how she is with *you*."

"What the hell does that mean?" I shoot back, sharper than I intended.

He stares at me. Long. Measured. I just made a guy kiss pavement for disrespecting him and won't fall into the same mistake now myself.

Rafail levels me with a look. We've been best friends for as long as I can remember, but right now, I'm reminded that he's a little older, and he has younger siblings he's raised. He crosses his arms on his chest.

"Are we going to have an honest conversation? Or are you going to take everything personally?"

My spine stiffens. I let out a long, slow breath.

Rafail continues. "You're wealthy. Powerful. Attractive. Women like that shit. They're drawn to it. And as your brother—and frankly, your boss—I need to make sure she likes you for the right reasons."

"And what are those?" I ask, jaw tight.

He tilts his head. "See? You're not even sure yourself."

And I don't answer because I'm not. Everything about this —about her—feels confusing and unsteady and charged in ways I don't know how to handle.

"Does she support who you are? Do you even know if your values align? Is there real chemistry? 'Cause the most perfect person on the damn planet can be in front of you, but if there's no spark—no fire—it's dead on arrival."

"Yeah, I got it." I rake a hand through my hair. "Answer to those questions? I don't fucking know. I really don't."

"Maybe you don't need to know right now," he says more gently. "Just make your decisions. Protect what's yours. And then? Let the rest come as it comes."

It sounds good on paper. Real good. But it's a hell of a lot harder when your heart—and someone else's—is on the line. What do I even have to offer her?

I go looking for her. But Ruthie's not where I left her.

Zoya is though.

"Where's Ruthie?"

I don't even think to check the tracker app—she was right here. I pull it up now.

"Sorry," Zoya says, grimacing like a kid who knows they've screwed up. "She said she had to get to work. I tried to get her to stay, but she said her job was important."

"Did you even check her?" My voice cuts sharp, too sharp, and Zoya flinches.

I want to be the one who takes care of her. The one who keeps her safe. "What the fuck did she do with her ankle?"

The room behind me shifts. Rafail's pissed at how I'm talking to his sister. His presence is like a storm building, suffocating us with an undercurrent of danger. I sigh. "Sorry, it's not your fault."

"It isn't," Rafail repeats. Then he turns his attention to Matvei and while they talk shop, I make plans to get the hell out of here so I can track Ruthie down, check on her, and give her hell for taking off.

Matvei is back working in the office. I can hear the quiet hum of his laptop. I know he's not just working but plotting, likely staring at video footage that would make anyone else tremble. He's the one who keeps things in line, the tactical mind behind this war.

The war—it's not just about the Irish anymore. It's about power, survival, and keeping the Kopolov family at the top. The Irish have been bold—too bold—and they think they can break us. They've stirred up more than a few dark corners of this city and aligned themselves with forces that threaten our stability. I've seen the intel, the whispers in the shadows—it's bigger than we thought.

The Irish are targeting our supply routes, cutting us off from resources, trying to weaken our grip. But it's the personal vendettas that make it dangerous—betrayal runs deeper when it's in your own blood.

Then there's the pressure on Matvei. He's the one who has to keep everything together and make sure the enemies don't slip through our fingers. I feel the weight of the decision that's been thrust onto him, a war he didn't ask for but is now bound to lead. The stakes are high—more than just the family's wealth is on the line. This is about territory, about loyalty, and about control. Violence is inevitable, and when it comes, it will be brutal.

Outside, the tension in the streets has been escalating. People talk, and every whisper feels like a threat. Those who are loyal to the Kopolovs are on edge, unsure of what's coming next. We've been forced to make alliances with people we wouldn't normally trust, and every meeting, every handshaking deal, feels like a moment where one wrong move could spark an all-out war.

The calm before the storm. I can almost taste it in the air—the anticipation, the fear, the certainty that we are standing on the edge of something we won't be able to stop. Rafail's anger, Matvei's cool control, and my own uncertainty about how much longer we can keep this balance… it all feeds into the dread. The war is coming, and it's going to tear apart everything and everyone I love.

CHAPTER 14

MAYBE I RAN. I knew Vadka would be pissed that I left without talking to him, but I don't want him to feel responsible for me. Why does that make me so damn uncomfortable?

I call my mother to check in on her, or maybe it's to remind myself that I have other responsibilities, that I don't need someone to help me shoulder my burdens.

But my mom is taking a nap, and they tell me she's stable.

So I go straight to the bar, a little early for my shift. Predictable, maybe. Stupid. But I need to clear my head because I'm starting to feel like I need Vadka like I need air, and that *freaks me out*.

He's not gonna be happy. But after I talked to Zoya, I needed to leave.

Zoya—kind, ever-pragmatic Zoya—told me the truth. About losing her parents. About feeling broken and soft and unsure. And she looked me in the eye like she saw right through me. "You think love is supposed to look tidy after loss? After death?"

I didn't respond, because I didn't have an answer.

Do I?

"He's not the same man he was before," she said gently. "He loves Luka. I believe that with my whole heart. And I do think he loves you, but I don't think that's new, Ruthie. He's loved you for years."

It feels dismissive and hurtful, even though I know sweet Zoya wouldn't hurt a flea. What she's doing is trying to make sure *I* don't get hurt.

"Listen, Ruthie," she said softly. "I'm just not sure he can love you in the way you need. Or deserve. You two are... very different people."

God, she's so right.

"I'm not saying it's wrong," she added quickly. "Don't mistake me. I think, in a lot of ways, it's very right, and my romance-loving heart wants nothing more than to see the two of you together. But I don't want you to make a decision in the heat of grief or lust or guilt. Not when it could hurt you. Because if it goes wrong between you and Vadka, it's not just you who gets hurt. Luka does too."

I thought about that, really thought about it. I can't just show up at their house, day after day, and then... not come anymore if something happens between Vadka and me.

Children need consistency, routine, structure. I'm not one to offer that.

She sighed. "He's your connection to your sister, and that might color your judgment. I don't mean that cruelly..."

But I get it. I get it so clearly that it aches. Can I let this... infatuation? Lust? Love? Whatever it is—can I let it cloud my relationship with my nephew? With Mariah's son?

It would be a grave, unforgivable mistake.

And yeah, Zoya's right—we're different. On paper, maybe even wrong for each other. But when people say I don't belong in the Kopolov Bratva... why does that hurt?

Maybe because here—here with him—I feel close to her. Maybe because part of me believes she'd want me to have this... if this is something real.

So I went to work. No warning. No long goodbye. Zoya said they could've talked for hours, and I didn't have that kind of time to waste.

I strapped on the walking boot they gave me, had my ankle wrapped, took my over-the-counter meds, and got my ass behind the wheel. All I wanted was the comfort of routine. Familiar faces. The rhythm of my world.

But none of it helps. Everything reminds me of him. I want security and comfort, and I have none of it.

I double-checked security like I always do, but this time, I had three uniformed men with me. I don't usually need that. But today? I do.

Seeing the regulars helps.

Faces light up at the sight of me, their warmth, their familiarity. It's easy to smile, to exchange pleasantries, to be part of the laughter that fills the room. The chatter is light, the air thick with laughter. I can pretend to be okay, pretend I'm fine as I sip my drink, my smile perfectly placed.

But the longer I stand here, the more my ankle protests. It started as a dull throb, just a mild annoyance, but now it's a sharp pain, biting through my every step. I wince, trying to hide it, trying to focus on the faces around me, but the pain is insistent, crawling up my leg with each movement.

"Ruthie, you okay?" The voice is familiar, soft, a friend, and I nod, forcing a smile. But the ache is there, pulling at my attention, twisting in my gut.

"Yeah, just tired," I lie, shifting my weight from one foot to the other, trying to alleviate the pressure on my ankle. "It's been a long day."

"Do you need a seat?" she asks, concern edging her tone. She's seen me like this before when the exhaustion starts to show but tonight is different. The pain is worse than usual, sharp and relentless.

"No, I'm fine." I try to wave it off, but the moment the words leave my mouth, my ankle screams in protest.

I suck in a breath, trying not to make a scene.

A couple of hours pass, but the ache is only growing. The room feels smaller with each minute, the laughter and warmth now distant as the throb in my ankle grows more unbearable.

By the end of the night, my body is screaming for relief. The nausea from the pain crawls up my throat, and my exhaustion weighs heavily on me. I glance around at the faces, the smiles, but they feel like they're from a world I no longer want to be part of.

I can't go back to that empty, hollow apartment. It's quiet there—too quiet. Cold, with nothing to fill it—just walls that feel like they're closing in on me. No laughter. No warmth. Just silence.

I start to gather my things, my energy for small talk completely drained. I hear someone mention driving me home, but I quickly shake my head. "I'm good," I say, trying to force some semblance of normalcy into my voice. "I just need to get home."

But I don't want to go to my apartment.

I want *his* home. I want the sounds of Luka's laughter echoing in the halls, filling every room with a kind of warmth I haven't felt in so long. His joy is unguarded, pure. It's the kind of noise that brings life to a space and makes it feel full. His tiny hands clapping, his giggles bubbling up like a song, even when he's getting into trouble. That chaos, that beautiful mess... it's everything I want in my life right now.

But more than anything, I want him.

I want *Vadka*.

The thought of him, of his presence, settles like a weight in my chest. He's not just a man; he's stability. He's the kind of person who makes everything feel like it's okay, like it's safe. I think about the way he moves in a room—quiet, controlled, yet there's an intensity to him that makes it hard to ignore. But it's not just his strength that calls to me. It's the moments when he's vulnerable, when the sharp edges soften, even just for a second. When he looks at me, and there's something in his eyes that's raw and unspoken.

I miss him.

I don't realize I've spoken out loud until my friend's voice breaks the silence. "You sure you don't want a ride?"

"No," I mutter, louder than I meant. "I'm fine. Really." But it's a lie. It's always a lie.

I can't shake the ache in my chest—the deep, almost aching desire to be with him. To be in his presence again.

I don't want to be alone tonight. Not in my apartment. Not with this pain.

"I'll be okay," I force out, offering another weak smile before I turn, my steps slow and deliberate, but with each one, the weight of my wanting for him grows heavier. I want Vadka's home, I want Luka's laughter, and above all, I want *him*.

But the road home feels too long tonight.

Pulling out my phone, I see texts from Vadka—predictably pissed, sharp and possessive. I don't answer texts at work, so I respond as I make my way out.

> I had to work. You were busy. You knew I had to go in. Relax.

> **Vadka**
> If you knew what the doctor told me about being on your feet, you wouldn't be telling me to relax.

HE PROBABLY WANTED to tack on *young lady* at the end. Stern. Overbearing. Bossy.

You told me I was safe, Vadka. You told me I had security with me. And you'd protect me too.

Vadka
So?

So I'm fine.

Vadka
Good. And you're coming home with me.

I hear someone in front of me clearing his throat, and when I look up, I nearly drop my phone.

I swallow hard. "Yes. I'll come back to your place tonight."

But we're *not* having sex. I don't say that part out loud. Not because I don't want to, but because it always complicates things, and I don't want to fuck this up.

When I hobble toward the door, he picks me up like it's his right. Like the ground never deserved me to begin with.

No words. Just arms—hard, possessive, final. I try to squirm, but it's useless. He's all muscle and control, and I'm... not.

"Vadka—"

"Shh."

He brings me home.

"No more, Ruthie. No more running," he says when he cuts the engine.

"Do I look like I can run with this ridiculous boot strapped to me?"

"You know what I mean."

Warmth settles into my chest at the sight of the neatly trimmed hedges my sister picked out and the rows of bright yellow and pink pansies.

"I'm carrying you in."

"I get the feeling that you *like* carrying me," I say, almost scoffing, trying to play it all off as a joke, when he sobers.

"I do like carrying you. Feels like carrying a doll..." He smirks. "That could bite me if she wanted to."

"I could arrange that," I mutter. He winks at me, and it sends my pulse racing straight between my thighs before he sets me on the edge of a table like I'm made of glass, like he's afraid something might already be broken.

Then he... kneels.

I freeze. Not because I'm scared—though maybe I should be —but because Vadka doesn't kneel for anyone. But he does for me.

He peels my boot off with surgical precision, fingers methodical, terrifyingly gentle. I'm reminded of him cradling his son in his big, capable hands.

Those hands could crush bone. They probably *have*.

But not mine.

I hiss when the pressure hits the worst of the swelling.

"I'm so sorry," he whispers. "I didn't mean to hurt you."

I don't respond, and he blows out a breath. His jaw ticks.

"Didn't say you could walk on it," he mutters, like my pain offends him. Like my defiance is personal. "You should've rested. If you'd stayed, I would've told you that." His voice is low, taut with restraint. "Should've kept off it. Elevated it."

"It's my ankle," I murmur. "Not a bullet wound."

He doesn't answer. Just sinks down, slow and deliberate, until his mouth hovers over the bruised skin.

Then—

A kiss. Barely there. A flicker of heat over the ache. Reverent. Possessive. Like he's marking it.

I freeze. "You're crossing a line."

He lifts his gaze. Cold fire. Shadowed hunger.

"No," he says. "You're not afraid enough."

He taps pills into my palm—careful and exact.

"Take them," he says.

I do what he says and don't protest. I'm tired, and there's no need to. It's time for me to trust him, to know that he'll take care of me.

I'm starting to get used to this.

There's a quiet buzz from his phone. He checks it, then silences it immediately. I glance over. Alarm icon.

"What was that?"

"Reminder to time your pain meds. I don't want you to get behind on these."

I blink. "You're tracking when I take my meds?"

He shrugs. I look away, unexpectedly emotional, and swallow hard.

The meds kick in fast—heat blooming under my skin, safety masquerading as surrender. I feel the edges soften, the ache dim. Everything blurs at the corners.

But I don't stop watching him.

Even as my body melts into the couch.

Even as my eyes begin to close.

Because his eyes haven't left me once.

And whatever's happening between us—it's not mercy.

It's a storm waiting to claim me.

I remember the weight of his arms around me, the way he lowered me into soft sheets like I'm something breakable. It's all so comforting, so familiar.

When I wake up, I look around me quickly.

Did I sleep in the guest room?

No. There he is.

I'm in his bed. The pain meds have worn off, but my ankle feels better. I wriggle it a bit. Healing.

So I roll over and look at him.

He's still asleep, his face unguarded. For once, I can just... look.

God, he's beautiful. He looks so young like this. The lines between his brows are soft, his lips parted, full and just slightly pink like Luka's. When he shifts the pillow in his sleep, his tattoos and muscles ripple under the blankets, and I love every inch of him.

I love him. I do. There's no use in denying it anymore.

I think about what Zoya said, and I'm... proud of us. That we didn't give in last night. Because looking at him now? God, I want to. Who wouldn't?

And then I make a decision.

I reach for his phone. Text the nanny.

> We won't be needing you today.

Scratch that. *I* won't. The swelling's already gone down, and this?

This is where I want to be.

I stare at the phone.

The message is sent. The choice made.

I won't be needing her today.

Because I need this. Him. The quiet. The illusion. This small, would-be family.

He shifts, muscles flexing beneath the sheet, a sound low in his throat. His lashes flutter, and then—those eyes. Storm clouds, waking.

And seeing me.

I expect the armor to slam back into place. It always does. But not this time. Not when he sees I'm still here. Still in his bed. Still watching him like he's something I've earned.

"You stayed," he says, his voice rough with sleep and something deeper.

I nod, suddenly shy. "Didn't feel like going anywhere."

A silence blooms, heavy with all the words we haven't dared say.

Then—he reaches for me.

His palm finds my cheek, rough fingers tracing over my skin like he's learning it. Like he needs to.

"How'd you sleep?"

"Like a baby."

He pulls me closer, mouth brushing mine with reverence, not hunger. But I feel the tremble in his hand. The restraint. The war he's still fighting.

"You don't know what I am, Ruthie."

I look him in the eyes, cup his rough jaw in my hand, and whisper, "Then show me. Stop hiding behind the mask." I sigh. "I know what you are with me."

And that *ignites* him.

He rolls me onto my back like I'm something fragile, something to be cradled and consumed all at once. His mouth finds my throat, my collarbone, the curve of my breast— slow, worshipful, desperate.

"You don't get to leave me," he growls, forehead to mine. "You don't get to light a fire and walk away." He kisses my forehead. "Tell me to stop." He breathes against my skin.

I press my knees around him instead, careful not to hurt the ankle.

"I won't tell you to stop."

The kiss that follows is molten—melting every defense, every fear, every wall he's ever built. He slides inside me like it means something, like it's the only thing that has ever meant anything. His forehead presses to mine, his hands caging my face like a vow.

"I don't want to lose you," he whispers, voice cracking. He doesn't speak what we're both thinking: *like her.*

I dig my fingers into his back, anchoring myself to the truth of it.

"Then don't let go." His hips still every few strokes as if he's trying to hold himself together.

And we fall.

God, we fall.

His rhythm is slow and deep, like he's trying to memorize how I break. I meet every thrust with a gasp and moan, a plea.

We shatter together. And then the world stills, and our mingled breath slows. He stays.

When we're tangled in each other afterward—sweat cooling, breath syncing—he doesn't pull away. He holds me tighter.

"Stay," he says into my hair, his voice barely a sound. "Just... stay."

I nod against his chest, eyes burning.

"I want to."

I mean it. God, I mean it.

But then the phone rings.

Not his.

Mine.

My mother's contact flashes on the screen.

And I know.

I sit up, the sheets falling. My skin instantly pebbles at the loss of his heat as Vadka is instantly alert, already reaching for his pants.

I answer.

"Mom?"

But it's not her voice that answers—it's the nurse—shaky and urgent. But I can hear my mom screaming in the background.

"Ruthie, help me. I've been attacked."

Attacked?

"I'm coming," I say, already moving.

"No," Vadka orders, stepping in front of me. "*We're* coming. But we're not bringing Luka."

His voice is different now. Sharp. Cold. Dangerous.

"Rafail," he says, his call already connected. "You're taking my boy. Ruthie and I—"

"We're going in," I finish, pulling on yesterday's clothes with trembling hands.

The warmth is gone now.

But the fire between us?

Still burns. And now it has something to protect.

CHAPTER 15

RUTHIE

Mom's voice rises before I even round the corner. Slurred, frantic, a storm brewing behind the locked ward doors. My stomach knots the second I hear it—

"Whore! You brought him here? You brought him?"

She sees Vadka and sees every man who ever ruined her. Doesn't matter that he's still as stone, jaw carved from control, arms crossed like he's ready to end the building but won't. Her rage isn't about logic. It never was.

I move fast. "Mom—"

She lunges, fingernails like claws, her voice splitting the air. I don't flinch. Not even when her hand cracks across my cheek so hard my teeth clack together.

Then—he's there.

Vadka lifts me like I weigh nothing. Not rough, not violent. But absolute.

He places me behind him, like a shield being sheathed, and turns to her with that death-quiet voice.

"You strike her again," he says, "and I'll make sure you're restrained. You will *not* like that."

"Fuck you," she spits.

He steps forward.

She recoils.

"She's not your punching bag. Not anymore. She doesn't owe you forgiveness just because your cage has padded walls."

The nurse is calling security. Mom's screaming now, but I can't hear it. My cheek burns, but my ears are ringing with a different sound—

Another slap. The same hand, less wrinkled. My mother's voice. *"Tears again? You think crying gets you out of this?"*

I'm six again. The walls blur.

And then—

Vadka turns. And everything fades but him.

He looks down at me, his hands clenched, trying not to touch me wrong. "Ruthie."

My lip trembles.

Shit. I don't want to cry again.

He doesn't speak again until we're in the cafeteria, the air sterile and too bright.

"Thought she said *she* was attacked."

I roll my eyes. "Seems she said she was, but what really happened was one of her staff tried to force her to get therapy."

There's a vending machine, soft-serve ice cream in front of me, half-melted. He pushes it there like it's a peace offering. Or maybe a truce.

I can't look at him. I just keep swirling the spoon in it.

"You were shaking," he says finally. Not a question.

I nod, barely.

"You don't shake."

"Yeah." My voice scrapes. "Parents really bring out the best in you, don't they?"

Silence stretches. He sits back in the too-small folding chair, his hands clasped in front of him.

"I remember the first time my father hit me," he says. "It was just an accident. I dropped a drink and made a mess of the floor. I was five."

I glance up. His gaze is steady. Not soft, but not cold.

"I thought it meant I was wrong. Later, I realized—he was the one who lost control. Not me."

Something in me cracks. The spoon clinks against the plastic. "So... what? We just do better?"

"Yes." He says it like it's the only truth that matters. "We break the pattern. Or it eats us alive."

I shake my head. "That sounds nice on a fortune cookie, but we're not saints, Vadka."

His jaw tightens, but he doesn't argue. He leans in instead. "You didn't deserve that. And I will never let anyone touch you like that again."

I whisper it before I can stop myself. "I like when *you* touch me."

His breath halts. The ice cream in his hand melts untouched.

"I like when *you* dominate me," I say lower with a soft smile. "Not because I'm weak. But because I trust you not to destroy me." I can barely breathe. Why is it so hard for me to be honest and open like this?

"I like it too," he adds. His voice dips rough. "When it's you. When I know you respect me. When you give me yourself willingly."

My chest feels tight.

He reaches across the table and wipes a streak of soft-serve off my hand with his thumb. Heat coils between us.

We've both been hit. Scarred. Trained to flinch.

But right now?

We're choosing something else.

Not perfect. Not pure.

Just better.

And maybe... that's enough to start.

CHAPTER 16

RUTHIE

THE FIRST TIME I walk back into the Wolf and Moon after the slap, my skin still feels raw.

Not from her. Not really.

From him.

From the way he lifted me like I was something precious and fragile—something that needed saving. Like I mattered. Like he cared.

Which is fucking dangerous. Caring is a liability in our world, and I know better.

Still, I throw myself into the chaos behind the bar like it's armor. Glasses clink. Orders barked. Neon haze and too-loud bass. The old rhythm returns, but it doesn't feel the same. Something under my skin itches now... like he's watching.

And he is.

Vadka's shadow is stitched into every corner. I don't even have to turn. I feel him in the way the hair on the back of my neck stands when the door opens. In the slight shift of weight when a man too dangerous to be ignored enters a room.

He watches me.

Always.

From across the floor. From the corner booth where he pretends he's not guarding me. Silent sentinel in a black shirt and darker eyes, tracking my every move. Not interfering. Just... there.

For days, that's all it is.

Work. Watch. Avoid.

He doesn't touch me. Doesn't speak. Just sends texts at night that haunt my phone and keep me up late.

> **Vadka**
> You look tired tonight. Eat something.
>
> The Irish haven't made a move. Doesn't
> mean they're not planning.
>
> I don't like the bartender who wears the
> gold chain. He watches your ass too long.

I don't respond to most. Sometimes I send a photo of the shitty food I finally ate. Once, a middle finger emoji when he got too protective.

But the truth?

I read every one over and over and over again.

And twice, I go to his place. No sex. His eyes never drop from mine. His shoulders tighten like he's holding himself back from touching me. Like the space between us is an edge he doesn't dare cross.

Until he does.

It's a Thursday night when the bar starts to feel too small.

The Irish have been quiet for too long. Everyone's tense... waiting for something to explode. I wipe down the counter harder than I need to, and the glass nearly slips out of my hand.

Then I feel it.

That shift in the air. Like lightning about to strike.

I look up.

He's here.

Vadka moves through the bar with purpose.

Uh-oh. Eyes locked on mine. Dressed in black. No jacket. Sleeves rolled up to his forearms, veins tight under skin. That jaw's clenched and hair tousled like he's been running his hands through it too long, thinking too much.

He doesn't smile. Doesn't nod.

Just stalks.

Straight to the end of the bar. No words.

I try to speak. I do.

"You weren't here tonight. Just your lackeys," I say, my voice too sharp, too deflective.

His eyes narrow on me as his gaze drags over me. "Been super fucking busy hunting," he growls. "Tracking."

He doesn't say it out loud, but I know it isn't animals he's hunting or tracking. "You wore the red shirt." His voice is clipped.

I look down. Yeah. I did. Tight. Cropped. Ridiculous. I don't know why I put it on.

Yes, I do.

His eyes go darker. "Come with me."

"Bar's busy," I snap.

"You're not the only one here," he says without looking. "They'll cover."

Like he planned this. Like he knew.

My heart starts to hammer. "Vadka—"

But he's already moving. Not asking.

Taking.

I hesitate for half a breath.

Then I follow.

The back hallway smells like spilled beer and cheap cleanser. The storage closet is open, dim light spilling from above. I barely step inside before the door slams shut behind me—and then his mouth is on mine.

There's no preamble. No pretense. Just *need*. I make a sound low in my throat, half moan, half plea, when his hands find my waist. My ribs. My throat. Rough but reverent, like he's been starving, and I'm the only thing that'll keep him alive.

I gasp, and he drinks it in. My skin prickles with awareness, and my heart thumps madly in my chest.

"Two fucking weeks," he growls against my mouth. "Two weeks pretending we're not circling each other like wolves. Two fucking weeks pretending you don't want to be with me."

I dig my fingers into his chest. "I needed some time, some distance. It was too much too soon," I say, but even as I protest, it sounds like a silly, pathetic protest.

He groans, low and feral, and spins me to the wall. His thigh presses between mine, pinning me. His mouth on my neck now, teeth scraping, followed by tongue soothing.

"You want me to stop?" he whispers against my skin. "Too much, too soon?"

"Are you mocking me?"

His hands tighten on my ass, punishing. "I asked you a question. Stop?"

I shake my head. "Don't you fucking dare."

His hand slips under my shirt, palm dragging up my stomach. Slow. Deliberate. Testing.

"You're fire," he mutters. "But I'll take the burn."

His mouth is everywhere—my collarbone, the line of my jaw, the edge of my bra. He pulls my shirt up with one hand and cups me with the other, thumb dragging over my nipple until I'm gasping. Someone could come in and see us, but the knowledge that it's possible only drives my need further.

Maybe I'll get fired. Maybe I won't.

I grab his belt, yanking him closer. "I've wanted this," I pant. "Since the first time you told me no."

His laugh is low, wicked. "You love pushing me."

"Maybe I like feeling the resistance."

He growls, and it's a sound that coils heat low in my belly. Then his hand is sliding down, fingers under my waistband. No teasing now. Just claiming.

"You're so fucking wet," he breathes out, stunned. "*Fuck.*"

"Of course I'm wet," I hiss. "You're *Vadka.*"

Oh god, I said that out loud?

That undoes him.

He pushes my panties aside and slips two fingers in, dragging a gasp out of me like it's oxygen. His other hand braces beside my head, muscles flexed, holding himself back.

"You like this?" he murmurs.

"Yes—"

"*Say it.*"

"*No.*"

His palm slaps against my ass so hard I'm up on my toes, hissing in breath and half begging for more. He presses the heel of his hand to my pussy, and I whimper. Circling, he holds his hand right there as pressure and need mount.

"Tell me you like it."

"I like when you—*fuck*—control me."

He slides his fingers into my panties again and curls them low inside me. I nearly scream.

"You trust me," he says. Not a question. A fact, and a reverent one.

I nod wildly. "Yes. Yes, dammit, I do."

He kisses me again, hard and filthy, and I come undone in his hand, pulsing around him while he whispers against my skin.

"*Mine.*"

When I slump, he catches me.

When I breathe, it's with him.

And when I finally open my eyes, he's watching me like I just gave him something precious.

His thumb brushes my cheek. Gentle. Terrifying.

"You're *mine*, Ruthie."

I should argue. Should bite. Should fight back.

But instead—I nod.

Because maybe I already was.

Vadka's phone dings with a text. He shows me the screen.

Matvei
Come to the house. It's urgent. Bring Ruthie

CHAPTER 17

THE THUMB DRIVE CLICKS OPEN.

Matvei doesn't speak at first. He just leans back in the metal chair and stares, his lips pressed in a solid line, breathing heavily.

I don't breathe. Ruthie doesn't move.

Matvei gestures to the screen.

"Not just targets," he says, voice flat. "It's a full family map. All Bratva branches. Children. Lovers. Everyone tied to the old bloodlines."

I feel it before I see it, a cold rush behind my ribs.

And then—there it is. Her name.

Ruth Wexler.

Under a red header that reads:

Purge the Line. Erase the Heirs.

I sit back like I've been punched.

"Fuck," I whisper. "They don't want a fucking war. They want a genocide."

I lean forward, eyes locked on the screen like I can kill it with a stare. My hands are fists on my knees. "This isn't... new. This isn't in retaliation for what you did, is it?"

Matvei swallows. "Worse. There's surveillance footage. Luka and the nanny walking. Timestamps after our last sweep."

I'm on my feet.

The air changes.

"They're watching Luka," I whisper. "They're fucking watching *Luka*."

"I'll leave you to it. Let me know what you want from me."

Matvei knows better than to argue, and he leaves.

The door clicks shut.

Silence swells between us, thick and brutal.

Ruthie runs her hands through her hair. "We need to pull everyone into a secure location. Lockdown. Total sweep. No movement unless—"

"No."

She blinks. "No?"

I shake my head at her. "You want to turn my son's life into a prison because you're afraid?"

"No," she snaps. "Because I'm not a fucking idiot, Vadka. Because he's a kid. Because they've got his face on a list—"

"They won't touch him."

Her laugh is sharp and bitter. "You don't know that."

"*I* do. Because I'm going to end this before it gets to him."

She throws her arms in the air. "You don't get to gamble his life to prove how powerful you are."

I glare at her. "And you don't get to dictate tactics because you're scared of losing again. We can't hide like sitting fucking ducks. Do you have any idea how hard it is to hide with a child?"

We stare at each other like enemies. Like lovers. Like two creatures who can't decide whether to tear each other apart or protect the other with our last breath.

She swallows hard. "Then use *me*," she says suddenly.

I feel my body go deadly still.

She goes on, even as she looks afraid. "I'm on the list. Let *me* draw them out. Use me as bait."

"*No.*"

"It's the cleanest way—"

My voice slices through the air. "You're not bait. You're *mine*. And *I* don't trade what's mine."

"Vadka." Her voice cracks. "You'd rather die protecting your fucking pride than live with your family safe."

"No. God, Ruthie, no." My voice is low, lethal. "You still don't get it. This isn't about fear. *This is war.*"

I move toward her.

She stands her ground.

"They killed my wife. I won't let them hurt my son or you." My voice breaks. "I can't. I *won't*. Not again."

I reach for her and kiss her hard, bruising, a punishment we both crave. I pull back and press my forehead to hers. "Don't you understand? If I had it to do over again, I wouldn't have hid with Mariah. I wouldn't have taken her and run. I would've come earlier and taken bigger fucking guns with me. I would have slaughtered every motherfucker who even thought about touching her." I kiss her temple. "Just like I would for you, Ruthie."

I want her, right here, right now. In my bed. Under my protection. Tethered to me in a way that can't be undone.

I bite her lip, and she groans. "Tonight, baby," I whisper. "Come back tonight. Come back every night. I want you in my bed. I want you to be mine. For now, we need to go back to the bar to set up a surveillance sweep."

CHAPTER 18

RUTHIE

"Agreed." I realize that might've sounded like I was agreeing to everything. "To the *surveillance* sweep," I clarify.

He only growls at me, low and unnerving, as he gestures for us to head out.

After the surveillance sweep, the bar feels hollow. No music. No crowd.

"I don't know how to do this," I admit.

"Do what?"

"Live on the edge, watching."

He walks up behind me.

Doesn't touch.

Just breathes.

"No one will hurt you," he says. "Not while I'm breathing."

"But what if *you* stop breathing, Vadka?" I turn to face him. "What then?"

It feels like we don't have the promise of tomorrow, that we can't hold onto any future together, and all we have is right here, right now.

"Ruthie," he whispers, shaking his head.

No build-up.

No sweetness.

Just collision.

His mouth crashes to mine. Teeth, tongue, heat. My shirt tears —literally rips under his fingers. I claw at his belt. His hands are rough, greedy, sliding up under my bra, down my spine, grabbing like he needs to feel me to believe I'm still here.

We stumble back into the dark corner behind the bar. No time. No care.

I shove bottles off the counter. They crash to the floor. He lifts me like I weigh nothing, slams me against the wood, and kisses me so hard it bruises.

"You want this?" he grits.

"*Always.*"

He grinds against me, and I'm already soaked, already shaking.

"This isn't gentle."

"Good," I pant. "I don't want gentle. I want real."

He groans. Fingers on zippers, fabric aside, skin on skin, and I groan.

Then he's inside me.

No ceremony. No softness. Just need.

It's brutal. It's broken. It's two people trying to survive each other.

I meet him thrust for thrust. Bite his shoulder, dig my nails into his back like I'm marking him.

We don't whisper promises.

We don't say I love you.

We just burn.

And when I come, it's not a moan—it's a sob. It rips out of me, loud and raw and real.

He follows seconds later, forehead against mine, breath shattered.

We stay there. Tangled. Silent.

Then he pulls away.

And I know.

We're not okay.

I try to fix my shirt, but it's ruined. Doesn't matter. I find my coat, my fingers numb.

He doesn't speak.

Neither do I.

He wordlessly holds my head against his shoulder, running his hand down the length of my back.

My eyes land on the calendar behind him, pinned to the wall under advertisements, and a cold thread of fear washes through me.

Oh no.

It can't be... can it?

CHAPTER 19

I LOVE HAVING her here with me, and I wish I could find a way to make her stay. But it feels like caging a wild bird, flapping her wings, ready to escape the first chance the door to her cage opens.

And something's bothering her.

I thought we made peace at the bar, that she understood how much she means to me. But now I'm not so sure.

She's distant and quiet, her brow furrowed.

"You sure there isn't something you need to talk about?" We're on the couch in the living room. Luka's asleep after Ruthie read to him over and over again. Her ankle's better but still slightly tender to the touch and swollen, so she's elevated it beside her, leaning against me.

"Yes, fine," she says, but she's worrying her lip and looking far off in the distance while I ease her onto me, her head resting on my lap.

Wordlessly, I run my fingers through her hair. I've noticed she likes it. Slowly, I drag my fingers at her temples. Her hair is warm and soft and silky, on the shorter side, but full with a little wave. As I continue brushing through her hair, her eyelids flutter shut, and she covers her mouth as she yawns widely. "I'm so tired. It's weird. I'm never tired this early. I felt like I could've crawled right into bed with Luka and slept all night."

Frowning, I put my hand to her forehead and feel for a fever. Nothing.

"Oh my gosh, that was so sweet," she says on another wide yawn.

"What?"

"Testing my body temp by touching my forehead," she says with a hint of a smile. "Your dad side is showing, and it's so cute."

I tweak her nose. I'll give her *cute*.

A crash sounds from Luka's bedroom. Ruthie leaps to her feet, and I'm right beside her. I take off at a run and yank the door open.

But Luka's fast asleep. My gaze quickly assesses the situation before Ruthie points to where a fan fell from a window. "There," she says, whispering so as not to wake my son, who thankfully sleeps like the dead. "It was the fan."

While she checks on my sleeping son, I go to the window and peer out. There's nothing but hedges and green grass. It would be nearly impossible for someone to access Luka's room from there.

Still, I check in with the guards who monitor the perimeter.

"All clear," I whisper to Ruthie after I get their response. "Everything's fine. No signs of any intruders."

She nods, her eyelids fluttering closed as she leans against the doorframe, her face pressed to her forearm.

"I can't keep doing this," she whispers.

"I know. You won't be. I promise. You have to trust me... give me some time."

It won't solve anything for me to hose down anyone even remotely associated with the Irish clan who have set their sights on our destruction. Nothing. I've been waiting, testing, prepared to draw out our enemies and destroy anyone I need to.

But I promised Rafail I wouldn't act rashly. Pulling the trigger too soon could bring more violence to the Kopolovs. To my family.

So I wait, even as it kills me.

Her sweater's fallen off her shoulder, her bra strap thin and white against gently tanned skin. I bend and kiss the tiny rose tat she has there. Wordlessly, she turns and rests her head on my chest.

Luka rolls over in his sleep, and his eyes flutter open. "Mama," he whispers, half-drowsy, half pleading.

Ruthie makes a choking sound she quickly stifles before she sits on the edge of the bed and quietly runs her hand down his back. "Shh," she whispers. "Sleep, sweetie." He snuggles back under the covers, his eyes fluttering closed, warm and safely cocooned under the blanket. I watch, pretending my eyes haven't grown misty and it's normal to have to swallow ten times in as many seconds.

She loves him. She loves my son.

When he's softly snoring again, she looks my way, and I beckon to her.

"Tea?" she asks.

"I want something stronger than that," I admit, my adrenaline still pumping through me after the scare. "Go, sit on the couch. I'll get you the tea and a drink."

She's at least agreed to stay here until the danger passes. A part of me wonders if I've made a mistake forgoing the safe house for now, but how long can I contain them in a place like that?

My mind races as I get our drinks. I answer a text from Rafail, then load a few stray dishes in the dishwasher. I make Ruthie a cup of chamomile, the one she always drinks before bed, and pour myself a few fingers of an aged bourbon Mariah bought me for my last birthday.

Ruthie's head is drooping when I walk in, but she straightens up, her eyes barely open, and offers a smile like she wasn't just moments away from drifting off. "Let me guess," I tease, raising an eyebrow. "You're not sleepy. It's not bedtime yet, right?"

She gives me a sheepish smile and stifles another yawn. "You can't make me."

I kiss her forehead as I nestle down beside her and hand her the cup of tea. She wraps both hands around it with a sigh.

"I remember when Mariah bought that for you," she says, smiling at the bottle still in my hand while I sip my drink.

The mention of Mariah pulls me back, a familiar warmth stirring in my chest.

"I can still see her picking out that exact bottle, asking all these questions, trying to find something that would surprise you but you'd still enjoy."

I smile and sip, imagining Mariah with her bright eyes and infinite questions, asking anything and everything about the different types of drinks. "She was always good at finding little things that made me feel special," I say softly, my voice quieter now, caught between the memories of her laughter and the quiet absence that followed. "She did that for everyone."

"Yeah," Ruthie says softly, absentmindedly running her thumb along the handle of her teacup. "She did. And she was damn good at it, wasn't she?"

"She was."

It might be the first time we're sharing fond memories of Mariah like this since her death, the first time the two of us aren't fraught with grief or crying. We'll still cry. We'll still grieve. But being able to talk about memories of her makes bearing the weight of grief a bit easier.

Ruthie shifts and slides her ankle up, peering at it. "Let me see," I murmur. I shift so I can make room for her swollen ankle on my lap. I hold it gently in my hands and take a close look. "It's much better. The swelling's gone down, and the bruising's faded, hasn't it?"

She nods as I rub her ankle softly. "You'll be back on your feet in no time."

She lets out a small laugh, though it's laced with exhaustion. "You're spoiling me, Vadka."

Am I? I like that. I miss having someone to spoil. I love that Ruthie appreciates it.

I smile faintly, brushing a stray lock of hair from her face. "Someone should." I tug the lock of hair. "Not that you can't take care of yourself or anything."

"Thank you," she says with a laugh.

"Haven't heard from your mother. How is she?"

"Seems kind of the same." Ruthie looks off in the distance and bites her lip.

"Is anything bothering you?" I still can't shake the feeling that she's hiding something from me.

When she doesn't protest right away, I feel myself growing more suspicious. "Ruthie."

But she only shakes her head. "Just a lot on my mind right now. I think everything's okay."

She... thinks everything's okay.

Fair enough. I won't push her. I reach my hand to the back of her neck and massage her gently. Her eyes soften at the touch, a quiet moment between us. She sighs and leans back against me, her body settling into the comfort of the couch.

For a moment, everything outside the room fades. It's just us in the soft glow of a life that feels uncertain.

"You know," she starts, her voice quieter, as if she's carefully choosing her words. "Mariah... she was like a mother to me when my own mother started to... well, when the dementia started showing." She pauses, a shadow crossing her features. "She used to take me to get my favorite candy just because she knew I liked it, even when I didn't ask. She reminded me to do my homework and taught me how to drive. She didn't let me carry the weight of everything like I had to when my mom wasn't herself anymore."

I can feel her heartache in the way her body tenses slightly. I want to say something comforting, but I know no words will ease it. Instead, I just hold her tighter.

"It's almost like you lost more than a sister."

She lost her whole family, her support, her rock, in one fell swoop.

"Yeah," she murmurs. "But... she was always there, always looking out for me. Even when I didn't realize it." Her voice cracks a little. "She was everything I needed."

A heavy silence falls over us. The room is filled with nothing but the sound of our breathing and the gentle hum of the house settling around us. Out of habit, I click the video footage on my screen and see Luka peacefully sleeping.

Everything's at rest. Peaceful. *Right.*

I want to tell her to stay. I want to tell her she has a place with us, that she can move in, and that it will be good for Luka.

For *me.*

But I don't want to push her too fast, too soon.

She looks over my shoulder at the video of Luka and smiles. "Sweet boy."

After a few moments, Ruthie shifts again, turning her head slightly to look up at me. "How did you become such a good dad, Vadka?" she asks, her voice still tinged with that trace of sadness. "You had such a shitty example."

I shrug. "You're right, I did. I decided at an early age I wouldn't be who my father was. It was easy enough sometimes. Others, it was learned behavior I had to reverse." I shrug. "So I watched. I learned from the good ones. My uncle, for one. Even Rafail—he was like a father figure in his own way, especially after he had to become their guardian."

"You learned from Rafail?" she asks, her eyebrow arching in mild disbelief.

I smile and nod. "Yeah. He's rough around the edges, but he knows what matters."

Ruthie smiles at that, a soft, affectionate expression. "Well, it worked. Luka's lucky to have you."

"Lucky to have *us,*" I correct gently, nudging her with my shoulder.

She chuckles softly, her head leaning back against me. The weight of the world feels a little less heavy in these moments. I can feel her relaxing, her trust in me, in us, settling into something solid and grounding.

We sit there in silence for a while, the only sound the steady rhythm of our breathing, as if time has slowed down just for us. It's rare, these moments of peace.

But peace doesn't last. It never does.

The Irish are coming. Ruthie is hiding something from me. She's ready to run.

The sharp trill of my phone breaks through the calm. I glance at the screen, my stomach tightening. It's Rafail.

I swipe to answer. "Rafail," I say, keeping my voice steady.

Sometimes, words hit you with the knowledge that this... this is the moment that will change everything. I know it when I hear him. I know this is the moment that could threaten the entire annihilation of my family, the brotherhood.

"Vadka," Rafail says quickly, his tone low. "I need you. It's happening."

The words hit me like a punch to the gut. My fingers tighten around the phone, the calm I had just found with Ruthie slipping through my grip like sand. The reality of the situation crashes down on me.

The momentary peace we'd carved out was never meant to last. It was only the windswept calm before the storm, clearing the path for utter destruction. The war, the violence, the constant fight for survival... it all comes rushing back in a tidal wave.

I don't have time to process everything. Rafail's tone tells me that whatever is unfolding right now, it's urgent. It's already in motion, and I'm needed.

I have to keep Ruthie and Luka safe.

No matter what it takes.

No matter *what*.

I don't say anything immediately. My mind races, but I can already feel the shift in the room.

Ruthie and I are on the same wavelength. I glance at her, and her expression flickers, the calm demeanor she was holding onto faltering just a bit. But there's no panic. No fear. Just that steady resolve that she's always had when it's time to act.

"Come to the mansion. We're here now. Together, we can assess if it's time to assemble at the safe house."

The urgency in his voice is unmistakable. It's not just a call to action—it's a command. The weight of it presses down on me, suffocating the peaceful moment we had been stealing.

I hate running. I hate hiding. I want to come out with guns blazing and hose every motherfucker down who threatens the safety of Ruthie and Luka, but I know I have to act rationally.

So I'll do what Rafail says, and if I have to take them to the fucking safe house, I'll do it.

Ruthie's expression shifts subtly, though she tries to hold onto the calm. She exhales softly, her body language shifting like a wave rolling in, her spine straightening as if she's already stepping into a different role. There's no hesitation in her eyes, no questioning. She's ready.

Without a word, she meets my gaze, her silent resolve speaking volumes. She doesn't need to say anything. I see it in the way her shoulders square, in the quiet way she looks toward the door as though the reality of what's coming is already settling in.

I don't speak much either, the gravity of the situation pulling me into action. The leader. The protector. That's who I need to be. In the space between breaths, I rise, moving with purpose but still mindful of her injury. Gently, I help Ruthie to her feet, careful not to jar her ankle. She winces slightly but doesn't make a sound, as though any pain she feels is secondary to the urgency of the mission.

For a split second, before the chaos of the world outside intrudes again, Ruthie touches my arm—just a soft, fleeting contact, a silent reminder that in this madness, there is still something between us. Her fingers brush against my skin, and I catch her eyes—quiet, unspoken words hanging in the air.

It's a brief, precious moment where the world is on pause. A moment where we're not soldiers or leaders or anything but two people trying to hold on to whatever scraps of peace we can before everything crumbles again.

I can feel the warmth of her hand, the tenderness, and for just that brief instant, it's enough. This—us—is enough.

I don't waste any more time and move into the role I've trained myself to assume. The leader. The protector. Ruthie follows me with her eyes, her readiness clear in the way she subtly shifts her weight, preparing for what's next.

For a moment, we don't say anything. But that silence speaks volumes. It's a shared understanding between us.

It's time to go.

Ruthie's steps are purposeful, though softened by her injury. She's determined. I can see it in the set of her jaw, the way she holds herself. But in her eyes, there's something else—something fragile that we don't talk about, something that won't make it past this moment of quiet.

I glance at her one last time before we step into the unknown. Her expression is soft yet fierce, a balance of vulnerability and strength. It reminds me, for a fleeting moment, why I fight.

The mission calls, but this—this moment—will carry us through whatever comes next.

"We have to go," I whisper. "Come with me? Come with *us*, Ruthie." The question feels symbolic.

Her eyes are sharp but trusting when she nods. "Always."

CHAPTER 20

RUTHIE

Tension's rising, and while the rest of the guys I've known in the Kopolov family would be on edge, Vadka is steady. Calm. Determined and alert, but a rock.

And I would follow this man to the ends of the earth, I would.

"I have a bag already packed for you and Luka," he says. "Front hall closet. Are you good to get them?"

Of course he does.

The pain in my ankle has subsided enough by now. It's still there, but I know we have to move.

I nod, pushing through the lingering ache as I head for the closet. There's no time for hesitation, no room for weakness.

I can hear Vadka behind me, always present, always watching, ready for whatever comes next.

I find the bags in the closet right away—two duffel bags, one stuffed with folded clothes and toiletries, the other a few toys and various items that would occupy a little boy. I grab them from the closet, their weight solid in my hand, and turn to find him watching me, his expression unreadable, but his eyes soft. His gaze drops to Luka, still asleep, now nestled in his arms, the quiet, fragile peace a stark contrast to the world we're thrust into.

"You're doing good," Vadka says quietly, his voice low enough that only I can hear. I lean my head on his shoulder and look down at the sweet boy asleep in his arms. If I loved Vadka before now, watching him hold his son against his chest, looking down at him with unfettered love and affection, makes me love him even more.

I manage a faint smile, but inside, my heart feels like it's slamming against my chest. There's so much uncertainty ahead. So much that could go wrong. But I can't afford to let any of that show, not now, not in front of Luka.

I take a breath, steadying myself. "Let's go."

We move quickly, silently. Vadka's presence at my back is like a shield, his steady footsteps matching mine as we head toward the car. Luka stirs in his sleep but doesn't wake. The quiet rhythm of his breathing is a small comfort, a reminder of why we're doing all this. For him.

For our little family.

Our family.

By the time we arrive at the Kopolov estate, everything has shifted. The air is thick with the weight of what's to come, but there's a hushed reverence in the house as everyone gathers. The atmosphere is heavy with unspoken tension, but also something else—preparedness. This is what they've been waiting for, what they trained for.

After settling little Luka in bed, Vadka moves through the house with ease, a quiet authority about him as he greets everyone, checking in and making sure everything is in place. I can see the respect in the eyes of the men here. They trust him. They know he's the calm in the storm.

"Luka is having a hard time settling down," Vadka says in a low voice to me. "He woke up a little."

"Poor little guy. Let me bring him something to drink."

I move to the kitchen and prepare a warm cup of milk for him. It's a small act, but one that brings a little bit of peace in the midst of all the chaos, and it makes me feel good to mother him. As I hand him the cup, his sleepy eyes flutter open, and for a moment, it's just us—no guns, no violence, just him and me.

Luka sips the milk slowly, his little body curling against mine as I stroke his hair, whispering soft words of comfort. He doesn't ask questions, doesn't sense the danger. He just trusts me, like he trusts Vadka. And that's enough. For now, it's enough.

I watch his eyelids flutter closed.

I glance over at Vadka, who stands in the doorway, watching us with that protective, quiet intensity of his. His gaze softens as he sees me holding Luka, and I swear, for a moment, the world seems to slow down. All the noise, all the urgency, fades away, and I see him—really see him. Not as my brother-in-law, not as some guy in the Bratva. I see him as... *mine.*

His eyes are warm, but there's a hardness to them too. A resolve that comes from everything he's been through, everything he's seen. But in this moment, he's just Vadka. The man who's going to protect us, no matter what.

My heart swells with a mixture of love and gratitude. He walks over, his steps quiet, purposeful. He crouches down beside me, his hand gently brushing a strand of hair from my face. His touch is warm, grounding, and in this moment, with Luka in my arms and Vadka beside me, everything feels right.

For a brief moment, it's just the three of us, a family.

"Thank you," I whisper, my voice barely above a breath.

He doesn't answer with words. Instead, he simply presses his lips to my forehead, a soft, lingering kiss that speaks volumes. His strength, his steadiness—it's everything I need. Everything I didn't know I needed until now.

"Let's get some rest," he whispers. I'm exhausted.

I look around us as I follow him to the room. Back in the safe house, Rafail had apologized for putting the two of us in a room together.

Would they now? Will they be scandalized if we sleep in the same bed?

Does it matter?

We're in a bedroom on the first floor, probably so we can be close to Luka, and I don't have to use the stairs with this damn boot. Vadka takes our bags and opens the door for us. It's quiet and well-furnished, with a sturdy king-sized bed, simple but elegant furniture, and thick blinds to block out the light. The walls hum with stillness. A pause. A breath.

The bedding is a stunning navy-blue-and-white pattern, heavy and welcoming. That bed looks like heaven after a long day like today.

While he puts our bags away, I walk to the bathroom and wash up for bed. I come back and find him stripped to his boxers. *Squeee.* I feel like I get a sleepover with my boy crush. The sight of his bare chest, those smoldering eyes, his strong, well-trained body...He pats the bed beside him. "Bed, baby."

I stand awkwardly near the edge of the bed, my fingers working the buttons on my shirt. My hands shake more than I expected. Vadka watches from the bed, propped up on an elbow.

"You're still limping."

"I'm fine."

He doesn't answer but pushes off the bed and walks over to me. My fingers falter. One button left.

He brushes my hands aside. Wordless. Efficient. He undoes the last button and eases the fabric off my shoulder like he's done this a thousand times in his mind.

I don't breathe.

His hands are rough and scarred but precise. He doesn't linger when he shouldn't, at least not this time.

But I feel everything.

He reaches for the hem of my shirt next. Pauses.

I nod… barely.

He lifts it gently, tugging it over my head and discarding it. Then he kneels and undoes the straps of my ankle brace with care that has no place in this brutal world. Then he slides off my jeans, one leg at a time.

I would say there's nothing sexual about him undressing me, that he's taking care of me, that we're tired and ready to sleep. But I would be lying. Every interaction with him is sexual. Every breath he takes turns me on. The back of his hand on my thigh as he has me slide one foot out of the jeans at a time has me *molten*.

But I'm so damn tired, and so is he; I can see it in the lines of his face and weariness in his movement.

I should feel vulnerable standing in front of him like this. I don't. I feel… *seen*.

He pulls back the covers and motions for me to lie down. And when I climb in beside him, all warm and protective beside me, he tucks the blanket around me like I'm something precious.

Like I'm his.

"Sleep, baby," he says softly, bending to give me a chaste kiss. "We need rest."

Wordlessly, I lay my head on his chest. His arms encircle me, and I listen to the steady beating of his heart. I let myself relax under the reassuring weight of his arm around me. I sigh, close my eyes, and drift off to sleep.

I wake the next day to Vadka leaving the bed.

"Up and at 'em, Ruthie," he says with a grim smile. "We're training today."

"Training?"

"Training. We need to prepare."

CHAPTER 21

RUTHIE

THE STILLNESS IS DECEPTIVE. Even I know by now not to trust it.

A part of me longs for peace, for predictability, for a future that's clear and dependable. And a part of me wants *action*. I want to fight. I want to *defend*. I want to use my energy and whatever I have to offer to bring a fucking end to the pain and tragedy that's descended on this family. To Luka. To Vadka.

Outside the estate, the sun hangs low where the session's been planned. We've been practicing all day long. Not a real ambush—yet—but close enough. Vadka and Rafail made sure of that.

The men don't just need drills. They need to be ready. Ready like I'll have to be.

He stands near the back exit, already in tactical black, sleeves rolled, neck taut. Watching.

Mmm. I need a little wallet-size print of him to slide into my pocket, looking just like *that*.

Always watching.

The vest smells like him, leather and a hint of something spicy and woodsy. Too big across my shoulders, but I try to tighten it anyway. My fingers work the buckles too fast, too rough. I don't care.

I need the armor. Maybe could use another damn layer.

Sigh.

Outside, I can hear boots shifting in gravel, voices low and clipped. Controlled tension. Everyone knows what this is.

My own pulse is too loud in my ears.

I sense him before I hear him.

"Five minutes," he says from the doorway. His voice gentles when his eyes lock with mine. "You look adorable."

Adorable? Really?

I finish the last strap and force my body to stillness.

I wink at him. "You're not so bad yourself." His black outfit is outfitted with weapons. Scary sexy. I can't control the flutter in my heart or the need to step closer to him. To feel him.

"I'm ready."

He steps toward me, slow and deliberate. His presence fills the space like smoke—thick, suffocating, impossible to ignore, his eyes on mine unwavering. And I know right then, dressed in protective gear, on the cusp of practicing actual fucking combat, I've... never been happier.

Happy. He makes me happy.

And I realize that it's the first time I've felt more happiness than grief since my sister left this world. I blink so he doesn't see my shimmering eyes.

"You look like you don't want to do this."

I clear my throat and laugh it off. "Would rather be maybe on a beach in Maui, but this is fine. It'll do."

He smiles. Barely. "Good," he says. "Because it's time." He leans in closer. "And when this is all over, Ruthie? When we're at peace and safe again. I won't hold back."

Why does that make my pulse spike?

I shove past him, shoulder bumping his—hard. A challenge. "Didn't ask you to."

His gaze drags down my spine, and I know it—can feel it like heat at my back. It makes my skin prickle and my breath catch, even as I hate it. Hate him for making me feel anything but fear.

He follows. Of course he does.

Outside, everyone's assembling. Practice, they say. But is it really? Not with the way Vadka sets the tempo. Not with the threat breathing down our necks.

I reach for a pair of gloves, but he's already there. Close behind. *Too* close.

Turning to me, he adjusts a strap on my vest. Then another. His fingers graze my ribs, and I freeze.

Not just from the touch.

He could press harder. Pull tighter. He doesn't. He touches just enough to remind me who's in control—and how badly he wants me to feel it. I feel fully handled when he touches me like that, and I never knew how badly I craved it.

"You don't trust them yet," he murmurs, his breath brushing the curve of my ear.

It isn't just trust. I'm not one of them yet, not like my sister was and definitely not like he is.

"No," I say. "You know me." My voice is husky. "I don't trust anyone."

It's a lie though. I trust *him*.

I feel the shift in him—that pause—that inhale likc he's biting back something darker.

I turn my face toward him slowly. Our noses almost brush.

His hand lingers a second too long on my waist, then drops.

He steps back.

"Stay behind Zoya," he orders, all commander. My skin is prickly, and my god, I want him. *Now*. I'm *wet*. Wet, like a fucking Pavlovian dog at his command and presence. I might've been guilty as fuck falling in love with him, but I can say with absolute honesty that I *never* felt like this with him before. But now?

We stare at each other, and I hate how quiet it gets.

Because I'm not just gearing up for a training drill.

I push back the memory of my fears, of what I thought back at the bar and shake my head. I can't deal with that, not now. I have to compartmentalize. I have to deal with the present.

"No fucking around, Ruthie," he says, holding me by the front of the vest, two straps anchored in his fists. "You get me?" He doesn't blink... just bends down and holds my gaze. "If it turns real," he adds, "I'll get to you first."

I scoff. "Romantic." Even as my heart thumps madly in my chest.

He smirks.

"No." His voice drops, low and sharp. "Strategy."

"Sounds good, *Captain*."

He narrows his eyes at me. "Listen to me, woman. Behave yourself."

Thump.

"Or what?"

He slides a knuckle under my chin. "Or I'll have to make sure to teach you a lesson, won't I?"

Won't he? I melt like butter on a frying pan but manage to stand upright. Yay me.

We need to get this behind us. To get back on solid footing. To stop running from our enemies and establish... whatever comes next.

I gulp as Rafail starts shouting orders, and we fall into line. My stomach twists, but not from nerves. Not exactly.

There's a part of me trying not to feel.

Not now. Not here. Not while I'm counting days and pretending I'm not holding my breath.

CHAPTER 22

VADKA

We train for days, we listen to intel, and we scan our surroundings, but we're not ready. Nothing feels like it's enough. It never does, but this time, there's more weight to the uncertainty.

I can't keep Ruthie and Luka holed away, dependent on the Kopolovs for life. I tell myself it won't last forever, that we will find a way through the dangers and threats around us. I tell myself this is what it means to be at war. Uncertainty, waiting. Survival.

I promised her.

But a part of me loves every second of this, savors these precious, stolen moments where we're safe, and Ruthie can't run and hide. After a long day of training, I slide into bed beside her or bring her into the shower with me. I can't help being her caretaker. It's who I am, what I know, and it fills me with no small amount of comfort to know I can take care of her and Luka, even in small ways.

No one here questions that we share a room, and even though we don't talk about it, there's no wonder in anyone's eyes anymore about who we are and where we stand.

Three days into the training at the Kopolovs, Rafail invites me to the balcony for a drink. He pops the top off a beer and hands it to me. My body's tired from training hard, my muscles sore, but in a way that feels like a good day's work.

I sit beside him and take a long gulp.

"Where's Ruthie?" he asks quietly.

"With Zoya." Zoya wanted her to read over an essay or something.

Rafail leans back, his eyes assessing, but the glimmer of a smile on his lips. "What are your intentions with Ruthie?" As the *pakhan* of the Kopolov Bratva and my best friend, I know he has the right to ask.

But it still feels too personal, too sacred.

I look out over the balcony. The sun is setting, hints of gold and red touching the buildings that loom in the distance. The wind kicks up with a bite of cold, and somewhere not far from here, a dog barks. I sip my beer. Swallow. Lean forward with my forearms on my knees and meet his gaze.

"I love her, Rafail."

He nods. Waiting. I haven't answered his question.

I look down at the bottle as a bead of condensation rolls down the amber glass.

"And I know she loves me."

"Has she told you?"

"Yes."

Another beat passes.

"And her mother? What's the latest news with her?"

I shrug. "She's stable, for now, but declining. She's losing her memory, and that scares her. Makes her combative. But she's in good hands, it seems."

Ruthie doesn't know it, but I paid good fucking money to ensure that happened.

"Yeah."

"So this isn't just comfort, then. You're not slipping into her bed because it's warm and familiar. You're thinking about the future." Is he baiting me? I nod slowly, my shoulder tense.

"I didn't plan any of this, not with Ruthie. But the more I'm around her, I realize... she fits. *We* fit." I glance up at him. "She challenges me. Sees me. Doesn't flinch." I look away. "With Mariah, it was different, yeah, but *I* was different." I take another sip of beer. "Drives me fucking mad some days knowing I'd burn down the fucking city if it meant keeping her and Luka safe."

What I don't say out loud is that it scares me to lose any control, and Ruthie undoes me.

Rafail leans forward, his tone low. "And do you think that's enough? That you're ready to protect them, no matter the cost?"

I stare at the beer in my hands. "It's a start, isn't it?"

He watches me for a long moment, then looks beyond me, back at the house. "I think she's scared."

I look back at him, my gaze sharp. "What are you talking about?"

He purses his lips, thinking over his words before he responds. "Women need to know that you're all in, Vadka. You loved her sister first, and that's got to be something that's in the back of her mind. She doesn't want to be Mariah's replacement."

My voice is vehement, my temper rising. "Fuck, Rafail, she *isn't*."

He swivels his gaze to mine. Challenging. Hard. "Does *she* know that?"

Does she?

I never knew I could love someone again. But now, she's *everything*. Fucking *everything*.

Rafail stands. "Look, brother. It's my job to make sure my men are stable and secure, that they don't make decisions with a woman that could impact their loyalty to the Bratva."

We don't date casually and never have. It's all in with us, and for good reason.

"And it's my job to make sure that if you *are* all in, that you make it official. You know she has greater protection inside our family if you make her yours officially."

I nod. I do know it. I've thought about it. I don't give a fuck about what others might say, but I don't want to push Ruthie.

He taps his beer bottle to mine. "Tomorrow, I'm separating you two. We need a trial run to defend ourselves in the event of an attack. I need to see you in action, make sure your judgment isn't affected by your concern for Ruthie." His eyes grow distant, his lips turning down into a scowl that strikes fear in the hearts of anyone who crosses him.

"Rafail, for fuck's sake, you know—"

"I don't," he finishes, his tone hard. "I don't, but I need to."

I take another angry gulp of my drink, blood burning in my veins.

"An attack is coming," he says, his voice laced with warning. "Matvei says it's imminent."

Imminent.

I've known it, of course, but hearing the words out loud makes it seem so much more possible.

I lean back in my chair, my shoulders tense. My beer is still half full, untouched. Cold condensation drips to the floor.

Rafail watches me, hard and calculating. Loyal to the bone. He's watching to see if my judgment's clouded by grief.

"You're questioning me. Because, again, I've got something to lose."

A beat passes. He gulps the rest of his beer and looks out beyond. "That's exactly why I'm questioning it. Tomorrow, we have a trial. You'll take sector east. Ruthie goes with Semyon."

"Rafail—"

"No." His word is law. "Tomorrow, I separate you two. This is war, Vadka. They say she knows her way around a gun."

She does. Her sister taught her, and I agreed. In our world, it helps to be prepared.

Rafail continues. "You have to depend on your brothers to protect everyone. And *I* need to know your loyalty to the Bratva hasn't been diluted."

"You know I—"

He stands, his gaze sharp. "Words are cheap, brother," he says. His hand falls on my shoulder. "Fucking show me."

BUT WE DON'T GET a chance to execute. We suit up for it, we separate, and I do exactly what Rafail fucking tells me to do, but it's too late. The time has come. There are no more practice sessions.

The first scream doesn't come from the street.

It comes through the earpiece.

"Two black vans. East alley. Move. *Now.*" Ice churns in my veins.

Zoya's voice is calm, but I know what calm sounds like when you're terrified.

Luka's inside.

Zoya confirmed it on the comm not two minutes ago before the shit hit the fucking fan. But I haven't seen Ruthie in eight hours.

We planned it this way. We needed a trial, needed to practice how to take them on in the event of an ambush.

I slam the door behind me and run, gun already warm in my hand. My men fan out across the block, but my pulse only locks onto one point.

Please still be there. Please—

I round the corner, and it hits me like a fucking truck.

She's there.

Ruthie.

Too-big tactical vest thrown over a tank top, hair a mess, eyes pure fire. Oh god.

She's already outside, kneeling by Luka.

Luka?

When did he come out here? He wasn't supposed to be here.

She tucks him behind a dumpster. Her hand is steady on his shoulder, the other gripping a pistol like it's second nature. Her stance is wrong—she favors her ankle. Still hurt. Still moving.

Rafail was right. She *does* know her way around a gun.

When she sees me, she nods and smiles. Pretending everything's okay, that we're practicing just like we planned.

Luka waves. Then I know. She's doing this for him. We're playing a game. It's just a game.

But I see *everything*. And I know the second everything shifts. My blood simmers, and my instincts snap into place.

Three figures are coming from the alley. Tight formation. Coordinated.

Irish. Not Bratva. No colors, just quiet killers.

Not a fucking drill.

I don't think. I *move*.

"Get him down!" I scream at Ruthie.

Gun up, the first shot lands clean—center mass. The second hits the runner's thigh, and screams erupt. Luka curls tighter into Ruthie's side, her hand over his ears, his head against her chest.

She spins toward the shots, gun raised.

Then she looks at me.

Time stops..

Everything goes still. And *sharp*.

Her eyes find mine. Wide. Disbelieving. Hopeful.

And then—

She nods.

No time for words.

We move.

Two more men behind the fence. I signal with two fingers, then tilt left. She covers right. We flank like we've done this a hundred times.

But we haven't.

Not really. *This* was supposed to be our practice session, our trial run.

Still—our rhythm is perfect.

She drops one with a clean shoulder shot.

I finish him before he can scream.

Smoke and blood coat the air.

Backup swarms in between us—Matvei and Rodion, Rafail and his lieutenant.

We drag Luka behind the back entrance. Thank fuck the little guy didn't see what happened, didn't know this was *real*. I press his head into my chest and feel his tiny hands grip my shirt.

"You did good!" he says with a grin. My heart pounds so fast I'm dizzy. I don't trust myself to speak.

Ruthie slams the bolt shut behind us and leans back against the door.

She's breathing hard and sweat runs down her temple.

I hold Luka to me, feeling his warmth seep through my fingers, reassurance that he's okay.

"You did good, too, buddy," I finally manage to say, my voice hoarse.

"Yeah, so that wasn't supposed to go that way," she mutters.

I meet her eyes. "You did great."

She swallows. "You protected me."

I step close.

Her breath hitches.

"Of course I did."

Luka smiles up. "You said I did good, too, Papa?"

I fall to one knee and hold him to me. "*So* good, buddy. I'm so proud." My voice shakes. "You're a real hero."

The tenderness cracks something in me.

Sirens now, distant, and gunshots have stopped. Backup closing in and doing their job. We need to move... We need to get out of here.

I kiss her.

It's not violent this time but soft, reverent.

Luka hugs our legs, and we pull back. She cradles him, and I watch her wrap around him like she's always been his shield.

And something inside me *clicks*.

It was never supposed to be her.

But it *always* had to be her. She's mine, his—we're family, and we love each other. She loves him unconditionally, the way he deserves.

The door bursts open behind us—Matvei's voice is shouting instructions to burn the fucking Irish warehouse in the harbor to the ground. Send a message. Strike back.

I lift Luka into my arms. He's still oblivious to how real this got.

We're heading back to the Kopolovs'.

Ruthie follows, gun still in hand, her eyes still scanning.

We walk out as one.

And the Irish are going to *bleed*.

CHAPTER 23

W*E'RE* in the evacuation van, and Luka's asleep against my chest. He's still convinced it was a game, just like we told him. Miraculously shielded from the terror and danger.

For now. *Jesus.* For now.

Vadka is beside me, his fingers brushing mine on the seat.

Neither of us speaks. We both know how close of a call that was, how dangerous that could've been.

Vadka leans in just enough that our shoulders touch.

We park the van, and it's like we're moving in slow motion. Everything happens quickly, but not fast enough.

Through the front door. We don't have to ask Luka to be quiet because he knows intuitively. At first, he laces his fingers with mine, but his steps are slow, and timing is urgent. Wordlessly, Vadka swings him into his arms. My heart turns over in my chest.

I don't even realize I've been holding my breath until the front door locks behind us.

Click.

It's the sound of something final, like a trigger pulled.

Vadka moves us through the house to the room we've been staying in, with his usual quiet precision—checking windows, arming the system, making sure no one followed. His black shirt is smudged with soot and something darker. Luka's still in his arms, thumb in his mouth, his tiny fist curled in the fabric of Vadka's collar.

He hasn't let go since the ambush.

And neither have I.

We're safe. For now.

I sit on the edge of the couch and press my fingers to my temples. The whole world tilts slightly to the left.

I hear the sound of Vadka's boots. Then silence. Then—

A soft rustle.

He's wrapped Luka in a blanket and laid him down in his room next to ours. The boy doesn't stir. Just breathes deeply and slowly, like he's finally allowed to.

Vadka crouches in front of me, his knees wide and hands braced on either side of mine.

"You're shaking."

I open my mouth. Close it.

I don't have anything brave to say. No bite. No barbed-wire wit. I told him I wanted to run, told him I wanted to hide, but now the future ahead of us—for many reasons—seems uncertain and scary.

I just whisper, "I don't know how to come down."

He nods like he gets it. Of course he does. He's lived in war longer than I have.

"Then don't," he says. "Just sit. Let me."

He stands and walks into the kitchen. I expect him to disappear into tactical planning, into his endless storm of protective rage.

But instead—

He opens a cabinet, pulls out a box of pasta, and tosses it on the counter. Grabs a pan like it's a regular Tuesday.

"You're... making dinner?" I ask, voice still wrecked.

"You haven't eaten."

"I'm not hungry."

He gives me a look that would scare actual criminals. "Doesn't matter. You need to eat, baby."

Baby. *Sigh.* A bit of my invisible armor slides off me. I'm safe here. I'm with Vadka.

The water boils, and he works in silence. Measured, methodical. His sleeves are rolled up, arms dusted with flour by the time he's chopping something green and pretending he's not watching me through the corner of his eye.

"I didn't know you could cook," I murmur.

He shrugs. "Basic survival."

"Isn't that what takeout's for?"

He turns his head just enough for me to see the smirk.

It's barely there. But I feel it like sunlight on cold skin.

He plates it—two bowls, one smaller for Luka if he wakes—and brings it to me like it's sacred.

I take one bite and have to close my eyes.

It's not gourmet. Not even that well-seasoned.

But it's warm and delicious, and I *am* hungry.

He sits beside me, legs spread wide, one hand resting on the couch behind me like a bracket. Not touching. Just close enough that I can lean closer if I want.

So I do.

I sink against him, cheek to his shoulder. His other hand finds my thigh and stays there. Steady. Warm.

We eat in silence.

I let myself breathe.

I don't know how to tell him what I fear. We've already been through so much.

"Is it just us here?"

"Just us for now," he says. I can tell he hates this, and it isn't what he wanted. He's not the type to sit back when he can take the situation in hand himself, but he has to.

My stomach twists.

Probably the adrenaline crash, I guess.

Or the cold.

Or the weight of everything. Or...

I swallow hard and try to push it down.

But it comes back, sour and sharp, right behind my teeth.

I lurch up and make it to the bathroom just in time.

The nausea hits like a wave—one hand on the counter, the other clutching the side of the toilet.

My whole body trembles.

When I'm done, I sit back on the floor and press my head to the cool tile. My heart's racing, and my skin is clammy.

I hear the floorboards creak.

Vadka's voice is low. "Ruthie?"

"I'm fine," I rasp.

He doesn't believe me. Of course not. But he doesn't push, just brings me a glass of water and crouches beside me.

"Shit, I didn't think my cooking was *that* bad."

I give him a watery smile and sip.

He brushes the damp hair off my forehead and doesn't speak.

Just waits.

His silence is more tender than words would be.

"Could be a stomach bug," I mutter.

It's not. I know it's not. *God.*

"Could be." But his voice is tight now. "Shit timing." He's watching me too closely.

My mind starts calculating... counting back.

"Is Zoya coming home?" I ask, trying to keep my voice nonchalant like I didn't just vomit into the toilet and my period's late.

"Yeah, Zoya and Rafail will be here soon."

"I need—I need to make a call."

"What's going on? Ruthie—"

"Please. Just—give me a second."

He nods and steps back.

I grab my phone and slip into the room, wrapping a blanket around my shoulders. The screen glows in the dark.

Zoya.

She answers on the first ring.

"You okay?"

My voice is too quiet. Fragile.

"Can you maybe... Can you get me a... test?"

The silence on her end is immediate. Heavy.

Then—

"Pregnancy test?" she whispers.

I barely trust my voice. "Yeah."

"I'll be there in ten."

I hang up.

My hands are shaking again.

CHAPTER 24

VADKA

It's almost two a.m. when she finds me at the kitchen table.

She's barefoot, wearing one of my shirts again—she does it without asking now, and I fucking love that. It falls off one shoulder, her legs bare. Hair is a mess. Eyes sharp.

My god, she's beautiful.

She's beautiful in that way people whisper about. Hushed and reverent, a little awed. And I want her, I want her so fucking badly I'm instantly hard. But she didn't feel well earlier, and I don't want to push.

Zoya came home and dropped off supplies.

"Maps again?" she asks, leaning over the table.

"Trying to see what the next move will be," I say. "They're obviously not posturing anymore."

"No," she murmurs. "They want blood."

Her voice trembles. Just for a second.

I hate it.

"You think he's planning a coordinated hit?"

"Or a message," I say. "Something brutal. Public. The Undertaker is the Irish's most wanted. He wants a panic. A culling."

She sits down, legs pulled up on the chair, staring at the intel.

"Maybe we should... I dunno, scatter the assets. Move the kids out of state."

I shake my head. "They'll expect that. Roads'll be watched. They want us running."

She meets my eyes. "So what? We dig in and hope they miss?"

"We don't hope. We bait. We lead them where we want them. We control the field."

Her expression hardens. "You still want to fight this like it's honor versus power. Vadka—we have a child in the other room. We have more to lose now."

"I know what I have to lose." My voice comes out rough, too close to raw. "You think I don't consider all the possibilities?"

She sighs. "We're both trying to protect him. Just differently. It's two sides of the same coin."

She's not wrong.

I nod. Barely.

She shifts closer, and her knee touches mine under the table.

"I want you to win this war," she says quietly. "But I need to know you won't let pride bury us in the rubble. Maybe we leave, maybe we get new identities. Pack up and just... go. Somewhere safe. Somewhere they won't find us."

I shake my head and reach for her hand.

"Ruthie," I murmur. "I don't care about pride. I care about *you*. And you need to know, just like your sister did." It feels like progress to be able to say *your* sister without guilt, without pain so sharp I can't breathe. "If you're in with me, you're in the Kopolov Bratva. There's no escaping. We don't move, we don't hide, we don't make any choices in the future that don't impact every goddamn one of them."

She stills.

Eyes wide. Barely breathing.

I lean in closer. "And in return, that means you're one of them. One of *us*. It means every motherfucker in the Bratva protects you like their own. There isn't a need you have we don't meet. You'll be protected. Cared for." I swallow hard. "Family."

Because isn't that what this is all about, in the end? Love and family, friendship that crosses boundaries and knows no limits. Love and war, death and life.

She holds my gaze and rests her hand on mine. Then she reaches across the table and pulls the map toward her.

"Okay," she says. "Then let's plan it together."

It's not surrender.

It's something deeper.

Trust.

And it feels like she's made the decision to do something she hasn't spoken of, not yet, like she's facing a fear she's held onto that no longer holds her in its grip.

I want to ask her what it is, what she's afraid of, what she needs. But Ruthie values her independence, and I know by now this is part of her process. If I need her to trust me, I need to give her space to do things in her way, in her time.

She gets up and walks away for a little while. Says she's going to brush her teeth.

But she doesn't come back.

Not right away.

After ten minutes, I check the bedroom.

She's not there.

The bathroom light's still on. Shit. Is she okay?

I knock once. "Ruthie?" My voice is sharper than I intended. "*Ruthie?*"

No answer. I hear a sniff that sets my racing heart to ease, but not fully.

I open the door slowly.

She's standing in the middle of the room, barefoot on the tile.

Trembling.

She's holding a plastic stick like it just detonated in her hands.

And my heart *stops*.

Wait. *What?*

She looks up, and her lips part.

"It's positive, Vadka." And then she's crying. She blinks, and hot, fat tears roll down her cheeks. She sniffs, and I can't think straight.

I step forward, and she flinches—not back, but inward, like she's bracing for me to say something. Something cruel. Or shocked. Or distant.

But I don't.

I just stare at her.

At the firecracker of a woman I've burned for.

At the knife-sharp survivor who's carried more than any one soul should.

At the girl who never thought she'd get to be anything soft.

And now—she's carrying a future neither of us planned.

A child.

Ours.

She starts to say something. I can see it bubbling up—an apology, maybe, or a shield disguised as sarcasm, fear, or humor, but I cut her off.

Not with words.

With my arms.

I pull her into me. Tight. Fierce. Like she might disappear if I'm not careful. "A baby? My god, Ruthie. You're *pregnant, baby?*" I hold her so tight she gasps for breath, and I have to let her go a little.

She doesn't resist, just melts.

Right there in the bathroom, under cold light and warm silence, Ruthie lets go.

Her arms come around me. Her face buries into my chest, and she sobs.

"I didn't mean for it to happen," she whispers, her voice broken.

"I know." Of course this wasn't planned.

"I don't even know *how* it happened. I'm on birth control, but like... I don't know what I'm supposed to feel—"

"You don't have to know," I murmur. "We'll figure it out."

"We're still being hunted."

"I'll end it."

"You can't promise that."

I pull back just enough to look her in the eye.

"I can. And I will. Because now? This isn't just about bloodlines. Or Bratva. Or war."

I put her hand on my chest.

Let her feel what she's done to me.

"This is about *us*."

She breathes, deep and wrecked.

Then she leans up... and kisses me. I hold her face in my hands, my lips against hers, my heart so full I feel like I'm on cloud nine. *A baby.*

Then she pulls away and breaks into a fresh sob. She puts her head on my chest again and weeps deep, wracking sobs that shake her shoulders.

"Ruthie," I say softly. "Shh. This is going to work out. Do you want the baby? Is that what you're afraid of? Do you—"

"It's not that." She sniffs. "I just— How do I— This isn't right, Vadka." Her voice breaks, and she wails. "I took my sister's life, and it's not fair. This shouldn't *be me* having your baby. This should be *her. Mariah.* I came in after she wasn't here, and I... I took her life, and I'll never forgive myself for that."

"God, Ruthie. No, baby. *No.* C'mere."

I bend, scoop her up in my arms, and walk to the small leather loveseat nestled in the corner of the living room.

I sit on the loveseat and tuck her against me. I let her cry it out. I hold her to my chest and rock her gently, and when I blink, my own damn tears follow hers. I shake my head and try to put into words what my heart already knows.

"You didn't take *anything* that wasn't yours, Ruthie. Nothing. Let me ask you a question. If Mariah knew you were loved, so deeply, so fully, unconditionally? What would she say, baby?"

She sniffs. I run my hands through her hair.

"She would want me to be happy. She would want someone who... loved me."

"And I do, Ruthie. I love you so damn much. And this baby? Unexpected, yeah. But unwanted? Never, baby. *Never.*" I kiss her fiercely. "This little baby brings *new life.*"

She sighs. "It might take time for me to wrap my brain around this..."

I shrug. "Seems like you have, at least, what? Eight, eight and a half months?"

She smiles. "Yeah. We do." She straightens her shoulders.

"You better?" I ask, now that the sobbing's stopped and she looks lighter. Freer.

She nods. "I think so?"

"Good," I whisper, leaning in to kiss her. I've never wanted her so much in my life. She's carrying *my baby.* My woman, carrying my child. And I want her so fucking bad.

Then, as if we've been waiting for this moment for too long, I lean in and kiss her, slow at first, tasting the sweetness of her lips, the way she sighs into me, and it feels like everything falls away. It's not just the kiss—it's the promise. It's our baby. Our future. And it hits me harder than I ever expected.

And in that moment, the threats beyond the security of this place slip away. It's not just a kiss. It's a vow, a promise, our future. And it crashes over me with a wave I never saw coming.

Maybe we would've taken our time. Maybe we would've been slow and deliberate. Maybe we would've allowed our grief and fears to ebb away like sand on a shore until we found each other whole. But now we have a baby knit between us, an irrevocable tie to one another that makes who we are and what we mean together *immediate.*

We'll make this work. We have to.

She presses closer, her hands sliding to my chest, slow and certain, fingers splaying like she's trying to memorize the steady beating of my heart. I deepen the kiss, hungry for more, knowing that she's carrying my child. Her body melts into mine. Heat rises, and my cock aches to fill her, claim her, remind her who she is and who she belongs to.

I break away just enough to breathe, the words raw, my voice hoarse.

"God, I want you so fucking bad, Ruthie. So goddamn bad."

Her lips hint at a tease, curving upward, but her eyes are dark, her pupils wide with need and want, her fingers near desperate when she reaches for me again. "Then take me, *please.* All of me. I want you too."

She holds my hand, and I tug her toward the bedroom. There's nothing frantic in the way we move, no rush or desperation, just a quiet, simmering need that pulses between us.

I lower her onto the sheets. Pulse pounding. Cock throbbing. Spurred on by the knowledge that she needs this as badly as I do. For a second, I just look at her, laid out before me, her chest rising, her lips swollen from our kissing.

And she's fucking breathtaking. *Mine.*

I lower myself to her, gentle but certain, aware that her nerves are probably heightened, her body sensitive. I skim the curve of her waist, the fullness of her thighs, the swell of her hips. Her skin is fever-warm and rosy, and I trace every curve as if to memorize her. Her breath catches when my thumb grazes a hardened nipple covered in my soft tee. I lift it wordlessly and remove it so she's bared to me.

Her back arches into me as I take my time kissing, licking, sucking. Her shoulders and breasts, nipples and navel. Her body responds to every touch as if she's made for this, made for *me*. I take my time teasing and testing, savoring the connection and need.

I lower my mouth to her hips, yank off her panties, and spread her legs.

"Vadka," she whispers.

"Open," I order, nudging her thighs apart. "Spread your legs for me. Give me that sweet, wet cunt. I want to taste you."

Biting her lip, she holds my gaze as she spreads her legs, and I groan. Mother*fucker* she's wet and hot, and I fucking want her. I taste her clit and moan again, nuzzling the tip of my tongue in her center before I lap lazily. My eyes flutter closed in pleasure, and she moans my name as her fingers tangle in my hair.

She's *soaked*, glowing with heat, slick with want. My mouth waters. My cock throbs. Every ounce of control I've had unravels as I spread her legs wider and drop to my knees. I've tasted, and now I want to feast.

I press a kiss to her thigh reverently, then another, slower, higher, my hands spreading her wider as I settle between her legs. I love worshipping her like this. I love the way her breath catches, and she trembles. I love the way my rough, darker hands look against her soft, pale thighs as I spread her wide and inhale the scent of her sex.

I groan and hear her sharp inhale. I smell her arousal, sweet and heady, and when I finally lean back in to give her the faintest stroke of my tongue—just a tease—she gasps like she's been waiting for this forever.

"You're fucking perfect," I growl, my voice ragged, lips dragging over the sensitive, damp, delicate skin of her thigh. She arches, desperate, already panting. And then I *really* taste her.

One long, slow stroke, savoring the way she tastes on my tongue. I grind my mouth into her harder as her hips buck and her fingers tighten in my hair, pulling like she can't help herself. I nip her clit, just enough to make her hiss and her hips jerk.

"Be a good girl," I whisper into her thighs.

"Yes," she whispers, breathless. "Fuck *yes*."

I smile against her, then flatten my tongue and lick again, slow and deep, dipping into her and dragging upward, circling her clit in lazy, wet strokes. Her thighs tremble. I love it. I *want* her to come undone on my mouth. I want her to lose herself to me. It's vulnerable and erotic, and I'm fucking savoring every second.

I suck her clit into my mouth, gently at first, teasing her with the rhythm, then her whole body arches. I don't stop. I won't. I wrap my arms under her thighs and press her down, holding her in place as I work a slow, relentless rhythm.

My tongue flicks and swirls, strokes. My mouth devours. Worships. She's a fucking miracle, and I'm starving.

Her cries are sharper now, desperate and sweet and broken. She rolls her hips against me, chasing more—faster, deeper, harder—and I give it to her. I drag two fingers through her wet heat and curl them inside her. She *wails*, desperate and needy.

"My god, please don't stop. Please keep going, just like that," she says in a heated whisper, clutching me as if I'll keep her from drowning, and she's sinking lower.

Stop? I'm just getting started.

I drive my fingers in deep, tongue circling, lapping, until I feel her come apart. Her thighs clamp. Her stomach tightens. Her moans rise into a crescendo.

She *shatters*. My cock jerks. Her body writhes against me, her muscles contracting as she comes so fucking hard, pulsing around my fingers. I keep going, easing her through it, licking her softer now, gently, as she trembles and whimpers and clings to me.

And when she finally collapses, breathless and shaking, I kiss her one more time.

"I could do this all fucking night."

"Oh my god." She moans, wrecked. "I'd fucking die."

My chuckle is low and wicked as I slowly rise and strip off my clothes, my cock thick and straining between us.

"On your hands and knees. Tits down, ass up, spread wide for me, Ruthie."

I give her a good slap to the ass, and she squeals. My cock throbs at the sight of my handprint across her perfect ass cheek.

My name's still trembling on her lips when I rise, towering over her, breathing hard, cock swollen and aching with need. She looks up at me with glassy, thoroughly fucked eyes, lips parted, her skin glowing with sweat and satisfaction—and I'm not done with her. Not even close.

She scrambles to obey, still trembling as she turns over, arching for me, offering herself like something sacred and filthy all at once. Her ass is high, thighs parted just enough to make my breath catch. She's dripping. Flushed. Mine.

I palm her ass and give it a firm smack, watching it jiggle, loving the sound of her sharp gasp. A perfect little squeal. My twin handprints rise fast and red across her cheek, and I groan, barely restraining the urge to slam into her right then and there.

"You feel that, sweetheart?" I growl, rubbing where I struck her, soothing as much as I mark. "That's mine. This body? *Mine.*"

"Yes," she gasps out, pushing back into my hand. "Yours."

Pride swells in me. *No one* owns this woman without her consent, and she's *mine.*

I grab her hips, squeezing hard, angling her just right. My other hand trails up her spine, fingers curling into her hair, giving a gentle tug that pulls a needy moan from her throat.

"You want my cock, baby?" I whisper into her ear, bending over her back, voice dangerous and full of dark promise. "You want me to fill this tight little pussy while you whimper and beg and take every goddamn inch I give you?"

"Yes. Please," she cries. "Please, I need you—need you so

bad. I want you inside me. I need your cock. I need you to fuck me—hard. Deep. I want you to ruin me."

That's it. That's fucking it.

I grip her hips and slam into her in one smooth, ruthless thrust, burying myself to the hilt with a moan. She cries out, loud and raw, her fingers digging into the sheets as her body takes me, stretches for me, welcomes me.

"God damn," I hiss through my teeth, rocking back to watch her swallow me whole again. "You take me so fucking good. Just like that. Just like you were made to."

Her walls flutter around me, hot and tight, gripping me like a vice. I start to move, slow at first—deep, grinding thrusts that make her sob. I stay low over her, chest brushing her back, hand tangled in her hair, the other gripping her hip hard.

"I want you to remember this," I growl in her ear. "Every time you sit. Every time you walk. I want you sore and dripping with me."

She's panting into the sheets, and I love her like this— undone, used, and adored. I shift my angle, pistoning into her with increasing speed, driving deep, hitting the spot that makes her scream my name into the mattress.

"You're so fucking wet for me," I snarl, pounding into her. "Good girl. Let me feel that pretty pussy squeeze me while you come. Let me hear you scream."

And she does—screams, actually, her whole body seizing as she shatters again, tighter than ever, pulsing around me like she's trying to pull me deeper, like she never wants to let me go.

I groan loud, losing control, thrusting into her hard and fast... no restraint now, chasing my own edge. "Fuck, you're so perfect—"

I slam in one final time and spill into her, bliss claiming me, burying myself to the root, holding her down as I come so hard it feels like the world splits open.

We stay there—breathless, trembling, slick and soaked in each other. I stroke her spine, still inside her, keeping her grounded. I don't want to leave.

"You okay?" I murmur, pressing a kiss to the back of her neck.

She nods against the sheets, her voice hoarse but content. "More than okay."

I smile.

"You're not done," I promise, nipping at her shoulder. "Not even close."

CHAPTER 25

THE NIGHT AIR is colder than I expected.

Concrete beneath bare feet. Wind tugging at the hem of the shirt I stole from him again. My pulse still hasn't calmed down—not since the test. Not since I said the words out loud. Not since he fucked me boneless.

It's positive.

And he held me like I wasn't a mistake.

Now I can't sleep, not with the weight of everything bearing down on me.

I find him where I knew he'd be—on the roof. Silent. Still. A sniper rifle rests across his lap like a sleeping beast. His eyes are on the dark tree line beyond the estate walls. He doesn't flinch when I come up behind him.

"You're supposed to be resting," he says.

I wrap my arms around myself. "So are you."

He doesn't turn. Just pats the ledge beside him. I sit.

Quiet stretches between us.

"I didn't think this would be my life," I murmur. "This—hunted. Pregnant." I wink at him. "Wrapped up in a Bratva god's war plans."

"You're not wrapped up in it," he says. "You're at the center of it now."

That makes me laugh, bitter and small.

"I didn't want to matter this much."

His head turns just slightly, enough for me to see the muscle ticking in his jaw.

"You always did. Remember what Mariah used to tell you, Ruthie. Don't make yourself small for anyone. Not me, not even yourself."

I nod. He's right. I know he is.

We sit in silence again, and I lay my head on his shoulder. I like how it feels sitting with him like this.

Then, like a live wire—

"I'm scared," I whisper.

"Good." He finally looks at me. "That means you understand the stakes."

I meet his gaze. "And if I run?"

"I'll find you." He says it without heat. Without threat. Just fact. "But I don't think you will."

"Why not?"

He studies me for a long time. Then, "Because for the first time in your life, you've got something to protect that's bigger than your fear."

I look down at my hands, curled around the faint swell of my belly.

My throat closes. The wind moves between us, but he's warm beside me. Solid.

So I lean in. Instinctively, his arm comes around my shoulders. And for a moment, the war doesn't matter.

We sit like that until the sky turns gray.

I lie curled beside Vadka, more at peace than I have ever been in my life. His warmth seeps into my skin, calming the chaos in my veins, and for a moment, it feels like maybe—just maybe—we're safe. But I know it won't last. It can't. Not with the hounds of hell snapping at our heels. He says we're at war, but what does that even mean? What does war look like in this world?

I've lived close enough to this world that I thought I understood it. I told myself I knew what it was to be part of something dark, something brutal. But I was wrong. I didn't know. I still don't.

"I love you," he whispers, his lips brushing the curve of my ear. "I love you so much. Listen... if we had more time—if we could do this a different way—I would've done it right. But you're having a baby, and there's one thing I can tell you about the world I live in—things happen fast. We move fast. We don't have the luxury of slow decisions. We've got more on the line than the average human," he says, giving me that crooked smile that's equal parts apology and warning and so sweet and hot my chest warms.

I think of his little boy sleeping in the next room and the tiny life growing inside me. Our baby. A mix of both of us. "How do we protect them?" I ask, my voice wobbling with fear I can't hide. "I don't even know how to be a mother… You know I didn't have a good example, and you know why—"

"We don't do it alone," he cuts in, voice rough, almost growling. "We have family. Protection. Yeah, we're in danger—I won't sugarcoat it—but we're not in this alone. Look at Luka. Who took care of him when it was just us? When we needed someone?"

He's right. His brothers did. All of them. They stepped in, no hesitation. Because that's what family does. If there's one thing I've learned from being around his world, it's this: They protect each other with fire and fury.

People like to say it takes a village. But for the Kopolov Bratva, it takes an army.

His phone buzzes—once, twice, three times, harsh and insistent. A jarring reminder that his time isn't his own anymore. And because I'm with him now, neither is mine. He answers to Rafail. To the call. To the cause. And I'm only beginning to grasp what that means.

He glances down at the screen, brows knitting. "Zoya?" he says aloud, confusion slicing through the air like a blade. Not one of his brothers. That alone makes my stomach twist with dread.

He holds my gaze as he taps the answer button and puts it on speaker. "Zoya, I'm here. I'm with Ruthie."

Her voice is shattered, full of tears. "Vadka…" she sobs. I sit up straighter, my heartbeat pounding in my throat.

He stills beside me, his body going tense, every muscle drawn tight as steel wire. His voice drops, low and lethal. "What happened?"

"The warehouse," she chokes. "They attacked the warehouse. Rafail was there, Vadka. They all were—"

My hand flies to my mouth, and my heart slams against my ribs.

"Which warehouse?" he asks, terrifyingly calm.

"The one Semyon took over. Across from Anya's bakery. Near the wharf. It's in flames. No one's answering their phones. I ran… I found my phone, and I called you. You were the first— I didn't know who else—"

"I'm on my way. Stay calm. Where are you now?"

She tells him. He stands, looks me in the eyes, and it's like the air between us thickens, scorches.

"I have to go."

"I'll go with you—"

"No."

I flinch. He's never raised his voice to me before. But this man before me… he's something else now. An avenging angel, eyes blazing, fury radiating off him in waves so intense I almost step back. Even though I love him—god, I *love* him—I can barely breathe in the face of that storm.

He climbs onto the bed, kneeling so we're face to face, his hand reaching out.

"My son is in the next room. And you—you're carrying our baby." He points at me, deadly serious. "Protect them, Ruthie. That's your job. While I go find my brothers."

I reach out, pressing my palm to his chest. "I don't want you to go." My voice cracks. "There has to be another way. Someone else—"

"She called me. Because she trusts me. This is what it means."

Protection. Love. Loyalty. Family. And all the danger that comes with it.

I watch him arm himself—gun, blade, phone, keys. His whole body humming with violent purpose.

"Believe me when I tell you," he says, head down, not looking at me, "I don't want to leave you. But it's the only way to keep you safe right now. Do you understand me?"

"Yeah," I whisper. "Of course."

I grab his shirt, yank him down to me, and kiss him. Hard. Bruising. A kiss full of desperation and rage and aching love. I want to be the last thing he feels. The only thing he remembers.

"Come back to me," I command.

He bows his head, a vow in the dark. "I will, baby. I will."

But isn't that what they all say?

I watch him walk out that door, and I'm left clutching my

knees to my chest, nausea rolling through me in waves. Only this time, I'm not sure I can blame the pregnancy.

I need to do something. I can't sit here helpless. But I don't know how to help. I'm new to all of this. The Bratva, their ways, their war—I'm still learning. Still fumbling.

I place a hand on my belly and try to picture the life growing inside me. A piece of him. Of us. A little girl with his eyes, maybe. Full pink lips. Will she look like my sister? My nephew?

I rise quietly and walk to Luka's room. He's sprawled in bed, one arm flung above his head, sleeping deep and trustful. I kneel beside him, brushing his hair from his forehead.

"I miss you, Mariah," I whisper into the quiet. "We're at war now. Things aren't safe here."

I climb into his bed and slide under the blanket, curling myself around Luka's small body. Cocooning him. Protecting him with my presence, with my body.

"I don't know what else to do but this," I whisper. "I love Luka. I love Vadka. And I will protect them however I can."

I press a kiss to Luka's head, close my eyes, and beg for sleep. But when it comes, it's full of screams—my sister's cries, blood on the floor of the bar, and the sound of Vadka's sobs as he shattered.

CHAPTER 26

I TAKE the back roads to the warehouse, every twist and turn burned into my memory from nights like this. Nights when you don't call ahead. Nights when you don't wear your usual clothes or take your usual car.

I'm in the unmarked ride we keep parked three blocks from the south side alleyway, the one we use when shit's gone bad—no plates, no records, no connections. A burner phone presses against my hip, cold and small. Untraceable. Disposable. Just like we were trained to be.

My heart's pounding like it's trying to punch its way out of my chest. I'm trying—really trying—to get my mind ready for the worst. Blood. Carnage. Smoke so thick you taste it. My brothers, dead. It's always an ever-present concern, but now...

Sirens tear through the silence, a flash of lights heading for the wharf. For our warehouse, the one near Anya's bakery.

That location wasn't just luck—it was strategy. Smart and dangerous. Plenty of rivals wanted that spot, but Semyon made damn sure none of them ever touched it. And that decision, that little power move? That was the beginning of our slow, inevitable war with the Irish.

I take a mental inventory of the weapons on me. I've got enough firepower to drop twenty men before I even take a breath. And somehow, it still doesn't feel like enough. When the hell is it ever enough?

The road blurs beneath me, tires screaming against asphalt, and my mind flashes—just for a second—to Ruthie. Her cheeks flushed, her hands cupping my face like I was worth something. Her voice shaking when she said she loved me.

A baby. New life. Family.

Focus, I snarl to myself. *Don't lose your edge now.*

I smell the fire before I see it—sweet, smoky, with that slightly acrid bite that tells you this wasn't an accident. It reminds me of the bonfires we built as kids.

I park the car just beneath the old willow tree—out of sight. This spot was picked for discretion, and tonight, it earns its keep. From here, I can't see much—just enough smoke to know something's wrong. But I need to get closer. I need to see who's here, who's been here, and who the fuck might've done this.

If they touched my brothers... if they're dead...

But what I see when I round the corner isn't the inferno I imagined. The warehouse is still standing. It's... mostly intact. There's smoke, yeah, and a fire truck already ahead, but no billowing destruction, no collapsed beams or shattered windows. It doesn't make sense.

"What the fuck?" I mutter.

"Vadka?"

I whip around, hand twitching toward my weapon, but it's Rodion. He's stalking up behind me, face tight.

He looks as confused as I am. "What the fuck, brother? You all right? Were you inside?"

I shake my head once. "No. I got a call from Zoya. Said she couldn't reach you or the others. Said everyone was here."

Rodion goes still. His eyes narrow, dark and dangerous. "She said that?" His voice is low now, sharp-edged steel.

"Yeah," I grit out. "She said exactly that."

He swears under his breath. "She told me the same. Zoya? What the fuck? No... she wouldn't..."

She's always been honest. Loyal. Why the fuck would she lie?

"You know what we have to do," he says, his jaw clenched. His whole body's vibrating with fury he's barely containing. "Scout the premises. Find the others."

I nod. "I've got a burner on me. Didn't even bring my regular car."

"Same."

"You take south. I'll go north."

"On it."

When I turn the corner, I see Rafail talking to one of the firefighters, posture casual—but his eyes give him away. When he spots me, his expression shifts. Relief—tempered with suspicion.

I feel the same.

"You all right?" he asks, low enough that only I can hear.

"Yeah. I wasn't even here when it started. Were you?"

He shakes his head. "Nope." But his eyes flick toward the fire crew, and I know we're thinking the same thing—we say nothing to them. We don't reveal shit. They're not here for us.

"I found Rodion," I tell him. "He's safe. He's checking the south side, looking for Semyon and Matvei."

Rafail gives a tight nod, a muscle ticking in his jaw. He's calculating—running the same numbers I am. This was a setup. Why?

We start moving, slow and steady, tracking the perimeter as firefighters disappear inside with hoses and gear. Rafail steps closer and lowers his voice again.

"Scared the fuck out of me," he says, voice raw. "But you're all right."

"Yeah."

"And Ruthie? Luka?"

"They're fine," I whisper. "Safe."

His brow furrows. He doesn't like any of this. "I just saw Rodion. He got the same call. We all did."

While the flames die down under the weight of heavy hoses, Rafail pulls out his phone and clicks into the security feed. His face hardens.

"Surveillance is offline," he mutters. "Someone shut it off."

Inside job. That's not even a question.

We find Rodion, then Matvei and Semyon, all accounted for. And it doesn't take long to piece it together—we were all called. Every single one of us.

She summoned us.

"Why?" I growl.

"Pull up house surveillance," Rafail snaps, and Rodion yanks out the tablet and boots it up. We watch it together.

"Everything's fine," he mutters. "No breach, no alarms."

"Where the fuck is Zoya?" Rafail snarls.

"She's at the house," Semyon says.

Matvei shakes his head slowly, brows furrowing as he scans the room. "Something's not adding up."

"Nothing's fucking adding up," Rafail growls, his voice low and lethal. "Right. I'm gonna try Zoya's phone again—"

But it rings. And rings. And rings.

"Why would she bring us all here? What's the game?"

"I went to check on the house," Semyon says. "Video shows Ruthie walking into Luka's room. We don't have cameras in private bedrooms—privacy policy—but at every entrance, every exit, we do. And there's nothing. No mess. No signs of struggle. The guards are all where they're supposed to be. Everything is... still. Too still."

Rafail's brows draw together. "Vadka, where were you when she called?"

"I was at the house," I answer. "With Luka. With Ruthie. You?"

"I was heading to Wolf and Moon," Rafail says, voice clipped. "Supposed to meet Semyon there for a drink."

"Yeah," Semyon echoes. "I was on my way too. Then she called. Told me to come. I didn't know why everyone was here. Rafail was supposed to be meeting me."

Rafail nods slowly. "That's right."

"What the fuck? Are we being set up?"

"I was at home with Ember," Rodion says. "We just finished a FaceTime with Yana."

Yana. Their younger sister, currently in South Africa.

"Matvei?"

"I was out driving," he replies. "Testing the range on a new tracking mod we installed today. Anissa's asleep back at the house."

"If Zoya is really at the house, let's go find her. Let's see what the hell she's playing at."

That fleeting rush of relief I felt—seeing all of my brothers safe and accounted for—vanishes in an instant. Dissolves into nothing. Because something is off. Deeply off. And Zoya, sweet, loyal Zoya... she isn't clean.

We've been betrayed before. Mateo's parents. His brother. Later, we learned his parents were behind all of it.

I would've sworn on my last breath—Zoya would die before she betrayed us. Before she betrayed her brothers.

It can't be betrayal.

No.

It's strategy.

"She dragged us all here," I mutter. "Why would she do that?"

"Fuck," Rodion breathes out, eyes wide and wet. "To keep us safe. That's why. Something's about to happen. Something big. She knew. She was scared—"

Then Rafail's phone starts ringing. Over and over again.

"It says you're calling me," he mutters, confused.

"Fuck. That's gotta be Ruthie. I left my real phone at the house—I didn't want to be tracked. Got a burner on me."

He holds it up, grim. "Rafail."

It's Ruthie.

She's sobbing.

Her voice is cracked, broken glass. "At the bar, Rafail." She gasps. "Tell me you have him. Tell me he's with you."

Rafail locks eyes with me, his face stone. "Who, Ruthie?" he asks, voice like a blade.

"Vadka." Her voice cracks. "Tell me you have him."

"I'm here, baby," I say, my voice loud and raw. "I'm right here." I don't care who hears me. "I'm here. Are you okay?"

"I'm okay," she breathes out. "But... oh, Vadka. Where is everybody?"

"We're all here, Ruthie," I say. "Every one of us. We're safe. Are you okay?"

"I'm fine," she whispers. "I'm okay. What happened?"

"Listen, baby, we don't know what happened yet," I say out loud so she can hear me.

We're going back to the house.

We're questioning Zoya.

"I'll question Zoya," Rafail says, his voice cold steel. He's always had a soft spot for her—she's like a little sister to all of us—but now...

He waits.

"No answer?"

"Back to the house," Rafail barks. "Bring your women. Now."

He turns to Matvei. His expression is grave. "Check in, see what you can find on surveillance. I'll do the same. We meet back here. Clear?"

Matvei nods. "Yes, sir."

And I echo him silently. Because Rafail has spoken.

And when he speaks—it's law.

CHAPTER 27

RUTHIE

VADKA IS SAFE. And so is Luka.

The room's too quiet. Too still. The kind of silence that screams.

Vadka finds me, and the moment he does, he wraps his arms around me like I might disappear. I collapse into him, pressing my cheek against his chest. There's a steadiness there, a certainty—his body is warm and solid, his breath slow and even. My fingers trail across the worn leather of his jacket, then up to his jaw. He smells like cold air, burnt metal, and the lingering echo of gunpowder.

He's here. He's safe. But he's not okay. I can feel it in the way he holds me. The tension in his shoulders. The quiet concern in his eyes.

"What's on your mind?" I ask softly, pulling back just enough to see his face. "What happened? Why? I-I don't even know what I want you to answer first."

He doesn't speak right away. His jaw tightens before he finally says, "Have you seen Zoya?"

That catches me off guard. "No... I assumed she was here. She's not?"

He exhales, a breath that sounds too heavy for his lungs. "Her tracker says she is," he says, giving me a sad smile. "But she's nowhere to be found."

"Oh no... Is she okay? Did somebody—"

"We believe she's okay," he interrupts, his voice low, but there's no certainty there. "That call she made to me? She made it to all of us—all her brothers. We all showed up expecting... devastation. But all we found was silence."

"What? Why?" I whisper.

"That's the question, isn't it?" he murmurs. "Why. And the short answer is... we don't know."

None of us does.

"We need to find her," I say, my heart thudding. "Rafail must be losing his fucking mind."

"He is," Vadka replies, almost too quietly.

"I'm not even one of you guys, and I would be too," I admit.

"For now," he says, pulling back just enough to start stripping out of his clothes, "we need sleep. There's nothing more we can do tonight." He presses a kiss to my temple, soft, sorrowful.

Will it always be like this? Walking the edge between life and death, grief and survival, love and devastation. Fear. Hope. Loss. Life. The edges blur.

I fall into a deep, dreamless sleep.

But I wake again. And again. Each time with that same weight pressing down. Finally, I can't take it anymore—I push myself out of bed. Vadka's still asleep, fully clothed, softly snoring. He looks exhausted. My heart aches for him. I want to curl back beside him, but nausea wins.

I use the bathroom, splash water on my face, and check my phone. Google says I need protein. Fine. I quietly head downstairs. The house is quiet and somber. Still.

In the kitchen, I find a wedge of cheese and some crackers. The salty crackers settle my stomach. I'm just starting to feel human again when I hear footsteps behind me. I tense. Guards are stationed at the doors, and cameras monitor every angle—so I don't know who to expect.

But I definitely don't expect Zoya.

"Ruthie," she says softly, her voice raw, her eyes troubled.

"Are you all right?"

I nod, but her voice wobbles when she responds, "I will be."

"Sit," she says. "Did you take that test?"

I can't help the small smile tugging at my lips. Despite everything between us, despite the storm we're all wading through, her being here feels like a breath of something good.

"I did…"

She reaches for me. "And?"

I nod, this time grinning. I don't know how you're supposed

to tell people news like this. There's no guidebook for what we are, for how we live. But yeah.

"Don't tell the guys yet," I say quickly. "They'll go nuclear or something. But yeah... I'm having a baby. Vadka's, obviously," I add sheepishly.

Her gasp is immediate. "Oh my god," she whispers, throwing her arms around me so tightly I can barely breathe. "Oh my god, I'm so happy for you!" Her eyes shimmer with tears. "Another baby. Ruthie, your sister left us—she left this gaping hole in our lives. But now... now you're bringing new life into the world. This is amazing."

She kisses one cheek, then the other, and then hugs me again. "How are you feeling about all this?"

I pour myself some tea, still unsure. "I don't know. I mean... I'm happy. Scared. It's a lot."

"Sit down, sit down," she says, taking the tea from me and guiding me to the table. "But keep your voice down. If my brothers hear we're down here, it's going to turn into the third degree, and I am not ready for that."

I laugh softly. "You do owe them some kind of explanation."

"I know," she says, a hard edge to her tone. "And now I know for sure I did the right thing."

"What happened last night?" I ask, watching as she bites her lip and lowers herself into the seat beside me.

"I can't tell you everything," she says, eyes searching mine. "But I need you to cover for me. Can you do that?"

She's one of my best friends. I trust her with my life.

"Why?" I ask, wary.

"Eventually, I'll tell you," she says. "Or... maybe I won't. But you know... my brothers are at war with the Irish."

"I know."

"Yeah. Obviously."

"I know someone within their ranks," she says, her voice tight, guarded. "That's all I can tell you."

She pauses, eyes flickering away before finding mine again. "But it became very clear to me that the Irish were planning to hit this house. They were coming *here*, Ruthie."

Her voice wavers, then hardens.

"There wasn't enough protection to hold them back. Not here. Not last night. And I thought about Luka. I thought about you. And now—now I know I did the right thing. Especially with you carrying that baby."

She lowers her eyes, shame barely concealed in her next confession. "So I diverted them." I don't ask how she did that. I'm not sure I want to know.

Her voice drops to a whisper like she can't believe it herself.

"I knew Rafail was headed there, but I figured—I thought—I could pull him back in time. And I did."

She looks up at me then, like she wants to be absolved, like she's still unsure if she deserves it.

"So I told them to go to the warehouse. It was the furthest place from here that I could think of. I knew that if I told them all to go, it might scare them. But that would be a hell of a lot better than someone actually dying."

Her throat bobs as she swallows. "If they'd come here, the Irish would've killed them. If they'd gone to the bar, same story. Instead, I sent them on a wild goose chase."

Her mouth twists. "I knew we were safe here. Don't ask me how. I just... knew. And I knew the Irish wouldn't find them at the warehouse."

Zoya is sitting on a mountain of secrets, and I had no damn idea.

"All they know is that you lied to them," I say slowly, raising an eyebrow. "You sent them to the warehouse under false pretenses."

She meets my gaze without flinching. "Correct."

"They also believe you weren't here. Even though your tracker said otherwise," I add, my eyes pinning her to the spot.

"But you were," I murmur. "We were downstairs in the kitchen. Having..."

"A nightcap," she finishes, voice a breath against my skin. "I don't drink tea."

Of course she doesn't. Zoya's full of sharp edges and hidden softness, the kind of woman who sips hard liquor while looking like she's plotting an escape route.

"Thank you, Ruthie. I mean it. I swear, I have everyone's best interests at heart," she says.

"Even mine?" I ask, gently laying a hand over hers.

She exhales slowly, unsure. "I'm doing what I can to keep this family safe."

We fall into silence after that. A rare, comfortable one. We talk about the baby. Her brothers. She mentions Vadka—just his name, but it's enough to paint an entire story between them. Then, after a long beat, she bites her lip and nods, eyes downcast.

"He's going to ask you to marry him, Ruthie," she says, voice barely audible. "Maybe not now. But eventually. And it'll be the right thing to do. It'll give you a kind of protection and loyalty that being his girlfriend never could."

I nod slowly. "I've figured as much. Still… isn't it strange? Marrying my sister's husband?"

She shrugs like she's heard it all before. "As if that's never happened. The question isn't whether it's strange. The question is—is it right?"

I sit with that. Let it settle.

She's right. That's the only question that matters. And yeah —it is right.

Deep voices echo from the hallway—male, low, familiar.

Zoya sighs and leans back in her chair. "Here we go."

CHAPTER 28

"You saw her at the house?" I ask, locking eyes with Ruthie.

"Yep," she says, but there's something in her tone—something tight and stubborn. Her gaze is flinty. Wild horses couldn't drag the full truth out of her right now. But she's trusted me this far, followed me into darkness, taken my hand and leaped without asking where we'd land.

So I take her answer. And I nod.

"Ruthie saw her last night," I say to Rafail. "She's an eyewitness."

"Good thing I updated the biometrics," Matvei says with a dry smile.

"Yeah," Rafail replies softly. "Good thing."

Luka isn't paying attention—swinging his feet at the table like he hasn't a care in the world. He's drinking milk and eating cereal, completely oblivious to the war zone we're crawling out of. I ruffle his hair as Semyon walks in.

"We'll salvage what we can from the warehouse. Back to business as usual in a couple of weeks," Semyon says, practical and always five steps ahead.

"And we got word about the bar," he adds, his voice low. "Fucking battle scene."

We're all gathered now, coffee and tea in hand, trying to feel normal. Ruthie looks pale, her edges frayed. She's nibbling on crackers, sipping peppermint tea—says it helps.

"The Irish. Inner circle. McCarthy clan. Six of them. Gone."

Zoya's at the sink, scrubbing a dish like it holds the secrets to the universe. Her back's turned, but her silence is louder than words. If there's ever a poker face, she's wearing it now.

She insists she was home last night. Finally admitted there was gunfire at the bar, she heard shots, a friend of hers was there, and she knew we'd go. That she knew the Irish were gunning for us. So she steered us away—toward the warehouse. Called everyone out.

It's a flimsy story. But Rafail accepts it.

Matvei steps forward, drops a USB onto the table, and opens up files—photos and surveillance footage.

"Do I wanna know how you got these?" Rafail asks him.

Matvei just grins. "Nope."

We lean over the table, eyes glued to the images.

"The Irish are gone," Semyon mutters. "Can't imagine even The Undertaker—"

"These men were older," Matvei adds. "All branded. McCarthy loyalists. They didn't come to negotiate. They came to end us."

He taps the screen. "They had a plan. A full-on attack. On this house. But something—someone—derailed it."

Rafail speaks, his voice low and measured. "So what you're saying is... the ones who were supposed to kill us—are dead?"

There's a beat of stillness. Zoya rinses a pan, her expression unreadable.

"Yes," Matvei replies, sliding the last image across the table. "That's exactly what I'm saying."

Ruthie glances down at her phone and exhales sharply the moment it starts ringing, and her breath catches. "Oh no," she mutters, shaking her head, fingers trembling just slightly. "Not now. She's home..."

"I have to take this," she says, voice tight, eyes already flicking toward the hallway like she's looking for an escape. "But I swear to god, I feel like I'm gonna be sick."

I glance at the screen. It's her mother. Of all the shit timing...

"Give it to me," I say, already reaching. She doesn't argue— just places the phone in my hand with a kind of frantic relief before rushing off to the bathroom, one hand clutched over her mouth. Looks like morning sickness has come with a vengeance. Poor girl.

I answer, my voice low, cautious. "Hello?"

A woman's voice, professional but somber. "Looking for Ruthie?"

"She's...indisposed. Can I help you?"

"Yes, sir, her mother's taken a turn, and she's very sick. Asking for her daughter."

Christ.

That's the last thing Ruthie needs to hear right now. I swallow the thickness in my throat and try to keep my voice even. "We're coming."

She returns a few minutes later, pale and shaky, the edge of a napkin still clutched in one fist. "I don't want to go there," she says softly, shaking her head. "We've been through so much, Vadka."

I nod. "Luka's back at the house with Rafail. Polina called in something for you—anti-nausea. You're already looking steadier."

She leans into me, just enough that her shoulder brushes mine. Her voice is soft but sure. "But at least this time... I'm not alone."

"You're not," I say, threading my fingers through hers, grounding her. "We're gonna get through this, baby. Yeah, it's been hell. But at least we're not looking over our shoulders every five seconds. If Zoya is telling the truth, the Irish are done. That threat is gone. For now, at least."

I watch her eyes close for a beat. "Death's always brutal," I murmur. "But it could've been so much worse."

She nods, slow, silent.

"We're going to see your mother," I say. "Whatever happens in there—whatever she says, whatever she remembers or doesn't—it's not just you anymore. It's us. The two of us. Together."

She turns to me, her expression softening, some small piece of light returning to her face. "Of course."

I squeeze her hand. "Alright. Let's do this."

WE WALK TOGETHER, our fingers laced tight. Neither of us speaks, not as we reach the doors, not as the heaviness of what waits inside starts to press against our chests.

Then a voice calls out—bright, too loud, too cheerful.

"There's the happy couple!"

Ruthie freezes mid-step. Her brows lift in surprise and disbelief. "Mom?"

She lets go of my hand gently—not in panic, not in fear. Just careful. Controlled. She walks ahead toward the woman in the wheelchair stationed near the garden windows.

"I always said you two were meant to be," her mother says, her voice airy now, touched with something dreamlike. "Such a beautiful couple. Just look at you. Destined."

Her tone has changed—it's lighter, warmer. Caught somewhere between the present and a memory.

Ruthie kneels beside her, folding her hands in her lap, her movements small and delicate, like muscle memory from childhood. Maybe she wants to hold onto this, to keep the sweetness instead of the judgment and pain... even if there's a thread of delusion in it all.

"You're glowing, daughter," her mother whispers, eyes soft but startlingly focused. "Radiant."

And then—just for a breath—her voice dips, quiet and deliberate. "Ruthie."

Ruthie stares. Her voice barely comes out. "Mom?"

"Yes?" her mother answers, and for a beat—just one precious second—her gaze sharpens. It's clear. Present. Grounded in now. "Come here, sweetheart," she says seconds before she's overtaken by a vicious cough.

Ruthie hesitates for only a breath before stepping forward. Her mother wipes her eyes and takes a deep breath. Ruthie crouches beside her, and her mother leans in, whispering something low and private into her ear. I can't hear what she says, but I see the way Ruthie's cheeks flush with sudden heat.

"Mom," she says, half laughing, half reeling. "You didn't."

Her mother just smiles. That same mischievous spark from years ago flickers in her eyes—quick and knowing. "I knew," she says, this time louder, looking directly at me now. "I always knew who you were."

She reaches out, brushing her hand down Ruthie's arm with featherlight affection.

"He'll take care of you. You were supposed to find each other."

That's all she says. And then it's gone.

The light in her eyes dims. Her gaze slips away, drifting toward the ceiling like she's watching something only she can see. The edges of her smile melt, her mouth going slack. She begins to hum—low, tuneless, disconnected. A lullaby with no beginning, no end.

Ruthie doesn't cry. Her hand trembles slightly as she lays it gently over her mother's. I move to her, kneel beside her, and wrap my arm around her waist. She leans into it without a word.

Her mother's eyelids flutter closed. The lines in her face soften. She breathes out, slow and light, and for the first time, she looks peaceful. Childlike. Asleep.

"Let's go, baby," I whisper.

I rise first, offering my hand. She takes it, and I guide her up, placing my palm on the small of her back like I always do— protective, grounding. We walk in silence, each step echoing down the tiled hallway. As we near the exit, she whispers.

"You were supposed to find each other," she repeats, more to herself than to me. Like she's testing the truth of it.

I stop. Turn her toward me.

She looks up, eyes wide and glassy, mouth just barely trembling.

I cup her jaw gently, fingers steady against her cheek. "Finder's keepers," I say, firm and sure.

And I mean it. Every damn word.

EPILOGUE

THE CITY's all bright lights, honking horns, and chaos, and I'm somewhere in the middle of it, one eye on the traffic and the other smudging half-applied lipstick in the rearview mirror. The toddler car seat in the back is empty, a backpack half-zipped next to it, and my purse on the passenger seat is full of rolled up bills from the weekend bar shift. Chaos, yes, but beautiful chaos.

"Green light, asshole," I mutter, slapping the wheel when the truck ahead doesn't move fast enough.

As usual, I'm not wearing anything special. Black jeans, the kind that stretch at the belly and my leather jacket with the scuffed sleeve. My hair is still wet from a too-fast shower, already curling where it wants.

But when the sunlight hits the windshield just right, I glance at myself. And for a split second, I smirk. It's the smirk of a girl who survived grief and violence. Who buried

349

a sister and nearly buried herself. Who clawed her way into the arms of a Bratva warlord and didn't break.

Never thought I'd live long enough to be late for carpool.

The thought slips in like a joke, but my throat tightens anyway.

I pull up to the school curb fifteen minutes late. Teachers are already shepherding the last few kids to the gate. One of them—Miss Gina, with bright eyes and cropped gray curls—smiles when she sees me stride up the walkway.

"Ruthie! You just missed him. Your husband already picked him up."

I breathe a sigh of relief even as I blink. That word again.

Husband.

It should feel wrong. But it doesn't.

Instead, I lift one brow, shift the strap of my bag higher on my shoulder, and smile. "Oh. Right," I say smoothly, already pivoting. "It's his night."

Of course he came. Responsible, on top of things, competent as fuck. And *I love him.* I love him so damn much. I see him with Luka, and I just melt into a puddle, thinking *this man will be the father of my baby.* I couldn't ask for any better.

I drive home without music. The silence isn't heavy—just full.

Sometimes, I still expect ghosts in the corner. But this house —*our* house—is clean. Safe. No bloodstains on the floor. No memory of the night Mariah died. No shadows that reek of old grief.

When I open the front door, the smell of something warm and garlicky curls around me. The nausea has passed, and now I'm ravenous. Eating for two, after all.

Luka gives me a sleepy hug with a yawn before he disappears down the hall—he needs some downtime before early bed. My heart pinches.

But what stops me is the rest of it.

The table.

Lit candles. Not the scented kind either—the real, tall ones, dripping wax into elegant little dishes. The good plates. Actual napkins. Cloth ones, like you'd find in a restaurant.

The house is pristine. The cleaning crew must've come today. Everything is gleaming: floors buffed, windows smudge-free, the scent of citrus cleaner in the air. Vadka's motorcycle jacket is on the hook. His boots are lined up neatly at the door.

I step further in and freeze.

Because *he* is in the kitchen.

Wearing a dark long-sleeve tee. Sleeves pushed to his elbows. Hair wet from a recent shower, his jaw freshly shaved. He turns toward me with that heavy-lidded look of quiet approval that somehow still manages to make me feel bare.

There are plates on the table. One is covered in grilled salmon and wild rice pilaf, the other piled with things I vaguely recognize from the pregnancy app I downloaded two weeks ago and deleted three days later.

He catches me looking.

"I googled," he says simply, nodding at the food.

My mouth twitches. "I figured."

I drop my bag by the bench, shrug out of my jacket, and exhale. For once, I don't have to be anywhere. Don't have to watch my back. Don't have to handle everything alone.

He hands me a water glass. "Hydration's important."

I squint at him. "Are you... nesting?"

"No. I'm protecting my baby." He grins.

My brows lift, and I don't ask him which of us he means. "*Your* baby?"

He's already pulling out my chair. "Behave yourself, you little brat."

I laugh, but it's softer now. My fingers brush the side of the water glass. There's something in my chest—warm, expanding.

And when he sits beside me instead of across from me, when his thigh presses against mine like it's meant to, that warmth spreads like fire licking up dry wood.

We eat in silence for a while, save for the occasional clink of silverware. Outside, the streetlights hum to life. Somewhere down the block, a dog barks.

And then—quietly, reverently—he reaches across and rests his hand on my belly.

I freeze. My throat is tight.

His palm is broad, warm, grounding. He doesn't say anything. Doesn't look at me. Just watches his own hand cup over my rounded belly.

I let out a slow sigh. "I just don't know how I'm going to do this. I'm not sure I can be a good mother..."

His eyes lift to mine. "*I'm* sure about you. And you're not alone."

That's all he says.

It's all I need.

Because this isn't the man who once drank himself to sleep on the couch. This isn't the enforcer who puts bullets through skulls with no hesitation. This isn't even the grieving widower who used to flinch at the sight of me.

This is Vadka.

The man who sets the table and lights candles and researches superfoods while the city sleeps.

The man who rests his hand on my belly with reverence.

And somehow, impossibly, I believe him.

Later that night, when the dishes are done and Luka is fully asleep, I stand in front of the mirror, brushing my teeth. Vadka comes up behind me, arms snaking around my waist, one hand flattening over my stomach again.

I lean back into him.

He meets my eyes in the mirror.

Together, we look like something rebuilt. Something strong.

Something *unbroken.*

VADKA

The box said *Some Assembly Required.*

It lied.

The crib is spread out across the nursery floor—planks of pale wood, indecipherable screws, and vague instruction diagrams that look like ancient hieroglyphic writing. There's a manual on the floor, bent and abandoned after page four because it was clearly written by someone who's never touched a wrench in their life.

I kneel in front of the chaos, my brows drawn, one hand steadying a half-assembled side rail while the other tightens a bolt with clinical precision.

The nursery is almost done.

Behind me, Ruthie leans in the doorway with her arms folded across her belly. She's barefoot, wearing one of my T-shirts knotted at her hip, her hair messy and eyes impossibly soft. She hasn't said anything for the last few minutes—just watched. Quiet. Thoughtful.

"You're really doing it," she murmurs. "Bratva enforcer turned crib builder. We're in uncharted territory here."

I grunt but smile.

She steps forward, bare feet soundless on the rug. Her fingers trail along the top rail of the crib, then down to my shoulder.

"You know," she says, low and teasing, "the baby's not sleeping in here."

I blink. "What?"

She smiles like it's obvious. "We're not doing separate rooms. I'm not trekking across the house at two a.m. with a screaming infant while you pretend not to hear."

I raise a brow. "So we're what... putting the crib in our room?" What the fuck? How are we supposed to have any privacy?

She shakes her head. "Nope."

A beat. Then, gently, "Baby's in the room *with* us. Bassinet."

I stare at her for a second, then glance at the half-finished crib like it's betrayed me.

She laughs, her hand covering her mouth.

I growl low in my throat and sit back on my heels. "All that work, and now it's for show."

"You'll thank me later when you're the one getting up for the three a.m. feeding," she says sweetly.

I huff out a breath. "We're taking turns."

"Sure we are."

She steps closer and kneels beside me. I just watch her. The way her hand flattens instinctively over the curve of her belly. The way her breathing shifts when I lean in, like she feels me before I touch her.

I lift one hand and curl it around the back of her neck.

Pull her in slow.

No fire this time. No bruising heat or need sharpened by grief.

Just *quiet*.

My mouth brushes hers with reverence. Like she's something holy, and I'm unworthy.

Soft. Slow. Like the world can wait.

When I finally pull back, I press my forehead to hers, my voice little more than a rasp.

"Bassinet it is."

"I love you," she whispers.

I kiss her mouth, her neck, all the way down to her belly, then back up again. "And I love you."

ZOYA

Mariah taught me how to slip past the trackers. No one was better at it than she was—precise, paranoid, and a little brilliant. She never showed off, never put herself at risk, just quietly made sure she could vanish if she needed to. She was the only one who really knew how. Ruthie knows a little now, but not everything. Not like I do.

I took my phone, stuffed it into the hollow back of a teddy bear—one I kept around just for this purpose—and tucked it under the blanket on my bed. Then I grabbed my burner phone, checked the biometric nodules wired into the bracelet around my wrist, and slid the decoy ball into place.

Weapons check: solid.

Rafail might've been overprotective and overbearing, but he made damn sure I knew how to wield a gun.

They're coming.

And it's going to be a fucking massacre.

The Irish will kill them. Every one of them. And Ruthie's here. Luka's here. And tonight—of all fucking nights—Ruthie asked me to pick up a *pregnancy* test.

We don't have the firepower to hold them off. I don't have time to convince my brothers. But if I can disperse the Irish...

So I make a decision and call Rafail.

I hate lying to him. God, I don't think I've ever lied to him before.

But he's the first I call.

"On my way," he says, with no hesitation. "Heading to the warehouse. Lock the house down."

I breathe. Just for a second. Then I call everyone else. Trick them into staying safe. Trick them into not playing the hero and endangering the innocents.

Every call is short. Every answer is instant. They trust me.

I cannot—will not—betray that.

I slide into the car and speed toward the bar. I know what I'm going to see. I already know. And I don't want to.

But then—there they are. Every last bastard. When they see me, a big, bearded redhead grabs me and yanks me forward, his hand on my arm like a death grip. He'll kill him for this. He'll fucking kill him.

I can't move and open my mouth to scream when a deep, commanding voice cuts through the mayhem.

"Get your fucking hands off her."

The voice is low, deadly, a rasp of rage and fire.

It's him.

My heart crashes into my ribs.

The weight of his boots thuds like anvils. He draws his weapon... and down they fall. I knew it was coming, and still, I'm unprepared for the way they scream and beg for their lives, but he pulls the trigger without hesitation.

My god.

One. By. One.

They try to run. They beg. They bleed.

They trusted him. But he executes them—cold, methodical.

"For betraying me."

Bang.

"For your lies and theft."

For the last one—he doesn't rush it. He takes his time. Deliberate.

"For laying *fucking hands* on her."

When the last body falls, the blood puddling like oil around their boots, his phone rings.

He meets my gaze and holds up a single finger—silent, commanding. I sit back against the wall, my knees giving out. My breath catches in my throat, swallowing a scream.

Then he answers. "Yes."

A voice snarls on the other end. Irish. Raw. Angry.

"What happened?"

"Bad intel," he replies smoothly. "Handful of Russians here. I couldn't hold them back." His voice is thick with emotion, taut. "They're dead, boss. All of them. All our men. All who attacked."

The voice of the man on the line is shaking with rage and grief. It's real—his voice cracking under the weight of what just happened.

"Any survivors? Any witnesses? Anyone see what you did?"

"No."

He stares at me, and I hold his gaze as the voice carries on, relentless.

"Anyone feckin' alive?"

Me, *I'm* alive, and if his boss finds out I'm here, I'm *dead*.

His eyes lock onto mine, beautiful and devastating.

He crouches in front of me. Brushes his thumb across my cheek. He raises the phone to his mouth, and he answers with the finality of a guillotine.

"No. None."

THE END

BONUS EPILOGUE

WANT TO READ MORE OF VODKA AND RUTHIE'S STORY? SCAN THE QR CODE BELOW TO GET THE FREE BONUS EPILOGUE FOR *UNBROKEN: A DARK MAFIA SINGLE DAD ROMANCE*!

PREVIEW

UNBROKEN: A DARK MAFIA SINGLE DAD ROMANCE

Three years ago...

CHAPTER 1

I stare at the narrow space in the hedges, hardly able to believe my luck.

Is this really happening?

I've been lonely. Restless. Half-wild from being overprotected by my family. I know I'm the baby, but how long does that title last? Will I still be the baby when I'm twenty? Thirty? Forty?

I'm tired of being told what to do. Tired of being the good girl.

I don't want to be the good girl anymore.

I've watched my brothers get married—one after the other. All three of them. And my older sister has been married for years now.

It's like everyone's next season of life has started...but mine.

So tonight, it's time. Something has to change.

If nothing else, I need to prove to myself that I can carve out a private pocket of freedom—one nobody else knows about.

I wait until everyone is distracted. I made a beautiful dinner tonight and served it with a smile, like I always do.

They call me Baby Mama. Little Zoya. The one who likes to cook.

And I do love taking care of them. My oldest brother, Rafail, and his wife Polina. My nieces and nephews. Rodion and his fierce, brilliant wife, Ember. And now Semyon, who's clearly falling hard for Anya. They're not married yet, but it won't be long.

A sliver of moonlight catches the path ahead of me. It's early summer just outside Moscow, and the crickets chirp a quiet chorus.

It's beautiful. Desolate. And the rising heat adds to the thrill of doing something I shouldn't.

No one will find me tonight.

I've planned this too well. In my bedroom, there's a teddy bear propped on my bed. Hidden inside is the small monitor my brothers use to track me. I've tested my decoy three times now.

Once during a quick trip into the city.

The second time, I stayed inside but crept around the house to see if they'd notice.

The third? I snuck out for ice cream at a local street fair.

No one ever noticed.

We have guards at every exit and entrance, of course. My brothers monitor everything. They're not just overbearing but militant. I've never been out like *this* before. Not without a bodyguard trailing close behind.

Even at school, someone was always watching. Nobody dared approach the Kopolov family's precious princess. They knew if anyone tried anything—anything—my brothers would kill them.

Literally.

No one took the risk. So I stood alone at school dances while the shadows of my guards hovered nearby like grim sentinels.

I was lucky to have one friend. Just one. And she was the only one who ever helped me bend the rules.

"Zoya?" a voice whispers from just ahead.

"I'm here," I whisper back.

My heart pounds. I rub my clammy palms against the thighs of my fitted jeans. I'm nervous tonight. More than usual. But I'm also resolved.

Tonight, I'm doing something that would make my brothers lose their ever loving minds.

I'm going to a club.

I'm going to have a *drink*.

Unsupervised.

And God help me—I'm going to get kissed.

"You ready, baby?" my best friend Mia grins as she peeks around the corner. Her eyes widen when she takes me in.

"Zoya... you look gorgeous," she breathes. "No one would ever know who you are."

I give her a small, nervous smile.

This. This is how I want to live my life—with no one knowing who I am. The name, the title, the connections... I'm over it. I need something more.

And tonight, I've pulled out all the stops.

I'm wearing a fitted, low-cut red halter top that dips nearly to my navel. The color pops against my pale skin, bringing out my blue eyes and dark brown hair. My jeans hug every curve. Red heels give me just enough height to feel bold, and a tiny clutch completes the look. I've practiced walking, practiced my smile.

Now I step out through the hedges, just as I rehearsed. They're covered in ivy and nestled into the old stone wall behind the estate. Hidden. Secret. It's not my first attempt at escape, but this is the first one that feels real.

The dusky air wraps around me. Moonlight filters through the trees, and the buzz of crickets fills the silence. For a moment, I feel like Cinderella on her way to the ball.

We head to the club. Mia chatters beside me about some guy she's meeting tonight.

"Are you sure your cousin isn't coming?" she teases with a wink.

"Matvei?" I snort. "Are you serious? He's terrifying."

"And the only one of them who's single," she replies, waggling her eyebrows. "Your brothers are *so* hot."

"Ew. Gross, Mia. Stop."

She laughs, and I shake my head, still terrified—but I'm not backing down.

When we get there, I feel exposed. Unprotected.

Still, I remind myself—I need to try. I *have* to try.

So I take a drink.

I'm cautious. I don't accept anything from strangers. I don't leave my drink unattended. I'm not stupid.

I let my gaze wander, half wondering when Rafail will storm in here and drag me home.

But no one comes. No texts even ping my phone.

I let out a breath.

I'm getting away with it.

There's a man at the bar. Attractive. Older. Longish dark hair curls around his ears. Warm brown eyes. A dimple flashes when he smiles.

"Hello, beautiful," he says in a low voice. "Don't you look stunning tonight?"

I smile shyly. "Thank you."

Mia's already in the corner, tangled up in someone else's arms and tongue. God.

I'm alone—and for some reason, I'm starting to regret coming. I think of the house, imagine curling into my favorite chair with a hot cup of tea and a book.

That actually sounds better than this.

"Are you alone?" the man asks.

Is that a normal pickup line or should I be worried?

I shrug, noncommittal, and let the conversation carry us forward. He's friendly, easy to talk to. Probably in his mid-twenties, so younger than I thought but older than I am.

After a while, he leans closer.

"It's loud in here," he murmurs. "Let's go for a walk."

I hesitate. Definitely more dangerous.

I want to be kissed. Secretly. Recklessly. Like I'm a woman someone wants, and not just a girl someone wants to protect.

I glance toward Mia, trying to signal her, but she doesn't look up.

I nod.

As we head toward the door, I become aware of someone else watching me. There's a figure sitting alone at the corner of the bar, nursing a drink.

I can't see his face since it's cloaked in shadow but I can see the wide, powerful set of his shoulders. He's still. Focused.

And I can feel his eyes burning through me.

Me.

Why?

I note how big and thick his hands are, wrapped around a full pint of Guinness. Condensation rolls down the side of the glass, but he's not drinking it, not now. A prop? He just stares, like he's lost in thought—or maybe pretending to be.

"Come on," I murmur under my breath, watching him.

I *want* to believe this is normal. That I'm safe. But something in my gut whispers otherwise.

"It's going to get busy in here soon," says the man beside me. My companion. I don't even know his name.

If Rafail could see me now, he'd lose his shit. My oldest brother has always been more father than sibling. He became my guardian when I was just a child, and I've never disobeyed him.

Well. Until I started sneaking out.

We walk hand-in-hand down the quiet street, making small talk about the last movie we saw. Turns out he doesn't like thrillers the way I do, and he definitely doesn't read the romance novels I inhale, but we have a few in common. Still, this is boring the fuck out of me. Is this what women like? He's hot, he's nice enough I guess, he's smart... but I am totally disinterested.

We're approaching a streetlight when I suddenly realize I don't have my phone.

"Where is it?" I mutter, patting my pockets. "Strange. I always have it on me."

"I have to go back to the bar," I tell him. "I think I left my phone."

He grins and winks. "You didn't. I've got it right here."

He opens his palm and shows me my phone, resting there like a prize.

A chill of unease slides down my spine. How did he get that? I never let it out of my hand.

I swallow hard.

"You shouldn't have my phone," I say, trying to keep my voice steady. "Can I have it back, please?"

"I'll give it to you," he says with a wink, "in exchange for a kiss."

My heart jumps hard. I'm not sure if it's excitement or fear. I *wanted* a kiss.

Didn't I?

But now that he's closer, everything shifts. His teeth are slightly crooked. He smells faintly of garlic and onions. His knuckles are hairy. My attraction drains away fast.

Have I been that protected? That sheltered? Is this what it's like, meeting a man in the wild?

Am I broken?

"I'd like my phone back, please," I say again, softer this time. "I'm not ready to kiss you."

He crowds me suddenly, pressing me into a darkened door-frame. Above us, the clouds shift, moonlight breaking through in a silvery wash across the sky.

He leans in, mouth slightly parted, and for one crazy, wild second, I'm convinced he's a werewolf. That he's about to bare his teeth and bite, or throw back his head and howl into the night.

I shiver.

I've read too many books.

"No," I say more firmly. "Not now."

My voice leaves room for a maybe, but that doesn't matter. Not now. Not like this.

I put more force in my tone. "Give me my phone."

But he doesn't.

Panic claws at my chest.

Fuck.

Shit.

Fuck.

Why did I do this? Why did I want to be alone? Why did I have to leave my brothers? Why did I have to prove anything to anyone?

I won't scream. I can't panic. My pride won't let me. But I'm cornered. Vulnerable. And this man is too close.

"Come here," he murmurs, voice low and greasy. "Don't be afraid. I'll make sure you like it."

"I said *no*," I snap, louder this time, clearer.

His face twists with anger. "I bought you a fucking drink, and you can't even give me a kiss?"

He lets my phone fall to the ground. It hits hard ,and I wince.

"Give me a fucking kiss," he growls and shoves me back against the wall.

My brothers taught me self-defense. They taught me how to shoot. But right now, every lesson vanishes. My mind blanks.

Do I kick him? Scream? Elbow him in the face?

And then—

"You'll leave her the fuck alone now."

The voice comes from behind us. Thick Irish accent. Cold. Dangerous.

"You do what I say by the count of three, or I'll slice your fecking throat. Try me."

The man holding me jolts and spins. "Who the fuck are you?"

The stranger steps into the light. Late twenties, maybe early thirties. At least a ten, twelve years older than I am. Tall. Still. Radiating power and calm like a storm waiting to break.

Even in the dim moonlight, his blue eyes glint like cut sapphires. A five o'clock shadow shades his jaw. A scar cuts through one eyebrow. Ink curls around his collarbone and disappears beneath his shirt.

This is the man I saw inside the bar. Watching.

Now he steps forward, anchoring his hands on his hips. Broad, solid, capable hands.

I swallow.

"You heard what I said," he murmurs in that accent. Blows out a breath. "I don't repeat myself."

There's something about his presence and confidence that tells me he's someone used to recognition, used to fear. But this man doesn't know him.

Should I?

He wasn't just watching. He was waiting.

When the man doesn't back off fast enough, the Irishman strikes like lightning. One brutal punch. A twist of the wrist. A growled word in what might be Gaelic?

"I don't know how you Russians do things," he says coolly. "But where I come from, we don't kiss a woman who says no."

His grip clamps on the guy's collar, slamming him into the wall. I wince.

"Now, are you going to leave the poor lass alone, or do I need to teach you a lesson?"

His tone isn't raised, but it slices through the air.

"You stay the hell out of this—"

Whack.

A punch to the jaw. One to the gut. Another to the temple. The creep crumples to his knees.

The Irishman stands over him, blood on his knuckles and not a single hair out of place.

"Aye, so you see," he says with unnerving calm. "The chance for another choice is now gone. Get the fuck out of here before I end you."

I can't breathe. My chest is tight. My legs won't move. My brothers would react like this, *exactly* like this, before they beat him beyond recognition. No one fucks with a Kopolov woman.

But this...doesn't feel the way it would if my brothers were the ones delivering justice and protection.

The Irishman turns to me.

His voice gentles, his blue eyes glinting.

"You all right, lass?"

I swallow and nod. "You didn't have to save me," I whisper.

He smiles. A dimple appears in his cheek. My god, he's hot. So fucking Irish. Ruddy cheeks, dark brown curls around his ears. Those bright, terrifyingly blue eyes.

Something in them makes my stomach twist. Something I can't name.

"I suppose I came here for nothing, then, eh?" he says, cocking a grin. "Should've had the stupid fucking Guinness."

Then he reaches for my hand.

I flinch, but his touch is gentle. Soothing.

Wordlessly, he lifts my hand and presses a kiss across the knuckles.

Old-fashioned. Arresting.

"Thank you," I whisper.

"Now, lass," he says, his voice dropping low. "I don't know why you're here, but something tells me you *probably* shouldn't be."

He bends, picks up my phone. Miraculously, it's unharmed.

He taps something into the screen. "This is my number," he says. "I'll be around a bit. Not from around here, you know. Ireland. But I'm not heading back just yet."

He holds the phone out to show me. "You get into trouble, you call this number. See?"

Why is he protecting me? Why does he care?

I nod. "Okay," I whisper.

He flashes a grin—bright, devastating. My belly melts.

"Good girl," he says softly. "That's a good girl."

Then he leans in, hooks a finger under my chin. "Now go back inside. Find whoever you came with. Go home where it's safe, eh?"

I nod again and swallow hard.

Safe. Funny word, coming from him.

Because somehow, I know—

I've never been in more danger in my life.

WANT TO FIND OUT WHAT HAPPENS NEXT? ORDER YOUR COPY OF "UNREQUITED: A DARK MAFIA AGE GAP ROMANCE" BY SCANNING THE QR CODE BELOW. AVAILABLE ON AUGUST 29TH!

Fueled by dark chocolate and even darker coffee, USA Today bestselling author Jane Henry writes what she loves to read – character-driven, unputdownable romance featuring dominant alpha males and the powerful heroines who bring them to their knees. She's believed in the power of love and romance since Belle won over the beast, and finally decided to write love stories of her own.

Scan the QR Code below to receive Jane's Newsletter & be notified of upcoming new releases & special offers!

Be sure to visit me at www.janehenryromance.com, too!

www.ingramcontent.com/pod-product-compliance
Lightning Source LLC
Chambersburg PA
CBHW070557300726
48975CB00006B/1621